MW00780963

DETACHED
Lover

Cover Design: by Triv ilovedesignsbytriv@gmail.com

Printed in the United States of America
Keen Vision Publishing, LLC
www.publishwithKVP.com
ISBN: 978-1-955316-77-4

DETACHED
Lover

a novel by

Adrienne Denise

KEEN VISION PUBLISHING

Prologue

♡♡♡

Tasia had never seen her father so angry. She didn't know how far he would go, but she was afraid. She frantically took a shower and quickly threw on the dirty clothes she saw on her bedroom floor. She didn't care what she put on. Tasia had to get away from her father — fast. Earlier, he had demanded her car keys and phone, so she grabbed the items, jetted downstairs to the kitchen to relinquish them as requested. It was just her luck, her father was sitting at the kitchen table with his palms over his face. She slowly and quietly placed the items on the table, as far away from him as possible, and headed to the front door before she got his attention.

Screeeech. Tasia heard her father push his chair away from the table. Within seconds, he was on her heels and his hand was aggressively wrapped around the back of her neck. He was much bigger than Tasia, so she knew there was no way to fight him back. Tasia's body gave way to her father's pull, and soon, they were face to face. His eyes pierced into her eyes hatefully.

"Where the hell do you think you are going? You're so damn disrespectful! I told you to give *ME* your keys and phone. You threw them on the table for me like I'm a got damn dog! You don't deserve shit I do for you!" He spat angrily. Tasia did not reply. Tears flowed down her face steadily. She tried to look away, but her father grabbed her by the neck of her shirt, and forced her to look at him. *"You know what? Fuck it! You want to leave so bad? Go!"* He drug her from the foyer and slung Tasia out of the front door. "Stay your ass out here until I decide to let you back in!"

Tasia cried and struggled to stand to her feet as the door slammed behind him. She didn't know what to do. Her neck was in pain from where he had grabbed her, but nothing ached more than her heart. In despair, Tasia crumpled down on the front steps of her home and cried for what seemed like eternity. As the sun set, the temperature dropped and Tasia began to shiver. She paced back and forth on the porch, rubbing her hands together swiftly, then rubbing them on her body to stay warm. A car approached the entrance, and Tasia was relieved when she realized it was her mother. She waived faintly to her mother. Instead of parking in the garage, her mother swiftly pulled into the front entrance of their home.

"Tasia, why are you out here in the cold?" Gabrielle Ingram grabbed her daughter and rubbed her back soothingly.

"He-he-he-he kicked me out." Tasia sobbed in her

mother's arms.

"Come on." Mrs. Ingram exhaled with frustration as she unlocked the front door. "Go upstairs to your room. I will talk with your father." She instructed Tasia before they walked in the house. Tasia walked in the house cautiously. She didn't see her father in the kitchen or living room, so she assumed he was upstairs and hesitated before walking up, allowing her mother to lead the way. Mrs. Ingram looked at her daughter sorrowfully and took her by the hand. Once they made it to the upstairs landing, she let go of Tasia's hand, and motioned her towards her bedroom before walking down the hall to find her husband. Tasia walked back into her room and closed the door. Within moments, she could hear her parents arguing loudly.

"Antonio, what happened? You were talking in circles when you called. Why did you kick her out?"

"Gabrielle, that girl has lost her fucking mind! The disrespect has gotten out of hand! She's seventeen but you let her go as she pleases! You wouldn't believe what I caught her doing when I got home from work! I couldn't stand the sight of her so I grabbed her ass by the—"

"*You did what?!* Antonio, what did I tell you about putting your hands on my child?! That's my baby!"

"Oh, she's definitely yours, Gab. ALL FUCKING YOURS!"

"Oh, you got something to say, Antonio? I hope you aren't about to part your lips to say a damn thing about that, because your record isn't scotch clean either!"

Tasia hated to hear them going back and forth. She grabbed her MP3 player, put her earphones in, and turned her music up as loud as it could go.

One

♡♡♡

lick-click-clack-clack. Anastasia, Tasia for short, pecked away feverishly at the keyboard on her MacBook Pro. Stopping to review her work, she slowly shook her head and let out a dramatic sigh. "I'm completely stumped!" She admitted out loud. Her phone rings, and she is irritated by the distraction until she sees Seth's name and face across the screen. A slight smirk spreads across her face as she answers the FaceTime. "Bae! How are you doing?"

"Better now," replied the handsome man smiling back at her.

Tasia and Seth had been dating for nearly three months, and the experience had been nothing short of pure bliss for Tasia. Seth was the type of man she had prayed would enter her life. He was a milk chocolate dream, standing six feet and four inches tall. Seth had a muscular build, the chiseled facial features of a Greek god, and sandy brown dreadlocks that draped over his shoulders. In addition to being attractive, he was funny, thoughtful, sincere, kind, God-fearing, and successful. To top it all off, the thirty-three-year-old entrepreneur was ready to pack up his bachelor life and build a family. He was everything a woman could ask for in a man.

Tasia was a hopeless romantic. She also couldn't wait to settle down and start her own family. The two seemed like a perfect match, but they were over 500 miles apart. Seth lived in St. Louis, MO, while Tasia resided in Atlanta, GA.

"Oh, is that right?" Tasia flashed a sexy smile.

"You know it!" Seth replied. "What are you doing?"

"Working on a lifestyle article. It's missing something, but I don't know what it is."

Seth gazed at her with admiration. "You'll figure it out. You always do. Did I forget to mention that you look absolutely beautiful today?"

Tasia blushed. "Boy, bye! I have on zero makeup, and my hair has been in this ponytail since yesterday."

"But I love when you wear your hair up in a ponytail. That shit is so sexy to me. I love seeing you in your natural state. But, hey, baby. I was just checking in on you. The store is getting pretty busy. Imma hit you up later."

After their FaceTime call ended, Tasia sat back in her lush pink desk chair and swirled around, smiling from ear to ear. "That's my baby!" she gushed. After a few moments had passed, she accepted that her creative juices weren't flowing and stepped away from her desk to find some inspiration. Being a writer for most of her life, she had mastered her writing process and knew she wouldn't get anything done if she tried to force it. Tasia was a writer for a small lifestyle magazine company that targeted adults ages twenty-one to thirty-four. She wrote articles about fashion, dating, culture, social media, décor, entrepreneurship, and world trends, and she was the Associate Editor for the celebrity gossip section at the company. Tasia also did freelance work on the side for different online websites. She made fantastic money doing what she loved and yearned to own a successful blogging company one day. Though only twenty-five, Tasia was a successful, well-known writer in Atlanta.

In addition to being a sought-after writer, she was a charismatic, fashionable socialite who had it going on in every way. Her beautiful features and slim-thick build turned heads wherever she went. Tasia had silky smooth chocolate skin, natural shoulder length hair, beautiful brown almond-shaped eyes, and stood at five feet, six inches without her heels.

It was almost noon, and Tasia was still in her pajamas. She decided to get dressed and go for a run in the park near her luxurious townhome. After her run, she planned to shower and head to her desk to take another stab at the article she had been working on.

Ping! Her phone sounded. It was a text message from Seth. He had sent her different articles about fashion, celebrity gossip, décor, and politics.

Bae, I don't know exactly what you're
writing about, but I hope this inspires you.

Tasia smiled at her phone and sent him three heart emojis.

Thank you, my love.

This is going to be my husband. Tasia thought to herself as she headed out the door. Seth always knew exactly what to do and say. Tasia loved that about him.

Three Months Earlier...

"Yo, I thought we were supposed to meet someone else here?" Seth asked Lisa after seeing that she was alone. Trap music blared through the speakers throughout the lounge.

"Yeah! My late ass cousin!" Lisa screamed over the music. "She just texted me and said she was pulling up. Knowing Tasia, that means she's about fifteen minutes away."

Seth chuckled. "That's cool. We just got here."

Lisa, who is Tasia's cousin, went to high school with Seth. Originally from Atlanta, Seth was visiting a family member in town, and Lisa invited him out with her and Tasia. They met at a hookah lounge in Downtown Atlanta to catch up. Lisa couldn't wait for Tasia to arrive. Her favorite cousin plus her high school bestie together in one room? She knew the three of them would have a blast together.

"So, what's new with you?" Lisa asked to pass the time. "Seems like I haven't seen you in forever."

"Bruh, it's 2017!" Seth laughed. "I haven't seen you since 2013. It has been a long ass time. But everything is everything, Lisa. I can't complain. The store is doing well. My day one, Chris, and I are finally seeing a profit and having consistent clientele. Everything is coming together, slowly but surely."

"That's wassup!" Lisa smiled. "I'm proud of you, Bro."

"Thank you, thank you!"

"What's the name of the store again? I gotta make sure I check you out when I slide through St. Louis!"

"Opulent Kicks STL. Damn, I thought you were following us on the gram?"

"Ooooo, I'm gonna fix that right now!" Lisa pulled out her phone to follow the store on Instagram."

"Niggas man!" Seth laughed and shook his head. "So, what about you? What's been going on in your world?"

"I got a new marketing gig. Everything is now on the up and up. I know it will be a struggle these first few months because I'm with a new company. But, it will pay off eventually."

"Okay, Miss Four Eyes," Seth joked. "I see you doing it big!"

"Oh, you wanna go there, McFatty?" Lisa joked back. "I grew up and said goodbye to those god-awful glasses." Lisa was no longer the scrawny, four-eyed girl from high school. She was now a curvy, caramel vixen with tons of sex appeal. Lisa was short but didn't let that stop her from rocking long box braids that fell inches beneath her full butt. Lisa had ass for days and wasn't shy about showing off her assets.

"Nigga, do you see me?!" She laughed as she did a whole spin for Seth.

"Girl, you aiight!" He laughed. "And, muthafucka, I ain't fat no more." Seth patted his abdomen. The fluffy stomach he had in high school was now rock-solid abs that showed slightly through his tight-fitted shirt.

"Man, I miss you," Lisa said as she caught her breath from laughing.

"Same, sis," Seth replied.

Seth and Lisa had shared a sibling-like bond since high school. Back then, Seth was the popular fat guy with the flyest clothes and freshest kicks, and Lisa was your typical nerd. One day after school, some students were bullying Lisa, and Seth took up for her. He threatened to beat their asses if they ever bothered Lisa again. Since then, the two became inseparable.

"Hey, my name is Patrice, and I'll be your waitress tonight. Y'all know what y'all want to order?" A beautiful, dark-skinned woman with a heavy southern accent approached Seth and Lisa, interrupting their walk down memory lane to take their orders.

"We'll order the hookah later, but can I get a Patrón with Sprite for now?" Lisa replied.

"And you?" Patricia asked Seth. He ordered a D'Ussé and coke.

"Aiight, sweetheart. I'll be back with y'all drinks." Patricia smiled as she sashayed towards the bar.

"Damn, I thought we were country! She got us beat!" Seth said as they both burst into laughter.

"Oh, shit! Look what the cat dragged in. There's my late ass cousin." Lisa said as she waved to get Tasia's attention. Seth's eyes darted to the lost woman searching for familiar faces in the crowd.

"Say, man! Why you never introduced me to your cousin?!" Seth inquired. Lisa wasn't paying him any attention.

"Tasia!" Lisa yelled over the music. *"Yo, Tasia! Over here!"*

Tasia was relieved when she finally noticed them but didn't rush to get to the table. She was feeling sexy and refused to be in a rush for anyone. Besides, she saw how Seth was looking at her. She decided to give him a show as she seductively tossed all 26 inches of her newly installed Peruvian Body-wave sew-in over her shoulders and strutted in their direction. Her face was beat, and her body looked amazing. She wore black, high-waist, faux leather pants, black thigh-high boots, a white corset, and finished it off with a red Gucci clutch.

"Sorry I'm late, you guys," She lied. "Please forgive me." Lisa got up to hug Tasia before she could sit down.

"Okay, cuz! I see you in that dress!" Tasia smiled as she checked her cousin out. Lisa wore a mustard, fitted, long-sleeve knit dress that showed off every curve she had been blessed with and paired the dress with brown ankle boots.

"Thank you, boo!" Lisa replied gleefully. "Tasia, this is my best friend from high school, Seth. Seth, meet my favorite cousin, Anastasia." They shook each other's hands and smiled.

The waitress brought Lisa and Seth drinks and asked Tasia if she wanted anything.

"I'll have a D'Ussé and coke," Tasia replied.

"I ordered the same thing!" Seth laughed.

"I can only drink brown," Tasia chuckled. "That white liquor is the devil."

"I feel the same way," Seth nodded his head in agreement. Without being obvious, Tasia was peeping Seth out. She thought he was handsome and fly as hell.

Seth wore a Gucci shirt, dark jeans, and the new Air Jordans that had just been released that week. Tasia was always attracted to a man who could match her fly.

The trio had fun that night. They ordered hookah, food, and bottles of Patrón and D'Ussé. Lisa and Tasia threw their drinks back, danced, and had a good time. Lisa had to go to the ladies' room and left Tasia and Seth alone. Since they didn't know each other that well, the space between them became awkardly quiet, so they both scrolled away on their phones. Seth didn't utter a word to Tasia, so she assumed he wasn't feeling her and decided to keep her distance for the rest of the night. Lisa's return came at the perfect time.

"*I know y'all lames ain't sleep!*" Lisa shouted.

"Hell naw," Seth replied as he looked up from his phone.

"Well, let's keep this turn-up going!" Lisa shouted as she grabbed another drink.

By the end of the night, they all had reached their liquor limit. When the lounge's house DJ started to play slow R&B songs, they took that as their cue to head out.

"Last call for alcohol!" Patricia shouted as she approached their table. "Can I get you guys another drink, or are you ready for your checks?"

"I think we are all good! It'll be one check," Seth replied as he gave the waitress his bank card without asking to see the ticket.

"Okayyyy, Mr. Baller!" Lisa joked.

"Thank you, Seth. That was nice of you," Tasia said smoothly. Seth grinned.

"Where are we off to next?!" Lisa asked. She was tipsy

and didn't want the night to end.

Tasia stood up, swaying back and forth, "If we go to another spot, I will probably fall asleep. It's damn near two in the morning!"

"Yeah, it is kinda late, Lisa," Seth laughed. Lisa playfully rolled her eyes.

"Lisa, can I stay with you? I'm not going to make it home." Tasia asked. Tasia's townhome was nearly thirty minutes away, while Lisa only lived a few blocks from the lounge. Moreover, Tasia wanted to avoid drinking and driving. If she stayed with Lisa, she would be close to her car when she sobered up the following day.

"Of course! I'll call an Uber." Lisa replied drunkenly.

When the Uber arrived, they piled in and made it to Lisa's two-bedroom apartment within minutes. Lisa told Seth he was welcome to stay and that he could sleep in her spare room. As soon as Anastasia entered the living room, she began unzipping her pants and unbuttoning her corset.

"Lisa! Can you give me some night clothes?" She shouted to Lisa who was in her room undressing. The entire time, Seth was standing near the couch frozen.

"Oh, my bad! I thought you were in the other room already." Tasia apologized.

Seth licked his lips and shook his head slowly. "Naw. I'm right here."

Still paying him no attention, Tasia walked right past him into Lisa's room. He stared at her from afar as she went through Lisa's clothes in search of a shirt and shorts to sleep in. Tasia knew Seth was checking her out, but she wasn't fazed in the least bit.

Lisa and Tasia slept in Lisa's bedroom. The following morning, Tasia came out of Lisa's room wearing only a shirt that barely covered her bottom. She headed toward the fridge to grab some water and was startled to see Seth sitting on the couch, watching TV.

"Shit!" Tasia grumbled. Seth looked at her in amusement. "I forgot you were here," Tasia said as she shuffled to Lisa's room to retrieve her shorts. "My bad, Seth. I barely had on clothes, and you startled me."

"Naw, you good," Seth replied coolly.

Tasia laughed. "Aye, we were lit last night!" Seth chuckled and agreed. She grabbed two bottles of water and then handed Seth a bottle.

"Aww, you're so nice. I appreciate it," Seth replied.

"No problem. Thank you for last night."

"It's no big deal. When you're with me, I'll always make sure you're straight, and I mean that."

"Oh really? Sounds good."

"Big facts."

Not knowing what to say next, Tasia flashed a sexy smile. "Well, Mr. Money Man, I'm headed back to sleep. I have a slight headache."

She went back into the bedroom to find Lisa scrolling on Instagram. "Soooo, do you think Seth is cute?" Lisa asked with a mischievous grin.

"Lisa, take your ass back to sleep." Tasia yawned.

"No, T. For real! You should talk to him. He's cute, stays to himself, about his business, no kids, and he got moneeyyy."

Tasia rolled her eyes and laughed at her cousin's impersonation. "Girl, he barely said two words to me

17

last night when you left us by ourselves. I don't think he's feeling me."

"Oh, I know he is!" Lisa interrupted. "Trust me."

"Lisa, I'm good. He's cute and all, but he is mad quiet and awkward as hell."

Tasia got comfortable in bed and dozed off to sleep for hours. Lisa was happy to see Tasia finally stirring around. "Damn, Tasia. You slept the whole day away."

"My bad, Lisa. I didn't realize I was that tired." Tasia yawned and stretched.

"Umm, clearly!" Lisa replied. "Well, Sleeping Beauty, you didn't get to tell your man goodbye."

"Bitch that is not my man! Lisa, you really need to cut it out." Tasia laughed.

"Okay, okay. But Seth did tell me to give you his number," Lisa grinned.

Tasia rolled her eyes and fought the smile trying to form at the corners of her lips. "I mean...you can send me his contact info or whatever."

"Or, whatever? Girl, bye. You're not fooling anyone. There. I just sent his info to your phone."

"Thank you," Tasia smiled. "Imma head on out. I need to shower and get my life in order. I can't believe I slept the whole day away." They said their goodbyes and promised to hang out again soon. When she got home, Tasia showered, made dinner, prepped for the work week ahead, and got into bed. As she got comfortable and waited to fall asleep, she scrolled through her Instagram feed and saw a picture Lisa had uploaded the night before. Tasia looked at the picture in confusion, shook her head, and commented, *LOL! I don't remember taking this!?* Then, Tasia looked harder at the picture to check Seth out. "Okay, Mr. Seth. You're kinda handsome." She said to herself. Then, she remembered that Lisa had sent her his number and that Seth had requested her to reach out. So, she saved Seth's number and sent him a text message.

Hey, this is Anastasia. It was great meeting you this weekend. I hope you had a safe flight.

Within seconds, Seth replied:

I'm surprised you hit me up.
I made it home safely not too long ago.

Why are you surprised?

Because you barely said anything to me...

Lol, you were giving me awkward vibes.

I didn't think you were feeling me,
so I observed you from afar.

And what did you conclude?
From your observation?

That I want you.

Tasia rolled her eyes and laughed.

Why is that?

Seconds after she replied, her phone began to ring. It was Seth.

Tasia hesitantly answered, and Seth chuckled, "Yo, you must think I'm crazy, don't you?"

"Hmmm, kinda," Tasia replied. She loved how his voice sounded on the phone but refused to get swept away so quickly.

"Nah. I'm not crazy. But I'm serious about that text, though. I hope you give me the pleasure of getting to know you. You're beautiful, and I can't stop thinking about you. I need you in my life."

Tasia sucked her teeth. "I'm pretty sure you tell this to every beautiful woman you're interested in."

"But you? You are more than beautiful. You're smart, outgoing, funny, and, excuse my language, you're fucking sexy. I know you've heard all this before, but I'm different. I want you to give me a chance." Seth confessed.

He was right. Tasia had heard all of this before, but she was intrigued by him and wanted to get to know him. He could be exactly what she needed. "If I give you a chance, you have to promise you will never hurt me and always be truthful." She replied seriously.

"I'll never hurt you. I will always keep it one hundred with you."

"Sounds good. And to be clear, you're single, right? No girlfriend or an ex you're still dealing with?"

"Baby, I'm single as a dollar bill. I'm looking for a wife, and that might be you."

Tasia laughed out loud. "Woah! You got the game sewed up, don't you?"

Seth chuckled, "I'm dead ass serious, though.

"Alright, Mr. Seth. I'll give you a chance to get to know me. Don't make me regret it!"

"Trust me. You won't."

The rest of the night, they talked about everything under the sun. They discussed their upbringings, family, friends, schooling, you name it. They learned they had so many similarities, including the death of their closest loved ones. He lost his mother in adolescence, and she lost her mother while attending college and then her brother shortly after graduating. They talked for hours, and she felt attached to him from that day forward.

Present Day...

Meek Mill's *Wins and Losses* blasted through Tasia's headphones as she ran through the park. For some odd reason, Meek's yelling in his music motivated her. His music was always her go-to when she needed a quick pick-me-up. After a good run, Tasia had a clear mind for creativity. Also, she couldn't wait to check out the articles Seth had sent her. She smiled to herself. She couldn't believe she had gotten so lucky.

Finishing the article was a breeze. After reading through her work again, Tasia closed her computer and dressed to meet her bestie, Kyle. They had been connected at the hip since grade school. They were like family and always showed up for each other. Over the years, they made sure that nothing got in between their bond. She couldn't wait to catch up with him.

They met at one of their favorite lounges near Edgewood called ATL Happy Hour. The ambiance was just right, and the weekday crowd was super chill. Kyle and Tasia met there a few times monthly to catch up, grab food, and smoke hookah. Tasia dressed casually for the occasion and threw on her black and blue Retro 1s, ripped dark blue jeans, and a Nipsey Hussle graphic t-shirt. She put her hair in a bun, picked out the perfect hoop earrings, and wore little to no makeup. Tasia lived fifteen minutes away from the lounge, but with Atlanta traffic, it took her forty-five minutes to get to the destination. She valeted her Jeep, and the security let her right in since she was a regular. Once inside, Tasia headed straight back to the pool table. She knew Kyle would be gambling.

"What up, Tasia?" Kyle chuckled when Tasia got close to the table. "You got here right in time." Clack! He hit the 8-ball into the pocket as Tasia sat at one of the high tables. "Shawty should be coming back in a few. I just ordered hookah." Kyle informed her before turning back to his opponent.

"Aye, my boy! Pay up!" Kyle shouted.

"C'mon, man! Best out of two?"

"No can do. Run me my money."

Kyle's opponent shrugged, then slid him a hundred-dollar bill.

"Right on, my boy. 'Preciate it!" Kyle said as he dapped him up.

"Cool, cool. See you next week, my G." The guy replied before heading to the door.

With his business settled for the day, Kyle turned his attention to his best friend. "Fuck you been on?" He inquired as he gave her a hug. "I ain't heard from you all day."

"Damn, Kyle! Hi! How are you today? You mad aggressive right now." Tasia checked him.

"Man, I'm just fucking with you." Kyle laughed. "You usually text me a million times to remind me about happy hour."

Just as Tasia was about to share how busy her day had been, a big booty waitress, who clearly had a thing

for Kyle, strutted to the table to deliver the hookah. Tasia wasn't at all shocked or bothered. All the ladies loved Kyle. He was good-looking, had a dope personality, and dressed well. Today, Kyle rocked a black Dior hoodie, slim-cut black jeans, and a pair of Yeezy's. He wore two iced-out Cuban links around his neck, and his red, shoulder-length locs were in a neat ponytail to the back. Kyle was 6 feet 2 inches tall, slim, and had a light brown complexion. His eyes were the prettiest shade of hazel, and women went crazy for them.

After he and the waitress exchanged words, the waitress finally acknowledged Tasia. "Hey, girl! Do you want your usual?" Tasia smiled and nodded yes. "Okay, I'll be right back with your drink, boo." Then, she strutted away just as seductively as she came.

Tasia sucked her teeth. "Damn! Little mama might need to make herself a drink. She was all over you, bruh. Thirsty, much?"

Kyle rubbed his goatee. "Shawty, I mean, what can I say? Bitches love the kid."

"*Nigga, please!*" Tasia laughed. She knew hanging out with Kyle was just the relaxation she needed. "But what's up, though? I haven't talked to you in a few days. What have you been up to?"

Kyle caught her up on everything he had been doing, including caring for his son, Kyle Jr. "His soccer game is this Saturday. You already know Jasmine gone be there." He shook his head.

"I'll be happy when she finds herself a man and stops giving you hell." Tasia rolled her eyes.

"Who are you telling? Junior is seven years old. We

haven't been together since he was four, and that bitch still be tripping! Tasia, the other night, shawty pulled up to the strip club on ya boi! I was watching Starr, throwing money, and Jasmine came out of nowhere talking mad crazy. The bitch gone tell me that the money I was throwing should be going to Junior and her. Then, she went on about how I need to stop drinking and all this other bullshit."

If nothing else, Kyle was an excellent storyteller, and Tasia couldn't stop laughing. "So what you say, man?" She asked.

"All I could do was laugh and ask why she was stalking me. I know one of them lame niggas told her I was there. The way I see it, she can't tell me shit about how to spend my money. Junior is with me more than her. I take care of my jit. Jas needs to move on like I did."

"Clearly!" Tasia agreed before she inhaled a pull of the hookah. Kyle had a new chick every month, and Tasia wasn't surprised that the flavor of the week was a stripper named Starr. She didn't even bother asking anything about her. Kyle would be tired of her by the end of the week and on to another chick. She was concerned about Jasmine. Her popping up was typical, but her behavior was becoming too much. She was tired of the drama she brought Kyle, but she knew to let him handle the situation his way.

The waitress returned with Tasia's D'Ussé and coke and a ten-piece chicken plate for Kyle. "Thank you, Ms. Lady." Kyle flashed a charming smile and rubbed her waistline as she put their order on the table.

The waitress blushed and smiled extra hard. "I'll be back to check on y'all in a few," she purred.

"You better!" Kyle replied mischievously.

Kyle's face changed when he saw a familiar face headed in his direction. "Aye, T. I need you to be cool and keep it playa." Tasia, eating one of his chicken wings, looked at him with confusion. "Darren is headed over here." Kyle informed her.

Two

Darren was Tasia's ex-boyfriend from almost two years ago. He had hurt her so badly that she had been celibate since they broke up. Tasia put the half-eaten chicken wing on a plate, wiped her hands with a napkin, and took a big gulp of her drink. Kyle shook his head and inhaled and exhaled deeply, hoping the night didn't turn left. Tasia was a hothead. Kyle knew she could go from 0 to 100 and pop off at any second. To top it off, her mouth was lethal.

"Be cool, shawty." Kyle practically begged her. Tasia replied with a fake smile and nodded her head sarcastically.

"Kyle! Good to see you, my dude!" Darren excitedly shouted as he dapped Kyle's hand.

"Wassup, man. Ain't seen you in a minute. How've you been?" Kyle asked coolly. Tasia plastered a fake smile on her face as the two exchanged updates and caught up on life.

Then, as if he had just realized she was sitting there, Darren turned in her direction. "What up, T? How have you been?"

She looked at him sourly. "I'm good." Tasia was intentionally short with him. It had been four hundred, twenty-eight days, twelve hours, thirty-six minutes, and twenty-eight seconds since a man made her climax, and the culprit was standing in her face, smiling as if they were cool. Their breakup forced her to promise to herself not to have sex until she met the one. It took all of Tasia's strength not to curse him out.

Puzzled by her dry response, Darren asked, "Dang, what's up with the hostility, T? I just wanted to say what's up to my people. I ain't mean to get nobody upset or nothing."

"I'm just trying to figure out what the hell you got on," Tasia said as she looked him up and down with disgust. He wore a black vest, a white V- neck t-shirt, a scarf around his neck, light blue, boot-cut Levi's, and square-toe dress shoes. Country, to say the least.

Darren was a handsome, caramel-toned man with a stocky build. He wore his long, curly hair braided back into a man-bun. She had met him a few years ago through Kyle's cousin, and they were together for over a year. She broke it off with him when she found out he was cheating on her with a girl who was away at college. As she stared at him, she couldn't believe he almost got away with cheating on her for so long. Memories of the night he broke her heart filled her mind as he stood before her, dressed like a backwoods, country bumpkin. *She could remember that night like it was yesterday...*

Tasia was leaving Darren's house when his friend, Justin, walked up the driveway. "Yo, Tiff! I'm coming in. You don't have to lock the door," Justin called out to her. Tasia's head swung around quickly. Justin realized he had made a big mistake, but it was too late.

"Hey, Ta- Ta-Tasia! Wassup?" Justin stumbled over his words. "My bad. Your hairstyle reminded me of my home girl from the west side. You look just like her from the back."

Tasia looked at him and cocked her head sideways. "But why would your homegirl be at D's house?"

Justin tried to laugh it off and diffuse the situation. "Man, T, I've been drinking. I'm a little faded right now. I'm tripping, sis."

Tasia instantly knew he was lying. "Cool, cool, cool." She replied calmly while still locking the door. When she walked past Justin, she intentionally shoved him out of her way to let him know he had fucked up. Justin knew the game was over but refused to tell Darren about his slip-up.

Tasia sped off to do some investigating. When she got home, she put on her detective hat and went to work. Tasia searched through all of Darren's social media pages in search of a woman named Tiffany or one who favored her. There was nothing in his friends' lists, so she narrowed her search to his comments and BINGO. Tasia found a comment from seven months prior from username: 404Teff_Baby. She had commented laughing and heart emojis under a picture of Darren that wasn't THAT funny or cute. Tasia rolled her eyes at their nerve, playing in her face, and clicked on 404Teff_Baby's page.

The name displayed was Teffanie Moore, which explained why Tasia couldn't find a Tiffany on Darren's friend list.

Tasia browsed Teffanie's page, but there wasn't much to see. She had very few photos of herself, and the pictures she had posted weren't anything to gawk at. Teffanie was a few shades lighter than Tasia. She wore basic glasses, had an average build, and had kitchen-sink, blonde streaks in her hair. One of the unimpressive selfies she posted had the caption: *On my way home to my boo.* Underneath, Darren had commented: *Can't wait,* with heart-eye emojis.

Tasia's eyes grew wide. "That trifling nigga!" She shouted in rage. "Oh, okay, Darren. I guess you like basic bitches now!" Tasia's detective work uncovered something even worse. A few weeks prior, Teffanie had posted a picture of herself lying in Darren's bed. The caption read: *His little secret…and that's how we gone keep it,* with hush and winking eye emojis.

"Oh, this bitch is bold!" Tasia shouted, even more enraged.

Her anger quickly dissolved into pain. Tasia tossed her phone to the floor, dropped to her knees, and let out a scream. "God, why me?" she cried. "I prayed for a good relationship. What's wrong with me?"

Typically, when they didn't spend the night together, Darren and Tasia would talk before they fell asleep. That night, Tasia cried herself to sleep and ignored Darren's calls. She didn't want to hear anything he had to say. Her mind was made up. Their relationship was over, and there was nothing he could say or do to change her mind. Tasia felt disgusted and foolish for not seeing the signs. "And to think that nigga was bold enough to have this woman around his friends?" Tasia said to herself. The thought of his friends calling her *sis* made her shudder. The entire time, they knew Darren was cheating on her and had been for months.

Tasia went back to check the timestamp of the photo of Teffanie in Darren's bed. She instantly remembered that it was the same weekend Darren had told her he was visiting relatives in Florida. She remembered that weekend vividly. They didn't talk much because Tasia intentionally didn't want to infringe on his family time. She scuffed at the thought. "He's fucking sick! How could he do this to me?"

After a few hours of tossing, turning, and crying, Tasia calmed down. She realized that though she had love for Darren, she wasn't in love with him. Their relationship was still relatively new at the time, and she had been done way worse in past relationships. She resolved that she would move on with grace and that it would be Darren's loss.

When Darren called the next day, Tasia decided to answer. "Hey, baby. Are you doing okay?" He asked, relieved to hear her voice. "I called you last night."

"So, who's Teffanie?" Tasia asked bluntly.

"Who?" Darren asked, dumbfounded.

"Teffanie. You know. The girl Justin thought I was last night when I left your house."

"Oh, Tefffff!" Darren responded as if the light bulb had just clicked on. *That man deserves an Oscar for this performance,* Tasia thought to herself. "Bae, that's Mike's homegirl. She comes by from time to time to play video games with us. I can see how Justin got y'all mixed up. Y'all kinda look alike. Same skin tone, around the same height." As he stuttered through his next lie, Tasia sent Darren screenshots of her detective work. There was complete silence as he began to read the text messages Tasia sent.

"Before you start stuttering through another fucking lie, save us both the time, nigga. You are a weak, lying, pathetic excuse for a man. I can't believe you really tried to play me. But we're good. You obviously like basic bitches, so I ain't never been your type! I'm done with you, fuck boy!"

"T, wait. Damn!" Darren tried to interrupt her, but Tasia was already seeing red. Kyle had always told him Tasia had a temper. He had experienced it before but had never felt her rage quite like this.

"Don't fucking cut me off, nigga! We have NOTHING left to discuss. The next time you think to call me, text me, drop by, or anything of the sort, DON'T!" Tasia ranted.

"Damn, T! Do you even love me? Can we please talk this out? I'm sorry, Anastasia. I effed up! Okay! Bad! But I want to work this out with you! I thought I could have my cake a-an-"

"Yo, my boy, can you hear? I don't give a fuck. Save your weak ass excuses for that bum-ass bitch, Teff. I'm not her. Pack my shit and put it on your porch. I'll grab it while you're at work." With that, Tasia disconnected the call.

When Tasia was upset, her classiness flew out the window. She was raised on the north side of Atlanta, GA., but her mother's family was from southwest Atlanta, aka the SWAT's. She had spent enough time with them to know how to stand her ground and let anyone know she meant business. Being disrespected in any way pulled out the aggression hidden deep within her. Tasia had fought for her respect her entire life and refused to let a mediocre man play with her heart.

Later that day, she headed toward Darren's with her music blasting. She rapped "I Know" by Yo Gotti as she sped down the highway. She wanted to get this over with as soon as possible. Tasia's "Fuck That Nigga" playlist was interrupted by a phone call from Darren. She abruptly hit ignore and turned the music up louder. Her all-black, four-door Jeep Wrangler vibrated as the music poured through the speakers and into her heart. Moments like this made her glad she didn't keep the Jeep model's original speakers.

She arrived at Darren's home, music still blasting. By this time, "Cut Her Off" by K-Camp was playing, and Tasia was bobbing her head along. She wasn't surprised to see he had missed work. Tasia opened the fence to his large backyard and saw three boxes labeled 'My One and Only' sitting neatly on the freshly stained, wooden back porch. She immediately rolled her eyes and sucked her teeth. As Tasia reached down to pick up the boxes, Darren's back door opened. She looked up to see him approaching her, holding a bouquet of white, red, and yellow roses and what appeared to be a letter.

"Hey, Boo," he said with puppy dog eyes.

"It's Anastasia." She corrected him.

Knowing this was his last chance to keep Tasia in his life, he ignored the comment and made his move. "Would you please hear me out? I know you don't want to talk to me, but I love you, Tasia. I was stupid, baby. I'm so sorry."

Tasia let out a loud, unruffled sigh. "Can you help me

put these boxes in my car?"

"Bae, I really don't want you to take your belongings. Your stuff belongs here. You belong here."

Tasia cackled loudly and reached to pick up her boxes. Realizing that she wouldn't be hearing him out any time soon, he stacked the boxes, put the letter and roses on top, and began walking towards her car. His shoulders sagged with defeat, but Tasia didn't care. After he put the boxes in her backseat, Tasia closed the back door, walked to the driver's side, and sat behind the wheel. Darren blocked her from closing the door by standing in front of it, gesturing for her to take the letter and roses.

"Darren, get the fuck out the way." She said, unamused.

"Tasia, please. If you won't take the flowers, at least read the letter." He said as he reached inside her jeep and put the letter on the dashboard.

Tasia looked him in the eyes, slowly reached for the letter, and ripped it into shreds. Still not breaking eye contact, she threw the shreds of his letter in his face. "Get the fuck out the way, Darren," she repeated. He looked at her in disbelief, stepped back, and allowed her to close her car door and drive away.

"*Dang, T. What's wrong with my clothes?*" Darren laughed, interrupting Tasia's trip down memory lane.

"What's not wrong with them?" She retorted. "By the way, how's Teff and your newborn?"

Darren let out an irritated sigh. "You still ain't let that hurt go?"

An appalled Tasia prepared to go off. Unfortunately, Kyle jumped in to save Darren from a mouth-lashing that had the potential to become more. "Yo, D! I think your order is ready. The waitress is looking for you."

Darren got the hint. "Preciate it, bro!" They dapped each other up as Darren turned to walk away. "I never stopped loving you," he said to Tasia before making his exit.

"Gah damn, T. I thought you were over him?" Kyle said, relieved that Darren took the hint and walked away.

"I am. I just don't understand how Darren moved on so fast. He has a whole family now, and I'm still single. And *HE* was the one who cheated. What type of shit is that?" Tasia replied with frustration.

"Don't trip, baby girl," Kyle comforted his friend. "The right one will come."

After her and Darren's breakup, Tasia had the worst luck with men. Every man she dated was worse than the one before. Once, she dated a man with a child, and he argued with his baby mama over money every other week. She tried dating a bad boy and realized she was not built for that life. Then, there was the forty-plus-year-old mama's boy, the weird *OMG-I-Just-Love-your-skin* white man, and Mr.CanIUseYourCarMineIsInTheShop. Tasia had been with them all. No one seemed to fit the bill.

After ordering another round of lemon pepper wings and drinks, Kyle and Tasia ended their night and parted ways. Tasia drove in a daze all the way home. Running into Darren put her in such a bad mood that she began questioning her dating life. Tasia couldn't pinpoint when her romantic life became so lackluster. It wasn't like she couldn't get a man. Sadly, she just never met one who was worthy of her love.

Even though they were dating long-distance, she had hope for her and Seth. She saw the potential. Tasia could see herself with Seth. Tasia believed that God had sent Seth to her and that he was the one. He was perfect. She would be the one to blame if the relationship didn't work. She couldn't handle another failed relationship. Another heartbreak would send her into depression.

When she thought about it, her bad luck with men didn't surprise her. The first man who was supposed to love her and show her what it meant to be loved failed her miserably. So, she blamed him for all of her failed relationships. Tasia's heart was ice cold toward her dad. Tasia and her father had never had a great relationship. He never gave her the affection a father should give his daughter. Instead, he had always treated her like she was a chore. Her anger with her father soon dissipated into concern. She just realized she hadn't visited him in a while and needed to lay her eyes on him.

She placed him in a nursing home a few months ago because his health drastically declined. The doctors told her he didn't have much time to live and, eventually, all his organs would shut down. Tasia felt terrible that he was going through so much pain, but she never shed a tear over his condition. She felt as if his karma was finally catching up to him. Tasia didn't have love for her dad but vowed to care for him because he didn't have any family, and his friends refused to visit him. It was tough, but Tasia truly believed in treating others how she wanted to be treated. She couldn't believe that God allowed her to witness the slow and painful death of the man who had put her through hell all her life. Tasia dreaded the day the doctors would call to inform her that her father had died. She didn't know if she would cry or rejoice. That thought alone made her feel horrible. *"This is so fucked up,"* Tasia sighed to herself as she parked in her garage.

Three

♡♡♡

"Last call for Boarding A," the airline broadcasted over the speaker.

"Tasia, are you excited about this weekend?" Lisa asked. She was standing in line behind Tasia as they waited to board their flight.

"Hmmm. A little bit," Tasia replied nonchalantly. She giggled as Lisa jokingly shoved her with her carry-on bag. "Okay, okay!" Tasia laughed. "Yes, girl! I'm excited to see my boo thang."

"That's more like it! And to think, you acted as if you didn't like him."

"Dang, Lisa! Can a girl play hard to get?" The two of them looked at each other and laughed.

Tasia and Lisa were headed to St. Louis for Tasia's birthday. Seth had bought them both plane tickets to visit him, and Tasia was excited to kick off a new chapter of life with her boo. Her college roommate and sorority sister,

Morgan, would also be in town for her job's convention, and they had planned to meet for dinner during Tasia's visit. Tasia's feet tapped with anticipation as she thought about the details of the weekend ahead.

"*Ladies and gentlemen, welcome to St. Louis. The time is now 5 pm. It is a crisp 35-degree day here in The Gateway to the Midwest, so make sure you are dressed warmly. Please remain in your seat with your seatbelt fastened. We will be landing shortly....*" The pilot's announcement faded out. Tasia pulled out her hand mirror to freshen up her makeup in preparation to see Seth. Giddiness rose in her as they walked off the plane and grabbed their suitcases. She could barely contain her excitement. Before she left Atlanta, she had decided to give Seth every inch of her body, and she began to fantasize about the number of orgasms he was going to give her.

"He should be pulling up in about ten minutes. Let's head to the front!" Lisa reported, breaking Tasia's daydream. They walked to the exit doors to wait for Seth, and the cold breeze from the October weather welcomed them to St. Louis.

It was Halloween weekend, and many people were dressed in costumes and spooky attire. Tasia chuckled as she watched a man dressed as Winnie the Pooh wave at all the children who passed by. After about five minutes, Seth called Tasia to let her know he had arrived.

"Here we come, bae. What are you driving?" She cooed.

"I'm in a blue Benz," Seth replied smoothly.

"Oh, okay," Tasia couldn't deny she was slightly impressed. "Honk your horn. We don't see you."

Lisa and Tasia heard rapid beeps nearby and noticed a blue, tiny, two-door hatchback Mercedes Benz. It was certainly different from what Tasia expected, mainly because Seth was so tall. It made her think of Shaquille O'Neal driving a Volkswagen Beetle, and she chuckled at the thought. Seth got out of the car and grabbed their bags. Lisa greeted him and climbed into the back seat as Seth and Tasia embraced each other.

"You cannot park there! Drive through lane only! Please get back into your vehicle!" The airport security yelled. Tasia and Seth quickly got into the car as other drivers blared their horns.

"Thank you for picking us up," Tasia said once they were all in the car.

"No problem, bae." Seth flashed Tasia a gorgeous smile. Suddenly, Lisa popped between them and rested her elbows on the compartment between the front seats.

"Now, why is your big ass in this small ass car?" Lisa shouted.

"Lisa, sit back!" Tasia laughed. She knew it wouldn't be long before Lisa said what was really on her mind.

Seth chuckled but didn't seem embarrassed at all. "You see, this small ass car is a sportscar." He switched gears, ramped up the engine, and sped onto the highway, going over 100 mph.

"*SLOW DOWN! SLOW DOWN!*" Lisa and Tasia shouted. They were both exhilarated yet scared for their lives.

"Are y'all scared?" Seth was amused. "I don't want to hear nothing else about my small ass car because this little motherfucker got some power."

"I'm sorry! I'm sorry! Slow this thing down, please." Lisa laughed. "I ain't mean to underestimate your little go-cart!"

Seth laughed and shook his head at her. "What do y'all wanna do tonight? Grab food, go to a bar, chill, sleep? Tell me what y'all have in mind."

Lisa and Tasia looked at each other and agreed, "Grab food!"

"We can start the fun tomorrow." Tasia was excited to be in St. Louis but wanted to rest before her birthday festivities.

"Cool. Cool. While y'all eat, I have to help out at the store before closing. When I'm done, I'll meet back up with y'all."

Seth got off on the downtown exit, then pulled into a beautiful, gated condominium community. He punched in his code at the gate, drove into the parking deck, and parked in his assigned parking spot near the front entrance. He grabbed their bags and led them through his building's door to a large glass elevator. When they got to the highest floor, the 15th floor, Tasia and Lisa followed him down the hallway. Seth had one of the largest condos, so his door was at the end of the hall. They were pleasantly surprised he opened his door to reveal his lavish domain.

"*Welcome home, ladies!*" Seth shouted. He showed them where to find their rooms in his over 2,000 sq. ft. condo. There were three bedrooms, two bathrooms, and a patio with a sky-scrape view. It was the epitome of a bachelor's pad, with leather and suede furniture, 72-inch flat-screen TVs, and sports paraphernalia on every wall. He had a beautiful leather and wood buffet in the living room that showcased hookah, top-shelf liquor, and labeled jars of weed.

After taking Lisa to her room with her luggage, he took Tasia by the hand to his bedroom, where she would stay. Seth's room was just as masculine as the rest of the house. He had a huge California king bed with a black and white leather headboard framed with LED lights that glowed light blue. He had a black, suede comforter coupled with black and white leather decorative pillows and shams. In the corner was a matching black and white leather sofa, and against a wall, a matching dresser with a large mirror. On the walls were pictures of popular retro Air Jordans. The large, green bamboo tree in the corner added just the right balance to his room. One wall of his bedroom was completely glass, and he had hung up suede black-out curtains for privacy. In the middle were French doors that led to the patio. The view was breathtaking; you could see the St. Louis Arch from his bedroom door. Tasia looked around and was impressed with his taste. Seth's room also had a large walk-in closet and bathroom with a glass shower, his and her sinks, and a nice-sized jacuzzi.

"Get comfortable. Make yourself at home." Seth said as he sat down her bags and wrapped his arms around her. "Imma have some food delivered to you, ladies. I'll be back shortly." He kissed Tasia on the forehead, flashed her a seductive smile, and walked out the door.

After ensuring the coast was clear, Tasia locked his bedroom door and began her detective work. She scaled the entire room for hidden cameras or female items. Tasia searched under his bed, in the dresser drawers, and on his nightstand. Next, she probed his bathroom, looking through the medicine cabinet, under the sink, and in the shower. Finally, Tasia searched his closet. After her search was complete, she took a deep breath and plopped down on his bed. Relieved that she found nothing alarming, she let her guard down and basked in the moment.

A few weeks ago, she was in a funk about her inadequate love life. Now she was lying in the bed of a man who flew her and her cousin out for her birthday weekend. "Thank you, God." She whispered before going into the bathroom to freshen up.

Seth had Italian food delivered, so Tasia and Lisa met in the living room for dinner. While stuffing their faces, Tasia got a text message from Seth. The store had received an early shipment of inventory, so he would be working late. Tasia was no stranger to hard work, so she didn't mind. "All good, boo." She texted back. "I'll see you later."

After they ate, Tasia and Lisa flipped through the TV apps, movies, and shows until they found a good movie. They laughed, helped themselves to some drinks, and talked until around eleven that evening.

"Honey, I am sleepy!" Lisa yawned. "Tell your man I tried to stay up for him, but auntie is tired!"

"Girl, you swear you're fifty," Tasia laughed. "But I'm with you. I'm about to go to sleep on him too."

"Yea, yea. I bet you are!" Lisa laughed. "Girl, you know you're about to stay up for your boo."

Tasia rolled her eyes. "Goodnight, heffa. And mind your business!" She said with a smirk.

"Oowee, yes, ma'am!" Lisa laughed as she sashayed to her room, snapping her fingers.

Tasia turned off the TV and living room lamps, then

headed to Seth's room. She pulled out her suitcase and found the perfect attire for their nightcap. Tasia unzipped the protective bag of her soft pink, lace Coco de Mer bralette and panty set with its matching, long see-through robe and laid them on the bed. After taking a long hot shower, she unscrewed her Coco Mademoiselle Chanel body oil and carefully massaged it into her skin. Once she was done, she slid into her lingerie and curled up on the bed with her phone. *Ping!* It was a message from Seth.

"Can I taste you tonight?"

"Damn right!" Tasia said out loud without responding to his text message. She would make him wait to ask her face-to-face. Tasia smiled and tucked her phone away. A few moments later, she heard the front door open and immediately positioned herself to appear asleep. Seth entered the room quietly and began lighting cream-colored candles in different areas. The smell of the amber and musk candles quickly filled the room. After hearing the bathroom door close, Tasia peeped at the room and took a deep breath. The glow from the candles gave the room a sensual ambiance, and there was no doubt Seth was trying to set the mood. Tasia's insides squirmed with anticipation. She was finally about to get what she desperately needed and planned to enjoy every second.

Seth stepped out of the bathroom, slipped on a pair of boxers from his top drawer, and rubbed lotion over his body. He stared at Tasia's silhouette, noticed her sexy lingerie, and smiled before sliding into the bed beside her. "Are you asleep?" he whispered as he gently kissed her neck and rubbed her waist. Tasia moved slightly, still pretending to be asleep. She was hot and ready but wanted to make him wait a little. He kissed her neck again, adding the slightest tongue movement. "Wake up, sleepy head." He nudged her softly. Tasia pressed her back against his body and seductively turned to face him.

"Hey, beautiful," Seth replied. Their eyes locked, and Tasia smiled shyly. "I've been thinking about you since I left earlier," Seth whispered as he played with the edge of her robe.

"Really now?" Tasia breathed as she ran her fingers across his jawline and down his neck before resting them on his chest.

"Can I have you?" Seth asked, barely able to keep himself together. As soon as Tasia nodded yes, he took her in his arms and kissed her lips deeply and slowly. He trailed kisses from her lips to her breast as he slowly removed her robe. Seth inhaled the light jasmine scent of Tasia's body oil and exhaled slowly. The warmth of his breath turned her on, and her body begged his lips to explore more of her. As if he could hear her thoughts, he gently unsnapped her bralette with one hand as his other hand caressed Tasia's exposed breast. Tasia moaned with delight, permitting him to go further. His lips replaced his hands on her breast, and he moved his tongue in circles around her nipple before taking it entirely in his mouth.

Wanting more access to her body, Seth repositioned her on her back and put a small pillow behind her head. He put his body between her legs and hovered over her, taking in the full view of her body. Tasia looked him in his eyes briefly before checking out the sight in front of her. Seth's body was chiseled, and the tattoos on his chest

44

turned her on even more. Seth reached down to kiss her, then kissed every part of her body. He trailed his tongue along the line of her panties against her stomach. She thought he would remove them, but he kissed her through her panties instead, which drove her crazy. Seth could taste her wetness through her lace panties and relieved her by moving them to the side.

"Can I taste you?" He asked, intentionally breathing on her sensitive, exposed body parts.

At this point, the waiting game was over, and Tasia couldn't take the teasing anymore. "Baby, please," she purred as she seductively bit her bottom lip.

Seth opened her legs as wide as they would go, slid his arms under her hips, pulled her close, and dived in tongue first. It took everything for Tasia not to scream with ectasy. She moaned and grinded against his face as his tongue explored every part of her. He twirled his tongue in circles, watching Tasia's body's response until he found her spot. After making his discovery, he stroked her with his tongue diligently until her body shook with pleasure. Finally, he came up for air, and Tasia was turned on by the sight of his face dripping with her juices. She leaned forward, wrapped her hands around his face, and pulled him close. They tongue kissed as Seth slid his fingers inside of her.

"Do you like this?" Seth asked seductively, not looking for a response. Her moans told him everything he needed to know. Seth removed his fingers from inside her and put them in his mouth as he reached into his nightstand for a condom. He dropped his boxers, stroked himself, and put on the condom. Tasia could see his size in the dim candlelight and couldn't wait to have him inside her. As if he could read her mind, he pushed her back on the bed, quickly grabbed her legs, and pulled her to the edge of the bed. "Are you ready for me?" He asked, teasing her by letting his body dangle between her legs as he hovered over her. He reached down and gave her a passionate kiss as she nodded yes. Then, he slowly guided himself inside her and let out a deep moan.

"Damn." He whispered. Tasia was tight, and he could feel her wetness through the condom. He was careful to pace himself. Once all of him was inside of her, he stroked her at a medium pace.

Tasia moaned continuously, and Seth took that as permission to quicken his pace. "Damn, baby, you're so tight!" He panted breathlessly. Careful not to enjoy himself too much and ignore her needs, he licked his thumb, placed it gently against her clitoris, and massaged her rapidly. Tasia was pleasantly overwhelmed by how good it felt and orgasmed while he was still inside of her.

The feeling of Tasia's insides throbbing drove Seth insane, but he wasn't ready for their dance to end. He quickly repositioned her legs, wrapped tightly around his waist, into a spread eagle position. Then, holding both her legs down as far as they would go, Seth thrust faster. When Tasia thought she couldn't take another thrust without exploding, he stopped, dropped to his knees, and lapped all her juices. As Tasia began to shudder with delight, he told her to turn around. Out of breath, Tasia flashed him a devilish grin – *doggy style was her favorite position.*

Tasia turned around seductively, arched her back, and looked back at Seth, beckoning him to have his way with her. Seth stared at the sight of her body open and ready for him. Then, he flashed a smile right back. "You gone spread them cheeks for me?" He asked. Tasia didn't reply, but she followed his instructions. He rewarded her by tongue kissing her clitoris before slowly inserting himself in her. Seth licked his thumb again, but this time, he used his wet finger to massage her other sweet spot. That turned Tasia on even more. She braced herself on the bed and bounced back on him. He held on to her waist to keep control and guide her.

"Oh, you like this, huh?" Seth grunted through his teeth. Tasia moaned back, barely able to respond. She felt him grow longer and harder inside her and knew he was close to his release. So she thrust her hips even harder and kept her back perfectly arched, so he felt every part of her tightness around him. Suddenly, Seth let out a loud moan, stumbled backward to get out of her, and then collapsed on the bed beside her.

Tasia lay flat on the bed and turned to face him. Satisfied, sticky, and sweaty, they looked at one another and laughed. Seth softly kissed her on her lips as he went to the bathroom. He returned with a warm washcloth and gently cleansed her, wiping away all the remaining juices. They lay beside each other in silence for a few moments before going back at it for round two. That night, Tasia knew Seth's neighbors knew both of their names. They went to sleep happy and exhausted.

The next morning, Tasia was awakened by the sensation of Seth kissing her inner thighs. Her moans filled the room as Seth found his way to her clitoris and began to swirl his tongue around it in different patterns.

She rotated her hips to match his rhythm until he made her cum.

"You are something else," Seth whispered as he kissed her. "We are going to have a lot of fun. Get up and get ready. We're about to hit the town."

Tasia blushed and kissed him back. "Let the celebrations begin," she said with a smile.

Seth threw on some loungewear and left the room to give Tasia space to get ready. She returned a few missed calls, then giddily jumped up to prepare for the day. Tasia was full of bliss, and it felt good. It had been a long time since someone had made her feel so special. She was falling in love, and she knew it. Reluctantly snapping out of her daydream, she replied to Morgan's birthday text. She couldn't wait to meet her soror at a lounge later that night. But for now, she would enjoy every second with her man. She made Seth's bed, showered, styled her hair, and put on some makeup. For today's festivities, she wore skin-tight blue jeans, a silk button-down blouse, blue thigh-high boots, and a faux fur jacket. She paired her outfit with silver accessories and a multi-colored Valentino clutch. Once dressed, she headed to the living room to join Lisa and Seth.

"*Happy birthday to you! Happy birthday to you! Happy birthday, Anastasia! Happy birthday to you!*" Lisa and Seth sang loudly as she entered the living room. Lisa held a birthday cake, and Seth grinned from ear to ear next to the kitchen countertop, garnished with a bouquet of white roses and balloons.

"Happy birthday, cousin! Make a wish and blow out your candles!" Lisa beamed. Tasia did just that.

"I wish I could have this feeling forever and that Seth is the one for me," she whispered as she blew out the candles. Seth and Lisa smiled at her as she blushed. "Thank you guys so much," Tasia said lightly. She was so overwhelmed by their love and celebration of her.

"Have a seat, bae. I've got something for you." Seth reached behind the counter and revealed a large white and gold gift bag with the words "Happy Birthday!" scripted across it. Tasia lit up like a little kid at Christmas. She hurried to sit on the sofa and smiled anxiously.

"Wait, wait, wait!" Lisa laughed. "Seth, I'm pretty sure your gift will top mine. You know you're rich and all. So, I'm going to give Tasia my gift first!" Tasia laughed. Lisa handed her a light blue box with a white ribbon wrapped tightly around it. Tasia removed the bow, and inside the box were a Tiffany's necklace and watch.

"Lisa, let me find out you got moneeyyyy!" They all laughed. "Thank you, Lisa. Thank you so much." Tasia said sincerely with tears in her eyes.

"Okay, is it my turn now?" Seth joked.

"Go ahead, Big Money Seth!" Lisa teased.

Tasia opened the gift bag from Seth and was at a loss for words. Inside was a Gucci tote bag, Dior perfume, diamond earrings with a matching bracelet, and a luxury black and white lingerie set. Tasia stood up and hugged him. "Seth...I love all of it. Thank you." She whispered as she hugged him tightly.

He hugged her back just as tight, looked at her, and smiled as he kissed her lips. "It's my pleasure, bae." He could tell that she and Lisa had some talking to do, so he retreated to his bedroom to get dressed and let them have their girl time. The minute his door closed, Lisa plopped beside Tasia on the sofa and began probing. "Soooo?" Lisa asked with her eyes stretched with excitement.

"What?" Tasia pretended she didn't know what Lisa meant.

"Girl quit playing with me! Spill it! Did y'all do the do or no?"

"A lady never tells."

"Bitch, please!" The two of them broke into loud laughter.

"Girrllll did we!" Tasia spilled, unable to hold in the details. "Baby, he licked me from the roota to the toota! And that dick game? Honeyyy!"

"What?! Not Seth! Girl, I'm shocked!" Lisa laughed.

"Shiddd! Me too!" Tasia laughed. "Lisa, he's everything I ever dreamed of in a man. Seth is going to be my husband one day. Look at how hard he is going; we're not even an official couple yet. I just know he's the one."

"Cuzzo, you deserve every bit of this. I'm so happy for you!" Lisa squealed.

"Alright, ladies! Let's hit the city!" Seth shouted as he walked out of his room into the living room. "We're going to this fly brunch spot. I know the owner, so we're going to have a good time."

Lisa and Tasia jumped up, grabbed their coats, and headed out of Seth's condo, excited about the adventure ahead.

Bruh, *seriously? Who didn't show up today?*" Seth shouted angrily into his cell phone. "We just talked about this in the meeting! How packed are we?" Tasia and Lisa glanced nervously at each other as Seth yelled furiously at the person on the other end of the call. "Well, you already know what I got going on today," he shouted. "Damn! Okay!" Seth ended the call and hit the steering wheel with frustration.

"Everything okay?" Tasia asked nervously. She had never seen Seth react so aggressively.

"Naw, T. It's not! We are short-staffed, and the store is packed with customers." He explained. "I'm sorry, bae, but I have to go in."

Tasia rubbed his hand that was on the console. "It's okay, bae. I understand you have to run your business."

"No. This isn't right. I had everything planned for us. Now, this." Seth fumed. Tasia remained silent. She was disappointed that their plans had been interrupted but understood that business could be unpredictable. She glanced at Lisa and smiled weakly.

"It'll be okay." Lisa mouthed back at her. Tasia nodded in response.

They pulled up to the two-story restaurant on the Southside of St. Louis, and the scenery was refreshing, very different from most of the buildings in the area. The landscaping was filled with lush, leafy green plants that complimented the dark tan color of the building. There were a few tables outside, and soulful music filled the air. At the valet booth were two handsome, chocolate men dressed in tan suits. The restaurant had a festive yet sophisticated feel that Tasia loved.

"What up, Sam! I'm just running in and out." Seth called out to one of the valet men.

"No problem, boss man. I'll watch the whip while you're inside." Sam replied as he took Seth's keys and opened Tasia's door.

A line of people was wrapping around the building, but Tasia and Lisa followed Seth to the front door. Seth greeted the security who warmly welcomed them into the restaurant. The ambiance was beautiful. It was filled with white and silver tables and booths. The restaurant had a flower wall for social media pictures, a DJ booth, two bars, and an upstairs VIP area. Seth saw one of the servers he knew and asked for Dre. The waitress went to search for him. Within minutes, the owner, Dre, came to the front and greeted Seth with open arms. Dre was an appealing older black man dressed in a tailored charcoal gray suit.

"Dre, this is my girl, Anastasia, and my sis, Lisa." Seth introduced them. "It's Tasia's birthday, but it's mad busy at the store. Can you show them a good time for me? I'll take care of the bill."

"Your money isn't good here." Dre waved Seth's hand away. "Don't worry. I'll take good care of your ladies."

"Man, I owe you one," Seth said as he handed Tasia his house keys and leaned over to kiss her. "See you later, birthday girl."

"Later," Tasia replied sadly. Dre instructed the waitress to escort Tasia and Lisa upstairs, which was less noisy and more intimate. The waitress sat them at a booth and gave them menus. For a moment, they sat in silence. Lisa could see the disappointment on her cousin's face and didn't want to say anything to make the situation worse.

"Where's your head?" Lisa asked cautiously. Tasia shrugged her shoulders. "It's your birthday, baby girl. Don't let this hiccup ruin it. His efforts count for something. I'm sure he would've stayed if the store wasn't packed."

"Yea, that's true," Tasia replied nonchalantly. "I wish he would have put his foot down. He's a businessman, so dating him won't be easy. But, I'm willing to make it work."

"Is he willing to make it work?" Lisa asked.

"I guess," Tasia replied with very little confidence.

"So what are y'all?" Lisa quizzed. "Are y'all a couple? Have you discussed children? Does he want something long-term? What about marriage? Wassup with y'all?"

"Damn, Lisa! Are you the Feds?" Tasia suddenly became annoyed with her questions. "I honestly don't know. I'm just going with the flow, following his lead since he's the man. We haven't made it official just yet, but

I know it's coming."

"Imma need you to get it together and ask him his real intentions. How can you think he's the one, and y'all haven't had these conversations yet?"

"Do you know something I don't know?" Tasia snapped.

"No. I just want you to be happy. Yes, Seth is my friend, but he is still a man. I want you to be sure before you give your heart completely to him. That's all I'm saying."

Tasia knew Lisa had a point, but it was her special day, so she refused to let anything bother her. She reminded herself that she had been flown out, got some good dick, and received beautiful gifts. She would live in the moment, but after this weekend, she and Seth had much to discuss.

Once the food and liquor were in their system, the mood lightened, and Tasia and Lisa had a great time. They caught up on life, discussed Tasia's plans for year 26, and laughed until their sides hurt. When they were ready, Seth sent an Uber to transport them back to his home.

"What you got up for the rest of the day?" Lisa asked. She and Tasia were lounging around Seth's condo, smoking hookah and watching TV in between naps.

"I'm going to catch up with Morgan at this nice spot downtown. You trying to come with?"

"Nah. You've spent the whole day with me. Go catch up with your soror."

Tasia smiled to herself. She knew Lisa didn't want to hear them gossiping and spilling tea all night.

"Have you heard from Seth? What is he doing tonight? I might kick it with him since you will be out with Morgan."

Tasia shrugged. "I hadn't heard from him since he

called to apologize for the 100th time earlier.

"You don't think he may have something up his sleeve for tonight?"

"Lisa, you know that if he had something planned, he would've hit me up by now."

Lisa agreed and shook her head.

Tasia rolled her eyes. "I guess it's the effort that counts, right?" She said sarcastically as she headed towards the bedroom to prepare for the night.

Tasia could feel herself getting frustrated. She refused to allow anything to put a damper on her birthday weekend, so she connected her phone to Seth's bedroom speaker system and played her favorite jams while she showered and pampered herself. As Tasia finished her makeup, her music was interrupted by a FaceTime call from Seth. She disconnected her phone and propped it up on her travel makeup box.

"What's up, Seth?" She answered dryly, not taking her eyes away from the mirror as she applied blush.

"Baby, I just wanted to say I was sorry again."

"It's all good. I understand you had to take care of business. It's all good." Tasia replied with a fake smile.

"Why are you putting on makeup? You about to step out tonight?"

"Yea, I'm going to a lounge with my soror, Morgan. She's in town on business and wanted to catch up."

"Aw dang. Wish I could have you on my arm tonight. I had dinner plans for us tonight but had to cancel the reservation since I'm working late."

"It's all good. Maybe another time."

Seth licked his lips seductively. "Well, I can't wait to

see you later."

"I'm sure," Tasia replied dully. "But look, I need to get off this phone. Gotta finish getting ready. See you later. She hung up before he could say another word.

Be safe tonight...

Seth texted her.

Be ready for this tongue later =)

He texted again. Tasia tossed her phone aside with annoyance. "The nerve of this nigga! Canceled plans but expecting some ass? Boy, bye!" She said under her breath. She didn't respond to any of his messages and immediately pushed him to the back of her mind. After she finished her makeup, she placed her hair into a messy bun. Then, Tasia slipped into a skintight silk gray dress. It had a low draping neckline that revealed her breast and the top of her flat stomach. The dress also had a high-cut slit that showed off her left thigh. She paired the dress with strappy heels. Elegant rhinestones adorned the entire six-inch heels. She wore a dainty silver necklace along with the new earrings and bracelet Seth had given her. Just as she sprayed her Chanel Chance perfume, she got a text message from Morgan, letting her know she was outside. Tasia grabbed her black trench coat and Louis Vuitton clutch and headed toward the front door. She looked herself over once more in the living room mirror, and she loved what she saw. Tasia was flawless.

"Morgaannnnn!" Tasia screamed as she threw her arms around her dear friend.

"Tasiaaaa!" Morgan replied, hugging her just as tightly. They were screaming and giddy like two schoolgirls. It had been so long since they saw each other, and Tasia couldn't wait to catch up. Morgan and Tasia met during their freshman college year in History 101 and didn't like each other when they first crossed paths. Morgan was a goody two shoes and volunteered to give her opinion every chance she got. Tasia thought she was a snob and wanted nothing to do with her. During their sophomore year, they both made the line to pledge the same sorority. While they were on line, their bond grew. Tasia realized that their differences made them better as friends than enemies. By the time they crossed the burning sands, Morgan and Tasia were inseparable. Junior year, they moved in together. When Tasia's mother died, Morgan never left her side. She helped Tasia get through some of her most challenging days. After the funeral, Tasia went into a deep depression and stayed in her room for almost three weeks. Day after day, Tasia sat in her pitch-black room, either sleeping or crying. She barely ate, bathed, or talked. At first, Morgan allowed her solitude. She checked on her periodically throughout the day to encourage her to eat or give her a shoulder to cry on. When Tasia did want to talk, Morgan listened as she expressed her hurt and grief. By day eighteen, Morgan couldn't take seeing her friend in that condition another day. She forced Tasia to leave the house and get back into a regular routine in society. Tasia always remembered what Morgan had done for her. Whatever ups and downs they may have, Morgan

will always and forever have a place in her heart.

"We have so much catching up to do, Tasia! First of all, you look amazing, darling!" Morgan said in her best snooty girl voice. The two of them laughed as Tasia pretended to model. "Did your man approve of this get-up?"

Tasia let out a big sigh. "Umm, about that."

"T, what did you do?" Morgan knew Tasia could be a hothead if pushed too far. So she was nervous to hear what had happened.

Tasia sucked her teeth while Morgan pulled off to head toward the lounge. "I didn't do anything except be myself and try to be open to new things. But, yet, here we are."

"So, what's the problem?"

"I don't want to sound unappreciative. But we haven't spent any time together. And we've done none of the things Seth claimed he had planned for my birthday." Tasia said with air quotes. "I'm grateful for the flight, the gifts, and all that. But where's the quality time? Do you know what I mean?"

Morgan understood Tasia's frustration. "I feel you, T! You want time with him, and you're not seeing any genuine effort."

"Bingo!" Tasia shouted.

"So, what's been his excuse?" Morgan asked.

Tasia filled her in on all the time conflicts with Seth's job. Morgan saw exactly why Tasia was concerned. They both wondered why he couldn't put his foot down as the owner.

"Well, we leave Monday morning. I don't know what will transpire within the next day or so, but for now, forget him. Fate put us in the same city at the same time, so we're going to have a damn good time!" Tasia shouted as she put her hands in the air and did a little twerk.

"*Yaaassss, Bitch! I know that's right!*" Morgan squealed and did a dance of her own. "My friend reviewed the lounge and told me the ambiance was to die for." *Classic Morgan.* Tasia thought to herself. Of course, Morgan had already gotten the scoop on the lounge. Morgan loved a good time. She was a little bougie, but Tasia loved that Morgan enjoyed the finer things in life. She actually reminded Tasia a lot of her mother. She worked hard for the good life she had and deserved it. Morgan was a beautiful girl and reminded you of a black life-size Barbie. She was built like a model, 5'9 in height, dark complexion, and her sister locs lay perfectly on her shoulders. Morgan wore a black cropped fur vest, an emerald green off-the-shoulder fitted dress that stopped mid-thigh, and over-the-knee black boots. Tasia smiled and admired her friend's beauty as they caught up on the ride to the lounge.

When they pulled up, Tasia took a moment to breathe in the view. It was breathtaking. The glass and steel lounge sat next to a lake. The lights from the lounge lit up the area, giving everything around it an elegant yet warm glow. A long black carpet stretched from the lounge door to the curb, where Morgan pulled up. A team of valets approached the car immediately and opened both doors. Morgan handed the keys to her white BMW X7 to the valet on her side and walked over to Tasia.

The inside of the lounge was just as gorgeous as the outside. It had ceiling-to-floor windows for guests to see the brilliant lake view while unwinding over dinner.

Pristine, tiered, grand waterfall chandeliers hung from the ceilings, and authentic bamboo plants were intentionally placed throughout the lounge. There were several seating options, swanky tables with plush chairs, a bar with tall bar stools that were dark bamboo and had deep brown, soft leather cushions, and there were large circular booths for big parties. In the middle of the lounge was a long, winding, white marble staircase with exquisite dark brown railing. The stairs led to the second floor of the lounge, where there was a DJ booth, a dance floor, and a few more booths for sitting. Soft R&B music played throughout the lounge.

The hostess in the foyer of the lounge confirmed their reservation, took their coats, and then escorted them to their table. Well-dressed gentlemen turned to watch as Tasia and Morgan strutted across the white marble floors. The hostess sat them at a table next to a window wall, handed them each a menu, and informed them a server would come by to take their orders shortly. Beside them was a booth filled with handsome bachelors. They smiled at Tasia and Morgan, and one even lifted a glass in their direction. Tasia and Morgan smiled at each other slyly and smoothly nodded back at the gentlemen before returning to their conversation.

"Morgan, this place is everything." Tasia sighed as they took in their surroundings.

"I know, right? And the view isn't too bad either." Morgan joked, nodding her head in the direction of the booth of bachelors.

Tasia giggled. "Honey, it ain't bad at all!" Tasia and Morgan laughed.

"Alright, T. Don't have Seth looking for me. I'm not trying to get you into any trouble!"

"The real question is, will you get in trouble enjoying this eye candy, I mean, view." Tasia teased.

"What do you mean?" Morgan laughed.

"No, ma'am! Don't even try it! You've gotten all up in my business. It's your turn. Spill it! I want to hear everything."

Tasia was relieved when Morgan began to share everything that was happening in her life. It kept her from thinking or talking about her situation with Seth. Even though she acted as if Seth's actions didn't bother her, she was really concerned. She checked her phone periodically to see if he had sent a new text message for her to read and ignore, but he had not reached out since earlier. She pushed her concerns to the back of her mind and forced herself to enjoy the evening.

The food and drinks were just as impressive as the scenery, a rare occurrence. Morgan and Tasia laughed and reminisced all night over exquisite food and beverages. When they were done with their meal, a few waitresses and hostesses came out with a piece of cake with candles and sang "Happy Birthday" to Tasia. Tasia and Morgan noticed the group of bachelors watching the celebration, and once the servers and hostesses left, two of the bachelors approached their table to introduce themselves. A tall, muscular, light-skinned man dressed in a perfectly tailored navy-blue suit spoke first.

"Good Evening, ladies. May I ask whose birthday it is?" he asked. Tasia smiled bashfully and daintily raised her index finger.

"Happy birthday, beautiful. May I?" He asked, reaching for Tasia's hand. Tasia put her hand in his, and he kissed it lightly. "May this year be your best yet."

"Well, aren't you a flirt?" Tasia teased as she returned her hand to her glass of wine and took a seductive sip.

"Not quite. However, I typically make my intentions known when I like what I see."

"So, you like what you see?" Morgan asked.

"We do." The other bachelor spoke up. He had a deep caramel complexion and wore his locs in a tight bun above the nape of his neck. He was also handsome and wore a hunter-green tailored suit that brought out the hazel color of his eyes. "We were headed upstairs to continue our night and wondered if you ladies would care to join us in our VIP booth. Of course, your drinks and anything else you require are on us."

"Oh, you just get right to the point, don't you?" Morgan laughed softly as she eyed Tasia to see if she was game.

"And it appears you prefer it that way." He quipped back at her. Morgan flashed him a seductive grin. She had always been attracted to bold men who could match wits with her. Their waitress came over with the check, and bachelor #1 pulled out his wallet and handed the waitress a black card.

"We will be taking care of their tickets. They will be joining us in VIP for the rest of the evening." Bachelor #1 replied.

"Very well, Mr. Laflin. Will you and Mr. Turner have your usual?" the waitress inquired.

"Yes, thank you very much." Mr. Laflin said as he turned his direction back to Tasia and Morgan.

"Do you think we are inclined to spend our evening with you because you took care of our check?" Tasia asked.

"Not at all," Mr. Laflin replied. "Consider it a birthday gift from a generous stranger who would love to make your acquaintance if you allowed."

"Do you all have first names, or should we also refer to you both by your surnames?" Morgan asked.

"Where are our manners?" Mr. Turner said. "I am Christian Turner, and this old rascal is my friend and business partner, Taylor Laflin."

"It's a pleasure to meet you both," Tasia said as they shook hands. "I am Anastasia, and this is my soror and dear friend, Morgan."

"Morgan and Anastasia, the pleasure is all ours," Taylor replied. "May we?"

After Morgan and Tasia nodded, both men pulled out their chairs and took them by the hand to escort them upstairs. The other bachelors at the booth had already left and gone upstairs. They were waiting for them in the VIP area when they reached the second floor.

"Gentlemen, this is Anastasia and Morgan. They will be joining us this evening. It is Anastasia's birthday, so let's show her how special she is." Taylor said as he flashed a charming smile in Anastasia's direction.

"To Anastasia!" one of the bachelors shouted as he raised his glass. Another bachelor had approached Tasia and Morgan with flutes of freshly poured champagne.

"*Anastasia!*" Morgan and the other bachelors shouted as they all raised their glasses. Tasia beamed with gratitude and nodded as she took a deep sip.

For the rest of the evening, Morgan and Tasia mingled with the other men and ladies that came up to accompany them as the night progressed. Tasia loved networking and meeting new people and made some really great connections that she couldn't wait to get back to Atlanta and explore. Taylor and Christian had a law firm, Laflin Turner and Associates, and frequented the lounge weekly. The entire group of bachelors was successful professionals with careers in finance, business, and education; a few were in the medical field. The women that joined them were equally successful and shared careers with similar backgrounds. Being around so much black excellence made Tasia smile. She was accustomed to being around the who's whos, and her new acquaintances were impressed with how many associates they shared. Morgan, who was always invigorated from being around other intelligent upper-class individuals, enjoyed herself as well. Throughout the night, she and Tasia found each other and ensured the other was okay. When they weren't talking with each other or mingling with the other individuals, they cozied up with Taylor and Christian.

Tasia was enjoying Taylor so much that Seth didn't cross her mind. They exchanged numbers, and both expressed excitement about getting to know each other more. Taylor invited Tasia to be his guest at a networking brunch hosted by a friend the following day, and Tasia agreed to meet him there if she was available.

It was nearly 1 am when the ladies decided to call it a night. Taylor and Christian escorted Morgan and Tasia to the foyer, made sure they got into their car fine and returned to their friends in VIP. Even though they were tired, Morgan and Tasia chatted the entire ride home about the grand time they had.

"Oh, Tasia. We have to do this again very soon!" Morgan said when they pulled up at Seth's condo.

"We do! It better not be another five hundred years before I see you again." Tasia threw her arms around her friend and gave her a tight hug.

"I love you, T. Enjoy the rest of your birthday!" Morgan said as she hugged Tasia tightly.

"*It's my birthday, biiiiiihhhhh!*" Tasia shouted as she hopped out of the car and twerked on the door.

Morgan joined her and twerked in the driver's seat. "*Ayyee, get it, bih!*" The ladies laughed and said their goodbyes once more. After Tasia entered the condo's front entrance, Morgan waved and drove away.

Five

♡♡♡

Anita Baker and Lisa's voices met Tasia as soon as she opened the door to Seth's condo. Lisa was singing "Sweet Love" to the top of her lungs as she ran a vacuum over the rug. The coffee table had been moved to the side.

"Hey, maid!" Tasia said in her best Joseline Hernandez impression. It was late, so she thought Lisa would be knocked out. She certainly did not expect her to be cleaning Seth's condo.

"Girl, it was so dusty in here. I couldn't help myself. How was your night? You and Morgan have fun?" Lisa asked, barely looking up at Tasia.

"It was cool. We had a good time." Tasia replied shortly. She didn't like the idea of Lisa cleaning her man's space. It felt awkward, but Tasia was careful not to jump to conclusions. She loved her cousin but felt like Lisa was doing the most by cleaning her man's house without consulting her. "So, you decided to be a housekeeper on vacation?"

"Just trying to help the homie out. I mean, Seth did fly us out here and take care of everything. I figured it was the least I could do." Lisa replied, still busy cleaning and humming along to Anita.

"So what did y'all do while I was gone?" Tasia coolly probed.

"Girl, nothing. I ordered a pizza from this spot called Imo's. It was good! Seth came in after I ate. We smoked some hookah, talked for a bit, and then he went to his room and passed out."

"Oh. I'm shocked you're not knocked out. Especially after eating a pizza." Tasia said suspiciously. "What time y'all smoked hookah?"

"Probably around midnight-ish," Lisa replied. "But enough about me! You're the birthday girl. I want to hear everything about your night!"

Making a mental note of Lisa's answers, Tasia told her about the lounge, the connections she made, and how much they enjoyed the evening. Lisa listened as she cleaned.

"Well, you deserved a beautiful night out. I'm so happy you enjoyed your birthday despite everything else," she said as she nodded toward Seth's room.

"Yeah. I am happy too. I'm going to get in bed. I'll see you in the morning, maid." Tasia joked as she turned to head toward Seth's room.

"Night-night!" Lisa replied cheerfully as she continued to clean. Tasia rolled her eyes. She couldn't understand why Lisa felt so comfortable cleaning another woman's man's house. It was a violation of so many female codes. Tasia felt like she should have been cleaning up, but there was no way she would do that for a man she had barely spent time with since her arrival.

Is Lisa trying to slide in on my man? Tasia wondered. *Maybe she's trying to show me up? It's possible that she secretly wants him for herself.* Tasia had never seen or heard of Lisa cleaning anyone's house. Especially not a man she was dealing with. Tasia silenced her thoughts and made another mental note to keep an eye on Seth and Lisa's interactions. Quietly entering Seth's room, Tasia tiptoed across the room to gather her things from her suitcase to get ready for bed.

While showering, she reflected on her day. Outside of Seth's lack of effort, she had actually enjoyed herself. *Why would he invite her to his city and not spend quality time with her? Why didn't he text to check on her throughout the night?* So many questions filled her mind, and eventually, she was turned off by the thought of Seth. She liked him as a person, but if they were going to make it official, Seth would have to put forth more effort. Rather than the lingerie she had planned on wearing for him, she opted for her black leggings and an oversized Atlanta Hawks t-shirt. She tied her hair in a ponytail and slid into bed beside Seth with her back turned.

Feeling her presence beside him, Seth began to move around in his sleep. Tasia laid still and pretended to be asleep. She felt Seth turn towards her and pull her body close to his chest. Tasia didn't move. Spooning her, Seth softly kissed the back of Tasia's neck. She felt her body warming and tingling at his touch, but Tasia remained strong and didn't move a muscle. "Bae, are you sleeping?" Seth asked as he lifted her shirt and planted kisses on her back. Tasia moved away from his kisses and moaned as if she was asleep.

"Bae?" Seth tried to wake her by rubbing her breast. Tasia moved away.

"I'm tired, Seth. Go to sleep." Tasia returned to her side of the bed, nestled herself in the covers, and pretended to be deep in sleep. She was determined to stand her ground and not give in to Seth. Getting the message, Seth kissed her on the cheek and rolled over to his side of the bed.

Rather than rolling over to see Seth, Tasia was greeted by a bouquet of red roses. The curtains had been opened, and the morning sunlight kissed her skin as she stretched and rubbed her eyes.

"Good Morning, sweetheart," Seth grinned as he entered the room.

"Morning, Seth. Thanks for the flowers, babe." Tasia said with a sleepy grin. She was still upset with Seth, but it appeared he was trying to make a step in the right direction. Tasia decided to soften her approach to him and see how he would amend yesterday's mishaps. Seth sat next to her on the bed and kissed her on the cheek.

"Tasia, I'm so sorry for this weekend." Seth's tone was so sincere. He looked deeply into her eyes as he apologized, searching for any sign that Tasia would forgive him. "Nothing went the way I expected. I wanted to spend every minute with you. But, unfortunately, I had no control over this weekend. I hope your heart will forgive me and allow me to make it up to you."

Tasia smiled. She was in awe of his heartfelt apology. "Well, what did you have in mind?"

Seth's face brightened. "Well, the store is closed today. I have a few things planned for us. It'll just be you and me."

"Hmmm. I think I would like that, Mr. Brown." Tasia teased.

"Good." Seth kissed her on the lips. "Get dressed."

Tasia stretched again, hopped out of bed, and pulled out her clothes for the day before jumping in the shower. After showering, she straightened her hair and put on her fitted knit black dress, black ankle boots, and the Gucci purse Seth gave her. Seth matched her and wore black jeans, black Timberland boots, a black sweater, a Gucci belt, a leather jacket, and a Cuban gold link. They looked at themselves in the mirror before leaving Seth's room.

"We look good together," Seth said as he wrapped his arm around her waist.

"We sure do." Tasia agreed.

Lisa had already left for the day. One of their friends from high school was in town, and Lisa went out to eat with him. Tasia sent Lisa a quick text to let her know they were also about to leave the house.

"I have to make one quick stop at the store before our day begins," Seth informed her when they got in the car. "Is that alright with you?"

Tasia sighed playfully. "I guess. Whew, I can't wait to see the place interrupting our time."

Seth laughed. "Well, I can't wait for you to see it. I hope it will be a part of our legacy someday."

Tasia picked up on the hint, but it wasn't enough to make her swoon. They still needed to have a serious conversation, and she would make that happen as soon as she returned to Atlanta.

The shoe store, or boutique as Seth called it, was only ten minutes away from his condo. It was located in a shopping center, and to Tasia's surprise, it was pretty dope. They had chandeliers, suede seats, glass walls, and neon lights that flickered behind the shoe cases. Tasia perused the store and was impressed to see the latest sneakers and sportswear.

"What do you think of the place?" Seth asked, attempting to sound humble.

Tasia laughed, "Seth, you already know what's up! This place is amazing." She walked around in awe. "I'm so proud of you, baby!" Seth grinned from ear to ear. After touring the establishment, Tasia understood why the store was always so busy. It made total sense that their exclusive inventory was in high demand in the city. Tasia knew there weren't any boutiques like Seth's store in St. Louis.

As she walked around the store, Seth disappeared into the back office area and returned with a pair of shoes. "I thought you would like these." He said as he gifted her a pair of Jordan Retro 1s that came out over her birthday weekend.

Tasia squealed, then walked over to one of the suede chairs to try her shoes on. "They fit perfectly!" She said as she stood to look in the mirror.

Seth walked up behind her and kissed her on her neck. "I knew they would. I can't wait to see what kinda fly shit you rock with them."

Looking at him in the mirror, she smiled. "I have a few ideas in mind."

"Well, if I'm not with you, send me plenty of pictures. Deal?"

"Deal." Tasia agreed.

"I know you're probably hungry. Are you ready to get out of here?"

"I'm starving!" Tasia replied dramatically. "Let's go." They got in Seth's car and rode to a brunch spot nearby. It wasn't as fancy as the brunch spot they visited on her birthday, but it was a beautiful quiet restaurant with friendly servers. Tasia's ill feelings toward Seth subsided as they laughed and talked over their meal. He seemed genuinely sorry about the weekend and worked hard to win her back. Tasia knew it was out of his hands and decided to let it go and focus on their future. After brunch, he took her to a shopping mall called Plaza Frontenac that had luxury brand stores. Tasia got items from Saks Fifth Avenue, Macy's, Neiman Marcus, and Louis Vuitton. Tasia was on cloud nine. Quality time with her boo and a mini shopping spree? What more could a girl ask for? "I can get used to this," Tasia whispered as she tried on a new dress.

After shopping, they returned to the car, and Seth loaded Tasia's bags in the back seat. "Enjoying yourself?" Seth asked once he got settled in the driver's seat.

"I am. Thank you for everything."

"The only thanks I need is that smile on your face. I want it to be permanent."

"Really now?" Tasia asked.

"Yes. I really want what we have going on to work. I can see a future with you. This is just the beginning. I want to spoil you, take good care of you, and give you everything you deserve."

Tasia leaned over and kissed him on the cheek. "I want those things too. I want all of that with you. I was hoping we could talk more about that soon."

Seth looked over at her and licked his lips. "Babe, I'm hungry again."

"Damn, big boy." Tasia joked. "We just ate not too long ago."

"I'm hungry for you, T."

"Is that right?"

"Damn right. Let's go back to the crib."

"What are you waiting for?" Tasia seductively rubbed Seth's knee and gently separated her thighs without taking her eyes off him. Seth bit his bottom lip and moaned under his breath. He accepted her invitation by pulling up her dress and sliding her panties to the side with his fingers. By the time they made it to Seth's condo, Tasia was ready to be devoured. They barely made it into Seth's bedroom before they started peeling each other's clothes off. Seth and Tasia made love to each other's bodies until they were exhausted and fell asleep entangled with each other.

Later that evening, Tasia was awakened by TV noises and figured Lisa was back. She threw on a shirt from Seth's drawer and headed to check on Lisa.

"Good Morning, sleepy head." Lisa joked. Tasia's hair was disheveled, so Lisa knew she had been playing around with Seth, sleeping, or both.

"Good morning! "Tasia grinned back.

"Girl, you know it's almost 6:30 pm?"

"What? For real? I had no idea it was that late."

"Yes, the day is almost over."

"Aww dang. And we got an early flight in the morning."

"Shoot, I didn't think about that. We should probably pack our things now and chill for the rest of the day."

"That's a good idea. Because someone isn't much of an early riser." Tasia teased Lisa. Lisa was notorious for going to bed early and sleeping in late.

"Aww, shut up!" The girls laughed before retreating to pack their things and lay out their clothes for the following day.

"Leaving me already?" A half-sleep Seth asked.

"Not quite. I'm preparing for our early morning flight." Tasia explained as she gathered her things and reorganized her suitcase.

"I'm sorry I slept the day away, babe. Did you have a good time?"

"It's okay. I figured you were tired. I enjoyed every second of our day." Tasia replied with a wink.

"Mmm...I did too." Seth replied as he licked his lips. "Thank you for being so understanding. Sundays are my only off days. I would have slept the day away if you weren't here."

"I understand, baby. Thank you for making an exception for me. I hope you will go into your work week well-rested."

"Not hardly! You put that work in on me earlier. A nigga is beat!"

Tasia laughed. "Hey, you wore me out too. I'm gonna sleep for a few days when I get back to Atlanta."

Once Tasia's bag was packed, she and Seth showered and went into the living room to catch up with Lisa. The three of them ordered dinner and enjoyed the rest of the evening in the condo. They watched movies, talked about their goals and plans for the remainder of the year, and Tasia laughed as Lisa and Seth teased each other about things that happened in high school.

After an evening well spent, Lisa headed to bed early, and Tasia and Seth followed suit. Seth and Tasia indulged in pillow talk about how much they would miss each other before going in for another rendezvous and falling asleep.

Monday morning, the ladies were up and ready to head back home. While Seth was taking their bags to the car, Tasia left a note on his bed that read, "To my man. Thank you for this weekend. Thanks for the gifts, hospitality, and, most of all…that dick, lol. Hope to see you soon, baby. Sincerely, Anastasia."

After everything was in the car, they headed toward the airport but got stuck in traffic. Tasia got antsy and was certain they would miss their flight. She hated waiting in the airport. Seth could see Tasia's anxiety rising and pulled out a bag of gummy bears from the center console.

"Ya'll want some edibles? Might help calm your nerves before the flight." He asked, dangling the bag from his hand. Without hesitation, Lisa grabbed a handful and ate three back-to-back. Tasia, on the other hand, was on the fence. She smoked weed occasionally but never indulged in edibles because she never knew how high she would get.

"Babe, it will be fine," Seth said as he handed Tasia the bag. Tasia grabbed three and ate them back to back, just as Lisa had done.

"I don't feel anything," Tasia said after a few minutes.

Seth laughed. "Don't worry. You will." They arrived at the airport with less than twenty minutes to spare. Seth and Tasia quickly said their goodbyes, and the ladies sped off to check their bags and get through TSA. After clearing the security check, they high-tailed it to their terminal, only to learn they still missed their flight. Fortunately, the next flight headed to Atlanta was leaving out in thirty minutes. Tasia was relieved they wouldn't have a long wait.

While waiting to board, Tasia felt the edibles kick in. Suddenly she was no longer at the airport but on a galaxy far from Planet Earth. Lisa, who had also begun to feel the effects of the edibles, was next to her, floating in midair. The two of them looked at each other and laughed.

"Bitch, I'm high." Tasia giggled as sweat beads formed on her forehead.

"We are now boarding Flight 1098 to Atlanta. If you are on standby, please approach the desk for your seat assignments." The airline announced over the speaker.

"Bitch, that's us. Let's go!" Lisa said, pulling Tasia by the hand. Since they missed their original flight, they could not sit together. They were rows apart. Tasia was stuck in a middle seat between an overweight white lady and a talkative older black man wearing a leather jacket.

Tasia began to sweat profusely before the plane took off. She took off her coat and fanned herself, but still could not cool off. Once the plane took off, the cooling system was fully powered, allowing the fan to release colder air. It helped a little, but not much. Tasia laid back and tried to sleep off the high, but it was still too hot to get comfortable. She asked the flight attendant for ice and water throughout the entire flight. The lady beside her asked if she was okay, and Tasia could only nod. The lady and the man in the leather jacket picked up that Tasia didn't want to be bothered, so they continued their conversation. Between their conversation, his leather jacket, and the lady's warm body, Tasia was getting hotter and more irritable by the second. She wanted to scream and yell for them to shut up, but she knew that wouldn't turn out well. So instead of yelling, she sat there miserably and gazed out the window.

"Ladies and gentlemen, welcome to Atlanta, Georgia," the pilot announced over the speaker.

Tasia exhaled deeply with relief. She was so happy she wore an all-black jumpsuit because her clothes were damp from sweating the entire flight. After getting off the plane, Tasia waited for Lisa. They burst into laughter when they saw each other.

"Girl, you look baaaad. What did they do to you up there?" Lisa laughed.

"Biiitch. I was stuck between Rosie O'Donnell and Shaft and they had plenty to discuss. I thought I had died and gone to hell I was so damn hot." Tasia said angrily. Lisa laughed so hard that Tasia couldn't help but crack up too. They laughed until tears rolled down their faces. They didn't even notice the people behind them trying to get around them.

"Tasia, let's get the hell out of these folks' way."

"Oh shit. My bad y'all." Tasia said to the group. Some of them smiled and went on their way. Others rolled their eyes and shook their heads at Lisa and Tasia.

The ladies took each other by the arm and collected their bags. "Lisa, I don't wanna be high no more. When is this shit gonna end?" Tasia asked.

"Hell, we ate three of them. Probably tomorrow."

"Tomorrow? That ain't gonna work. I got shit to do!"

"Well, you better drink some Pedialyte or something."

"Bet. I'll try that."

"Tasia, just go home and take a nap. You will be fine." Lisa laughed.

"This is exactly why I don't fuck with edibles."

Tasia caught an Uber home and was delighted when the driver drove into her neighborhood. She couldn't wait to take a cool shower and lay across her bed naked. As soon as Tasia opened her door, her cell phone rang. At first, she planned to ignore it until she got settled. Then, she thought it could be Seth checking on her. She smiled until she saw another familiar number flashing across her screen.

"Hello?" Tasia answered.

"Hi, may I speak with Anastasia Ingram?" a lady on the other end requested.

"Speaking. Who is this?" Tasia asked nervously.

"Good afternoon, Anastasia. This is Rebecca with Garden Manor Nursing Home, calling on behalf of your father. Do you have time to talk?" Anastasia took a seat on her couch and prepared herself for the worse.

Six

♡♡♡

ello? Ms. Ingram? Are you there?" Rebecca asked.

"I'm here." That was all Tasia could manage to say. She didn't know what Rebecca would tell her, but she braced herself for the worst.

"Ms. Ingram, we want to discuss your father's health. How soon can we schedule a meeting with you?" Rebecca inquired. Tasia already knew her father's health was declining; she thought this was the call she had feared receiving since the day she put him in the facility. She took a sigh of relief because her dad was still alive.

"What's wrong with his health now?" Tasia inquired. "Was he diagnosed with something new?"

"It is best that you discuss his health with Dr. Billups. He can better answer your questions and will be able to advise you on the best plan of action for your father." Rebecca replied kindly.

"Very well. I can come in tomorrow. What time slots do you have available?"

"Would 1 pm work for you?"

"Yes, that's fine."

"Thank you. We will see you tomorrow, Ms. Ingram. Have a good day."

"Good day, Rebecca."

Just like that, Tasia's high was blown. She dragged her bags into her bedroom, took a hot shower, put on pajamas, and lay in bed. Speaking with Rebecca put her in a somber mood for the rest of the day. Anxiety filled her body as she anticipated the bad news headed her way the following day. The worse part was even though she knew her father wasn't getting any better, she still didn't feel an ounce of remorse for him. She searched her childhood memories for one good memory with her father, something that would make her love him enough to feel sad, but she came up empty. That hurt her more than the thought of losing him. Tasia knew those who grew up without their father would probably think she was ungrateful. She didn't care. In fact, Tasia felt like her life would have been better without her father. Sure, he provided for the household, but he traumatized Tasia her entire life. He abused her emotionally, physically, and mentally and didn't seem to care. It was so bad that Tasia once thought about killing him. The only thing that stopped her was her fear of serving jail time and leaving her mother and brother behind. If there were a slight chance she could have gotten away with murdering him, she would have done so without hesitation. Even at a young age, she knew she didn't have a chance as a black girl in America. The judge would have thrown the book at her. Most people could never understand how children killed their parents without regret. Not Tasia. She understood their pain. Her hate for her father ran just as deep. Reminiscing on her childhood made her think of her mother and all the good times they shared. Tasia loved her mother dearly. She yearned for her mother's love, laughter, smile, wisdom, and patience.

Tasia spent the rest of the night crying. She wept until her throat was dry and her eyes became sore. The next morning was dreadful. She woke up with puffy red eyes and was in a bad mood. Her mind raced a mile a minute, nervous about the news she would get from the doctor about her father. She wasn't in the mental space to assemble another funeral, especially not alone, but she had to face reality. Her father was dying and would be leaving the earth sooner than she could imagine. Though Tasia dreaded visiting the nursing home, she knew she couldn't avoid it. So she threw on a pair of black jeans, a black Nike hoodie, and her black Retro 11s. She wore all black because, in her mind, Doomsday had arrived. She pulled her hair into a ponytail, put on her black Gucci shades, jumped in her Jeep, and headed toward the nursing home.

Garden Manor was the epitome of peace and tranquility. Passing it, you wouldn't even know it was a nursing home. The owners of the private facility intentionally made sure Garden Manor looked and felt like home. The manor's community stretched over nearly 10 acres of land. Every building of the facility was designed like a ranch and was built around a stunning lake. There was an assisted living community on the property called

Garden Homes. It was designed for elderly people who could still do most things independently. From the main parking lot, Tasia could see many walking around the lake, having picnics on the grass, or simply conversing with others in their community. Individuals with more severe cases were housed in the Thompson building, an area with an around-the-clock nursing staff. That's where her father was. Though it operated like a typical nursing home, you couldn't tell when you first walked in. Though the environment was sterile and smelled similar to a hospital, the design and interior were decorated like a ranch. It had wooden fixtures and welcoming, comfortable furniture. Every patient had their own room that included a living area with sofas, a small dinner table, a TV, and an extra bed for family members and guests who came to visit. Though she dreaded her visits there, she appreciated the facility's charm. It was the perfect place to take rest from the world. It was too perfect for her father. He deserved worse, but Tasia believed in karma. She wouldn't want to spend her last days in a cold, dark nursing home. So even though he deserved worse, Tasia put her father in the best nursing home Atlanta had to offer.

Tasia parked in front of The Thompson building, walked in, and sat in Dr. Billups' waiting area. After a few minutes, a family exited Dr. Billups' office, and the receptionist motioned for Tasia to enter.

Dr. Billups' office was just as warm and inviting as the rest of the facility. Pictures of his family and friends were on the wall, along with degrees and his license to practice. In addition, there was a picture of a cross with a scripture, John 3:16, inscribed. His office had a huge window, and the horse-printed curtains were pulled open, allowing brilliant sunlight to fill the office. When Tasia walked in, Dr. Billups was standing at a file cabinet near his desk.

"Ms. Ingram, hello! Come on in and have a seat." Dr. Billups was a handsome, older black man with kind eyes and a peaceful disposition. Years in the business had not hardened him. Though poised and intelligent, he was understanding and genuinely cared about his patients and their families. "How are you today?" He asked.

"I'm here," Tasia replied, her sunglasses still covering her eyes.

"I can't imagine how you must feel, Ms. Ingram." Dr. Billups replied compassionately.

"Just lay it on me, Dr. Billups. Things must be pretty bad if you all requested me to come in." Tasia said painfully.

"I wish I had better news about your father's condition. But the truth is, his health is declining rapidly." Dr. Billups shared. "In addition to diabetes, arthritis, lung disease, dementia, and immobility, Mr. Ingram's heart is failing." Tasia removed her shades and allowed Dr. Billups to see the sorrow and pain in her eyes.

"How much time does he have left?" Tasia asked, unsure how Dr. Billups' answer could change the circumstances in any way.

"It's hard to tell," Dr. Billups explained. "He could last months, or it could be days." Dr. Billups could tell Tasia wanted to get to the point, so he did his best to limit fluff or small talk. "We wanted you to be aware of everything since you are his Power of Attorney. We asked you to come in to sign off on a few documents. The most important one is about his life-sustaining treatment. You must inform us whether to continue life-sustaining treatment or withdraw it if there is nothing more we can do."

Tasia grabbed the papers swiftly, but Dr. Billups did not flinch or seem taken aback. "Can I take these home, review them, and decide how to move forward?"

"Of course, Ms. Ingram." Dr. Billups replied gently. "However, because of his condition, we need to hear back from you as soon as possible."

"Just give me a day or two," Tasia replied swiftly. "Can I see him today?"

"Absolutely. The nurses just brought him back to his room from the afternoon activity. He should be awake."

"Thank you for meeting with me. I appreciate your time."

"My pleasure, Ms. Ingram. Please don't hesitate to call us if you have questions about any of the documents."

Tasia nodded as she exited Dr. Billups' office and headed to room 219, where her father resided. She hesitated before knocking on the door. Then, finally, she knocked on the door and said his name before entering.

"Come in." Mr. Ingram said from the other side of the door.

Tasia walked in slowly. Mr. Ingram was watching the news on the television and slowly turned his head to see who had entered the room. "Bout time you came and showed your face." He said to Tasia before returning his attention to the news. Tasia shook her head, amazed. His illnesses had made him fragile and pale, but he was still a smart ass. Before her father became ill, he was about 240 lbs. Now he was barely 160 lbs. soaking wet. Tasia knew his condition was worsening, but seeing him in person gave her a visual of how he was literally withering away.

"How are they treating you here?" Tasia asked, completely ignoring his rude comment. He was already dying. She didn't feel the need to inflict any more cruelty on him.

"For the most part, they treating me alright. But, they won't let me have any snacks, and they always bringing some bullshit in here for me to eat. Can you go in the lobby and get me a soda and honeybun?"

"No. They aren't giving it to you for a reason. It will mess with your blood pressure and diabetes."

"I don't wanna hear that shit, Gabrielle! I want a damn honey bun and a soda!"

Tasia didn't bother correcting him. His dementia made him sometimes mistake her for her mother. It didn't help that Tasia was the spitting image of her mother. "You don't need it. And I'm not getting it for you." She replied calmly. Mr. Ingram responded by turning up the TV's volume as loud as it would go. Tasia walked over to the TV, turned it off, and sat in the chair next to his bed.

"How are you feeling?" She asked.

"Why don't you come visit me more often? You don't really care about me. You might as well bring me the honey bun and soda!" He shouted, completely ignoring her question.

"Daddy, I've been busy with work and other things ---"

"I don't give a damn! I bet my angel would bring me a honey bun and a soda."

Oh, great. Now the nigga is seeing angels, Tasia thought, growing annoyed. "Daddy, seriously, I've been very busy. I just got back in town yesterday, and ---"

"Stop lying!" Mr. Ingram shouted. "Now, all the shit I've done for you. I ---"

This time, Tasia cut him off. "What you've done for me? Please tell me what you've done for me! Abuse me? Curse me? Tear me down? Exactly what have you done for me? Please humor me, big fella!"

"Watch yourself!" Mr. Ingram shouted back. "You're an ungrateful bitch. Always have been. I did more for you than I should have! I took your ass to school and basketball practice and put food on the table. That's what the fuck I did!" Tasia wasn't phased one bit by her dad calling her a bitch. He had called her much worse. She stood to her feet and clapped her hands, giving him a sarcastic applause.

"Kudos to you, Daddy! You gave me stability. That's what you were supposed to do! What about love, affection, kindness, and niceness? What about that shit, huh? Don't you think I deserved that from you? You don't think I needed that?"

"Don't forget I paid for your schooling." Mr. Ingram said matter-of-factly. Completely unbothered by Tasia's other requests. Tasia knew she would never get through to her father. Even on his dying bed, he was still as evil as ever.

"Look around you, old man. You're literally dying. And who's here by your side? The one person you treated like shit! Despite all the pain you caused me, I'm still by your side!"

"Cause you owe me, Gabrielle! You owe me! All the shit I did for you and that girl. You owe me! You should be here!" He shouted.

Tasia didn't give a damn that he called her mother's name again. "No one owes you a damn thing! This sickness is your karma. You're going to suffer until you die."

"So be it! Being with you was even worse anyway." Mr. Ingram replied nonchalantly.

At this point, Tasia was in tears, fuming with hurt and pain. "All I ever wanted was love from you! Nothing more, nothing less! Even on your deathbed, you refuse to put your pride aside and apologize for treating me like shit!"

He looked her straight in the eyes and shrugged. "I'm not apologizing for shit. I treated you better than you deserved."

Tasia knew she was fighting a losing battle. She refused to say another word. She put on her shades and walked out of the room. On her way towards the front door, she grabbed a pen from her purse, skimmed through the documents, and signed all the necessary stuff about her father's final arrangements. She signed off on not giving him life-sustaining treatment. *If it's his time, it's just his damn time,* she thought to herself. With that, she gave the documents to the receptionist and ran as fast as her feet would carry her to her Jeep. Once inside, she let out a treacherous scream while slamming her hands on her steering wheel.

"Why, God!?" She screamed. "Why doesn't he love me? What did I ever do to him? Why does he hate me so damn much?" Tasia sped off and cried the entire way home. When she got home, she rolled the biggest blunts she could and smoked them in rotation until she passed out.

Seven

"So, what have you got planned for today?" Seth asked. "Bae, I already told you. I'm going to a Mardi Gras parade with a few friends from high school." Tasia replied.

"That's right, that's right. It totally slipped my mind. You better not be acting wild and flashing your boobs for beads."

"These boobs are only for you, baby," Tasia said, lifting up her shirt and shaking her breast for Seth over their FaceTime call.

"You damn right!" Seth laughed. "You are crazy as hell, but I wouldn't have it any other way."

"I bet you wouldn't." Tasia joked back. "Anyways, I have to finish getting ready before they get here to pick me up! There's no way I'll get done staring into those sexy eyes. I'll hit you up later."

"Okay, baby. Love you," Seth replied. Tasia looked at

the camera and gave Seth her full attention.

"You said what now?"

"Nothing, I-I-I didn't say anything." Seth looked away from the camera bashfully.

"You sure?" Tasia asked. "It sounded like you said you loved me."

"And if I did?"

"Well, the love can't be that real if you aren't willing to stand on what you said."

"Damn, T. okay. I did say it. I love you, okay? I love you, Anastasia Ingram."

"I love you too, Seth Brown."

"Do you really?"

"I do."

"Okay."

"Okay."

"Well, hit me up when you get back in."

"I'll do that."

Rather than finish getting dressed, Tasia took a moment to replay what had just happened in her mind. "Did that nigga just say he loved me?" She asked herself out loud. "Did I just say it back?" She had deep feelings for Seth, for sure. But she wasn't sure if she loved him. Over the last four months, Seth had been a listening ear and confidante throughout the process of dealing with her dad. Even after their previous encounter, Tasia had prioritized visiting Mr. Ingram once a week, especially since his condition had worsened and he was transferred to the hospice wing at Garden Manor. At this point, the doctors and nurses were just doing their best to keep him comfortable. Tasia knew that at any time, she would be getting that call. After her visits with her dad, Seth was always there to comfort her. His support made their bond even stronger. They hadn't seen each other since her birthday due to Seth's hectic holiday schedule with the store, but they made sure to talk to each other every day, morning, noon, and night. They were on FaceTime daily and knew each other's schedule by heart. Seth also took the initiative to take care of her monthly and self-care expenses. Still, Tasia wasn't sure if it was real love. They still weren't in an exclusive relationship, and honestly, it felt like Seth avoided the conversation.

Nevertheless, Tasia was loyal to him. She didn't date or see anyone else but him. Tasia typically made that mistake with men, but she felt like Seth was different. If she had done that for the wrong ones, could it be possible that this time, she was doing it for the right one? Thoughts about her love life circled through her mind until her phone rang. It was Brittany, no doubt checking to see if she was ready to go.

"What's up, Britt?" Tasia answered the phone coolly.

"Aht, aht. Don't "wassup Britt" me! Are you ready to go?" Britt laughed.

"Uhh, yeah. I'm just putting on a little makeup." Tasia lied.

"See there! I knew you were over there on some bullshit. We are 20 minutes out. You better hurry up!" Britt shouted.

"Okay, okay!" Tasia giggled. "I will be ready when y'all pull up."

"You better be! Byeeee." Britt hung up.

Tasia jumped up immediately. She didn't want to

be the reason they couldn't find a good parking spot in downtown Atlanta. Britt would never let her hear the end of it. It was a typical brisk February afternoon in Atlanta. Tasia knew she needed to dress accordingly if she wanted to stand in the cold weather for more than an hour. She styled her hair in an up-down curly hairstyle, wiggled into her distressed, skinny-cut blue jeans, slipped on a warm cream turtleneck, and accessorized with dainty gold necklaces. Tasia pulled out a soft brown leather jacket that perfectly matched her brown knee-high boots. She threw her phone, wallet, and lip gloss in her Gucci crossbody and sprayed perfume. Just as Tasia gave herself one final look over, a car horn blared outside her window, and Brittany had texted to let her know they were outside. "Perfect timing," Tasia whispered to herself. She grabbed a water bottle, set up her security system, and headed out the door to climb into Brittany's red Dodge Charger.

"Aye, turn up, turn up! Now the party can officially begin!" Britt shouted when she got in the car. Britt threw her arms in the air and let out another round of "ayeeeee" combined with some playful twerking. Britt was a beautiful girl. She had smooth, light brown skin, stood at about 5'3, and had a slim-athletic build. She had big green eyes that stretched wide when she was excited. Her naturally curly hair that she kept slayed was styled into a blonde pixie cut.

"*Wassup bitches!*" Tasia shouted back. "Ya'll ready to show Atlanta how to Mardi Gras?"

"*Hell yeah!*" Tracy and Brittany shouted back.

Tasia met Brittany during her freshmen year in high school. They were assigned to sit next to each other in homeroom and connected by joking on their classmates.

Their friendship grew as they went through high school, and they learned they had more in common than good jokes. Brittany was a good friend; they genuinely looked out for each other. Tracy, on the other hand, was a different story. Since Tasia and Britt met him their senior year in art class, Tracy was always the life of the party. He was always down for a good time. They all bonded over their love for the latest fashion and gossip. Even though Tasia enjoyed hanging out with him, she could only handle Tracy in small dosages. He wasn't the most dependable friend and stayed in drama with some woman's hood, down-low baby daddy. Tracy was deep chocolate and had almond-shaped eyes outlined with long, full, beautiful eyelashes. He was a little heavier but carried his weight well and always wore the most fashionable attire.

"Bitch, I just knew your ass wasn't going to be ready when we pulled up!" Tracy shouted to the backseat over the music.

"Honestly, I had just finished when y'all pulled up!" Tasia shouted back.

"See, I knew it!" Tracy laughed. "So y'all hoes ready to turn up or what?" He said as he held a bottle of Patrón in the air.

"Hell yeah!" Britt and Tasia shouted back. Tracy passed around shots of Patrón to start the day off right. Tasia took one shot but pulled out her rolled blunt and smoked for the rest of the ride. This turn-up session was just what the doctor ordered. She had so much on her mind. It felt good to let her hair down and forget everything.

Since many streets were blocked off for the parade route, they parked a few blocks away and walked to the heart of the festivities. As they got closer to the parade spot, the scenery changed. Seemingly overnight, Downtown Atlanta had transformed into Bourbon Street, New Orleans, on Fat Tuesday. Clusters of people poured in from different parking areas into the streets, some dressed in purple, green, and gold Mardi Gras regalia, while others wore regular everyday garb. People were laughing and having fun. Parents holding younger children by the hand smiled and pointed at different Mardi Gras sights. Influencers had their phones out, selfie sticks jutted out in front of them, snapping pictures and recording videos to share with their social media followers. The light posts in the streets had Mardi Gras flags hanging from them. Peddlers with countless green, purple, and gold Mardi Gras beads adorning their necks attempted to sell their souvenirs to passers-by. High-rise lofts and apartments in Downtown Atlanta had flags, lights, and Mardi Gras beads hanging from their balconies. Some of the residents were hosting Mardi Gras parties in their homes.

Different types of music poured into the streets from the various downtown establishments. Some residents and owners just had music playing on their patio and shouted, *"Laissez Les Bon Temps Rouler!"* to the crowd below. New Orleans-inspired food trucks and alcohol stands were lined along the curbs of the streets, and lines of people circled around them, hoping to indulge in the creole goodness. Some of Atlanta's local high school bands were participating in the parade, and band members in their marching attire were shuffling through the crowds, no doubt trying to enjoy the Mardi Gras experience before their performance began. A group of older gentlemen dressed in brown suits played New Orleans-style jazz music, using trumpets, saxophones, and trombones to breathe more excitement into the entire scene. There were even people dancing in the streets. Although Atlanta was not the home of the major Mardi Gras events, the city did a good job emulating the experience one would have in Mobile, AL, or New Orleans. Celebrities, influencers, and everyday Atlanta people came in from all over the city to partake in the Atlanta Mardi Gras experience.

Tasia inhaled and exhaled the carefree environment and smiled as they walked through the crowds enjoying Mardi Gras. She looked at her own attire and wished she had dressed more festively. She and Brittany were fly, per usual, but nothing about their look said, Mardi Gras. Tracy, however, took advantage of the opportunity. He wore gold metallic pants, a white hoodie, and customized Air Force 1s painted Mardi Gras colors. In addition, Tracy had Mardi Gras beads around his neck and wore a metallic gold, half-moon Mardi Gras mask adorned with purple and green feathers. As if he could read her mind, Tracy reached into his fanny pack and pulled out a fistful of Mardi Gras beads.

"I kinda figured y'all was gonna come out here acting basic. Baby, we in the NOLA for the night!" He shouted in his best drag queen voice. "Put these on, and at least try to look like y'all are here for a good time." Tasia and Britt rolled their eyes and laughed as they snatched the beads from his hand and put them around their necks.

"Ahem!" Britt cleared her throat and put her hands in the air to make an announcement to the crew, "Okay, bitches! Today, we are getting fucked up! Let's have a good time! The first round of drinks is on me."

"Damn, y'all know I'm a lightweight. Let's pace ourselves," Tasia said, already slightly tipsy.

"Oh, honey. If you were going to act like a grandma, you should've stayed your ass at home." Tracy shouted.

"Okay, okay, okay! Peer pressure is a bitch!" Tasia laughed. "Let's do it." All the while thinking to herself, peer pressure, my ass. Ain't no way I'm getting tore up in these Atlanta NOLA streets. She knew that after a while, Britt and Tracy would be too drunk to notice she was not drinking.

Their first drinks were Hennessy-infused daiquiris. They were so good everyone gulped them down quickly. Once the liquor kicked in, Tracy, Britt, and Tasia joined the crowds and danced with others in the streets. Everyone got hungry, so they picked a food truck to try and got in line. A group of white college frat boys were standing on the balcony above the food truck area and started shouting and cheering at them.

"Hey! You! The one in the brown!" one of them shouted below as they dangled some beads in the air.

"Oh shit, Tasia!" Britt shouted. "They calling you out!"

"Show us your boobs!" the frat boy continued.

Tasia laughed. "The fuck?"

"Do it! Do it! Do it!" Britt and Tracy began to chant.

"Y'all done lost y'all damn minds!" Tasia laughed at them. "I got a better idea."

"Aw, hell," Britt laughed.

"*SHOW ME YOUR DICK!*" Tasia yelled back up to the frat boy. The white boy pulled down his pants and boxers. He was poorly endowed but proudly swung his dick from side to side. Tasia and her friends laughed hysterically while his frat brothers cheered him on. Tasia shook her head but threw him some beads for being a good sport.

After grabbing more food and drinks, they hunted for a spot to enjoy their grub and watch the parade as it passed by. Tasia and Tracy had a hand grenade cocktail with their meal and agreed it was their last drink for the night. Meanwhile, Britt had gulped down her Hurricane cocktail before she ate and was looking around for another drink. Tasia drank water for the rest of her time at the parade to sober up. She wouldn't dare be seen drunk, stumbling around in public.

The trio partied until late into the night. Even after the parade, the streets were still abuzz, and people were patronizing the food trucks and the bars that had stayed open late to partner with the theme for the evening. They finally staggered back to the car around 2 am. Behind them, the party was still going on. However, Britt had reached her limit, and Tasia and Tracy knew it wouldn't be long before she was puking her guts out. They wanted to get her to the privacy of her own home before things got ugly.

"We know this bitch ain't driving us back home," Tasia teased. "You good to drive?" she asked Tracy.

"Yeah, I'm good. Let's ride. Put that hoe in the back seat." Tracy shook his head jokingly at Britt.

"I just wanna lay dowwwwnn." Britt whined.

"Okay, girl, come on." Tasia helped her into the back. "You sure you're good, Tracy? I'm pretty sober. I don't mind at all." Tracy nodded his head. Tasia got in on the passenger side, and Tracy flopped into the driver's seat.

For about two minutes, the car was completely silent as Tracy fumbled through the keys, even though he had just used the key fob to unlock the doors. Mid-search, he rested his head on the headrest and started to laugh.

"What's so damn funny? Don't tell me you lost the key." Tasia asked.

"Can a bitch have a little chuckle? Damn!" Tracy laughed.

"Are you sure you okay to drive? You tweaking my nigga." Tasia offered to drive again.

"Girl, gone on! I'm good. I can make it." Tracy rolled his eyes and sucked his teeth as he put the long-lost key in the ignition and started the car.

"Don't be getting an attitude with me. I just wanna make it home in one piece, bitch." Tasia snapped back.

Tracy pulled off quickly, nearly doing a burnout turning out of the parking lot. A few crowds were in the street, and they hurriedly moved out of their way, fearing getting hit. A few of them even flipped him off and yelled at the car. Tasia said a silent prayer under her breath. She wasn't confident Tracy was good to drive, but to avoid a scene, she let him drive. She had considered getting an Uber but didn't trust Tracy with Britt or Britt's car. Besides, he wasn't sloppy drunk, and both of them had stopped drinking hours ago.

Tracy navigated out of the downtown Atlanta area without a hitch, so Tasia relaxed a little bit. When they reached the light to get on the highway towards Tasia's house, Tasia turned to look in the backseat and checked on Britt. She was sleeping peacefully with her mouth wide opened, curled up in fetal position. Tasia shook her head and chuckled. *She's gonna feel like shit when she wakes up in the morning,* she thought to herself. Tasia turned around in her seat just in time to see Tracy swerve to dodge the guardrail getting onto the highway.

"What the fuck, bruh!" Tasia swung her head in his direction.

"Bwahahaha!" Tracy cackled. I just wanted to scare yo chicken ass.

"I didn't find that funny at all." An irritated Tasia replied. "I play about a lot of shit, but my life ain't one of them."

"Damn, you need to loosen up! I hope you get some dick or something when you get home." Tracy laughed as he continued to drive recklessly down the highway.

"Tracy, pull over! Right damn now!"

"Sit back, bitch! I got this!" He mashed the gas and rode the tail of the car in front of them before swerving into the right lane to pass them. The hard jerking of the vehicle shook Brittany from her sweet slumber. She sat up completely and rubbed her eyes.

"Tracy, let Tasia drive. I'm getting seasick back here."

"Girl, lay yo little ass back down. I got this up here."

"Brunnkkkk Brunnnkkkkk!" An oncoming 18-wheeler in the next lane blared at them. Tracy was driving in the middle of the lanes. He quickly swerved into the left lane, then back in the correct lane, just slightly missing a collision with the 18-wheeler.

"Arrrggghhh!!!" Tasia and Britt yelled. Tracy let out another hideous cackle and sped forward even faster after straightening the car in the correct lane.

"LET ME THE FUCK OUT RIGHT NOW! YOU'RE

TRYING TO KILL US!" Tasia screamed. Brittany was crying uncontrollably, pleading with Tracy to pull over. She got so discombobulated in the backseat that she began throwing up. Tracy was unbothered. In fact, their panicking fueled his laughter and reckless driving even more. He laughed with delight as he swerved in and out of lanes at high speed. By now, Tasia was infuriated.

"Yo, you're fucking sick. I don't know about you, but I love my life, and I'm not trying to die. Kill yourself on your own time. Pull the fuck over, Tracy!"

"Girl! Fuck you! Witcho lame ass!" Tracy pulled off the exit, almost hitting another car.

"Are you dumb? No, like, seriously, Tracy! Are you fucking dumb? This shit is not funny. You can't be that damn drunk. I know all that body fat has soaked up your liquor by now!"

"Fuck you, Tasia! Get the hell out of the car, party pooper." He pulled in front of her townhome, smashed the brakes hard, threw the car in park, and turned off the ignition. He almost hit Tasia's Jeep, and she looked at him as if he had lost his mind.

"Get out of the car, Britt. I will take you home! Tracy, you can get the fuck out of Britt's car and leave it right here."

"And how you expect me to get home, simple bitch?"

"I don't give a fuck if you walk! You ain't driving her car another inch!" Tasia quickly snatched Britt's car keys and jumped out of the car, slamming the door behind her. She walked to the backseat and helped Britt get out of the vehicle.

"Britt, you gone let her do me like this? Forreal, bitch?!"

Tracy yelled. Britt didn't say anything. She climbed out of the backseat and followed Tasia into her townhouse. "Oh, y'all some sensitive ass hoes! Y'all really gone leave me out here like this? Fuck y'all! I swear to God, imma kick the door in if y'all bitches leave me out here."

"Go straight to hell, Tracy!" Tasia yelled back at him. "If I was a man, I would beat the fuck out of you!" Tracy got out of the car and started to stumble toward them, asking them to stop playing. Tasia took that opportunity to lock Britt's car door. Once she and Britt were in the house, she locked her front door, set the alarm, and led Britt to her guest bathroom so she could get cleaned up. Tasia went into her closet to grab some tights, socks, and a slim-fit warm hoodie she knew Britt could fit. Tasia heard the shower going, so she walked into the guest bathroom and put the clothes on the sink for Britt.

After she ensured Britt had everything she needed, Tasia jumped in her shower to refresh herself, ignoring Tracy's drunk knocks at her front door. She knew if he persisted, her neighbors would call the police. Tasia didn't care. Once she washed off the night's festivities, she sat down with Britt, who had curled up on her plush, emerald green sofa in the living room.

"Did that shit really happen?" Britt asked. Britt had sobered up somewhere between seeing her life flash before her eyes and taking a warm shower. Tasia had sobered up before they left Downtown, but she was still livid about Tracy's reckless driving. She and Britt sat and rehashed the night's events, trying to understand when and why Tracy went left. They knew he could do the most, but they had never seen him act that way. He had stopped banging on the door, so Tasia figured he had called an Uber. Then, right when she was getting up to grab her keys to take Britt home, her phone began to ring. Tracy's name and picture flashed across the screen.

"What do you want, Tracy?" She answered with much hostility.

"I want my beads back. Bring them outside right now."

"Bitch, you still outside my muthafuckin' house?" Tasia was done entertaining Tracy. "Fuck you and these beads. You ain't getting shit back!"

She hung up the phone. Britt was appalled. "Did he pop a pill or something? Because he's bugging right now." Tracy began to blow up Tasia's phone. Every time she hit ignore, he called again. Finally, after about ten times, the calls ceased. Moments later, Tracy was banging on her door.

"*That's it! Imma beat his ass!*" Tasia walked towards her front door, unset the alarm, and twisted the doorknob before Brittany was able to pull her away from the door. Tasia was shaking with fury and wanted to fight Britt for trying to restrain her.

"Tasia, calm down. Please. Do not stoop to his level!" Britt knew Tasia well enough to know that if she had gotten to this level of anger, it would be hell to calm her down. Britt said a silent prayer and attempted to keep Tasia away from the door. Then, using her free hand, she called another mutual friend she and Tracy shared, Bryan, and begged him to come to pick up Tracy. Before Tasia could go off on Britt for keeping Tracy from a well-deserved beat-down, she got a FaceTime call from Kyle. One look at her face and Kyle immediately knew Tasia was upset.

"Yo, what's going on?" Kyle asked aggressively.

"Kyle, I swear to God! I'm finna beat Tracy's ass." *Bang! Bang!* Tracy banged on the door even harder.

"T, what's all that noise? What the fuck is going on, man?"

"That's Tracy's ass banging on my door for some fucking beads. Kyle, this bitch literally tried to kill Britt and me earlier, and now he's at my door! I'm about to hurt this nigga real bad!"

Kyle became enraged. "I'm headed your way." With that, he ended the FaceTime call.

"Oh shit! This isn't going to end well." Britt cried. She hoped Bryan would pick up Tracy in time, but it was a long shot since he lived on the other side of town. Tasia knew it was about to get really ugly for Tracy, but she was too livid to care. Kyle played no games when it came to the women in his life.

After a few minutes, the knocking ceased, and Tracy's calls began again. Tasia continued to hit ignore on his call. *Bang! Bang!*

"Yo, T! It's Kyle! Open up!" Brittany jumped up to open the door, and Kyle busted in looking around. "Where that fuck nigga at?" Kyle asked as Britt locked the door behind him.

"I don't know. He keeps calling me, then banging on the door when I don't answer."

"What the hell happened, Tasia?" Kyle inquired. Tasia and Britt filled him in on the details of the evening. The more they shared about the ride home, Kyle became infuriated.

"Fuck that! We are gonna take Britt home, and I'm going to find that nigga before the sun comes up!"

Bang! Bang! Everyone knew who was at the door. Britt jumped up to block Kyle from answering the door, but he gave her the scariest expression she had ever seen on a man's face. Tasia and Brittany both knew all hell was getting ready to break loose. Kyle was also a hothead and had been in plenty of fights throughout his lifetime. Tasia knew there was no point attempting to hold Kyle back. Besides, if Tracy had just gone home, he wouldn't get what was coming his way.

Kyle yanked the door open, and before a shocked Tracy could utter a word, Kyle grabbed him by his hoodie and shoved him back down the steps to Tasia's townhome.

"My nigga! You done saved me some gas tonight. So you wanna taunt muthafuckas?"

Tracy began pleading with him, "Kyle! Come on. It's not like that. It's just a misunderstanding." They all went to school together, so Tracy knew Kyle wasn't the one to mess with.

Kyle didn't respond. He cocked his arm back and plundered his fist into Tracy's face. Tracy grabbed his face and looked at Kyle in disbelief. "Did you really just hit me?" *Thud.* Kyle threw another punch that landed right in Tracy's eye.

"Come on, nigga! Fight back. You are a tough guy when it comes to the bitches but can't fight a real man." Kyle stepped back and allowed Tracy to get to his feet and fight back. Tracy stood up slowly, then rushed toward Kyle, attempting to catch him off guard. But Kyle was skilled at dirty street fighting. He swiftly moved out of the way, took a fighting stance, and dodged another punch from Tracy. "Damnit! I ain't know your big ass could move that fast!" Kyle chuckled before catching Tracy with two quick punches to the face. Tracy's lips were gushing with blood. But Tracy still wasn't ready to back down. He tried to tackle Kyle, but Kyle moved out of his reach quickly, grabbed the side of Tracy's hoodie, and swung him to the ground. Kyle kicked and stomped him as soon as Tracy's body made contact with the grass. Tracy balled up in a fetal position to block his face from Kyle's shoe. Kyle didn't care. He stomped and kicked at whatever body part his foot landed on. Just then, Bryan pulled up and jumped out of the car, running full speed to Tracy's rescue. Kyle spun around quickly to face Bryan, keeping his eyes on Tracy, who was cowering on the ground.

"Oh, you want some too?" Kyle asked Bryan.

"Naw, man. I don't want no drama with you. I heard what happened. I'm just here to take Tracy home."

"Bet! Collect ya bitch and be on your way 'fore I stomp both of y'all out!" Before walking back towards Tasia's door, Kyle bent down and whispered to Tracy in a low stern tone, "I bet yo bitch ass learned your lesson. Don't ever fuck with my people again. If it's a next time, it's gone be one to the dome." He kicked him one more good time and walked away smoothly without one strand of hair out of place.

"Britt! Tasia! Y'all ready to ride?" Kyle asked. Britt and Tasia grabbed their things, locked the door, and headed to Kyle's SUV. Bryan was still helping Tracy into his car. When Kyle passed them, he waved and smiled at Tracy as Tasia flipped him off.

Once they left the neighborhood, Tasia took a deep breath, giving Kyle a dap. That was her way of saying thank you. Kyle untucked his gun from his back and gave it to Tasia to put in the glove department, "I'm pretty sure that's the last time he'll harass y'all."

"I'm sure." Tasia agreed.

"Damn, Kyle, you still got them hands." Brittany piped in from the back seat.

"Damn, right, I do! Y'all hungry?"

"Hell yeah!" Tasia and Britt shouted.

"Alright, cool. Let's hit up this 24/7 soul food spot on the Westside called Big Mamas. Y'all gone sleep real good tonight after downing this food."

Tasia sat back and took a deep breath. The situation with Tracy had really taken a toll on her. Thanks to her relationship with her father, any drama with men took her from 0 to 100. Hearing him yell at her and experiencing that emotional abuse triggered her. There were moments in the car with Tracy when she felt she was back home living with her father. Despite how much she would tell him that his actions hurt her, he continued yelling or hurting her. Very much like Tracy did earlier. So many thoughts ran through her mind. *Why did men feel like it was okay to play with her emotions?* She started to feel overwhelmed and as if he could sense her spiraling, Kyle called her name.

"You straight, sis?"

"Yeah. I'm good."

"Don't let that shit shake you up. I'm gone always be here for you. Know that. And if that sissy come with any more drama, Imma handle him."

"I know, bruh." Tasia was extremely grateful for Kyle. She could count all the solid men in her life on one hand, and Kyle was definitely at the top of the list. She shook off the thoughts of Tracy and her dad. Instead, she thought about finally settling in at home and Facetiming Seth tomorrow to tell him everything that had transpired.

The next morning, Seth FaceTime called her before she got out of bed. She was too tired to wrap her hair the night before, so she had bed hair. He had woken up next to her before. Still, they weren't at the point in their relationship where she wanted him to see her disheveled, so she declined the FaceTime and called him regularly.

"That nigga must be lying beside you, huh?" Seth teased when he answered her call.

"Nah, bae! It ain't nothing like that. I was still in bed, so I look a mess." Tasia explained.

"Somebody must have had a good time last night," Seth replied.

"Seth...you don't even know the half of it." Tasia proceeded to tell him all the details of the night before and how it triggered some painful memories of her and her dad. Seth was angry but glad Kyle was there to defend her and Britt.

"Damn. I wish I could hold you right now. I knew when I heard your voice something wasn't right. I miss you, bae." Seth cooed.

"I miss you too. I wish we could be together right now." Tasia had finally gotten herself together and clicked the button to switch to FaceTime with Seth.

"You know what we need?" Seth's face was stern with concern but softened as he saw Tasia's face.

"What?" Tasia asked curiously.

"We need a vacation. We both have a lot on our plates, and the stress on your end has been even crazier. We need to get away and leave all our worries behind for a few days."

Tasia's mood brightened, and a smile spread across her face. "So, where do we want to go?" She had never been on vacation with a man before and was excited that her first time would be with Seth.

"I'm thinking Las Vegas? Everything will be on me! What do you think?"

"That sounds perfect."

"Okay, love. Let's shoot for the top of April. I'll have a lot of free time before we start planning for the summer shoe drops, and that will give us about six weeks to plan. I'm looking up first-class flights right now. I think we should leave out on a Thursday and then head home the following Monday or Tuesday."

"Sounds good to me!" Tasia replied gleefully. Seth continued to discuss flights while Tasia walked around in circles, twirling her hair and smiling from ear to ear. It had been almost four months since they had last seen each other, and she was in need of some loving.

"These flights are mad cheap. We might need to go ahead and book today." Seth informed her, interrupting her daydreams of walking on the strips in Las Vegas, looking delectable with her man on her side.

"Okay. That sounds like a good idea." Tasia agreed.

"Alright. Hold on. Let me get my debit card." Seth put the phone down. Tasia heard him in the background, scrambling to find his card. After a few minutes, he returned to their FaceTime call, his eyebrows furrowed with frustration.

"I need to put some cash in the bank, but I'm here at the store until closing. Shit! I'm not going to make it by five. Bae, could you buy the tickets? I'll send the money to you tomorrow through CashApp. We really need to jump on these tickets today."

"Uh, sure." Tasia obliged. Truthfully, she was appalled that Seth would ask her for the money to purchase the tickets. Tasia knew he was loaded and could pay her back. She wouldn't miss the $2,500. However, she would have rathered for him to wait and use his own money for the tickets. Tasia took a deep breath, decided not to fuss about it, and sent him the money.

"Good looking out, bae!" Seth exclaimed after informing Tasia that their tickets had been purchased. "I got you first thing tomorrow. I gotta head back to work, but I'm gonna check out some spots for us to stay in Vegas. I'll hit you up later. Love you."

"Okay. Talk to you later. Love you." Tasia replied dryly. Tasia couldn't put her finger on it, but something about that transaction didn't sit well with her. She knew she had trust issues with men, and for a good reason. So she brushed her intuition off and sent any doubts about Seth to the back of her mind. She refused to ruin her one opportunity to go on a vacation with her boo. "This trip is going to be different." She said out loud, forcing her gut to silence the alarm. "Seth is different. Everything is okay!"

Eight

♡♡♡

Anastasia, this will be the premiere Atlanta fashion event of the year! You are so lucky you get to cover it." Stephanie's face lit up over their Zoom call. It didn't take much to get her excited, but in the blogger world, Tasia was lucky to have coworkers who weren't secretly jealous and trying to sabotage her, so she welcomed Stephanie's excitement.

"Yes, I know!" Tasia replied as she sipped her Starbucks Strawberry Fizz Refresher. "I'm very excited. I've attended several fashion shows in Atlanta, but this one is major. Social media has been buzzing about this new designer group, and I can't wait to check out their threads and interview them before the show."

"Honey, yes!" Stephanie snapped her fingers twice and laughed. "You might even see a few pieces you like for yourself. I know how fly you like to get!" Tasia chuckled. Stephanie desperately wanted to be a black girl, but for a blonde white chick from Dawsonville, GA, she was pretty cool just the way she was. "So, what are you wearing tonight?"

"I don't know yet," Tasia shrugged. "I was thinking of doing something simple, a nice pantsuit, a dope graphic tee, and some sneakers."

"Oh, girl, you are going to look so good! Take plenty of pictures for me." Stephanie gushed.

"I will do that. Promise."

"Okay. So are you all set for tonight. Good to go on the questions and the who's who?"

"Absolutely! I'm all set!"

"Perfect! I can't wait to see what you write up for this event! I'm here to help in any way you need."

"Thanks, Stephanie. Talk with you soon!"

"Bye, Anastasia. Have fun, girlfriend!"

Tasia genuinely wished she shared Stephanie's excitement about the fashion event. She was grateful for the opportunity to go, but her dad's condition was constantly floating in the back of her mind. To make matters worse, they were two weeks away from their vacation, and Seth still hadn't updated her with an itinerary or sent her money back for the flights. She could no longer push back the doubts.

Tasia had too much on her mind, and her work plate was full of events she had covered in Atlanta the previous week. She knew she could go and do an amazing job, but she wouldn't be 100% present. So instead of half-stepping, she called her boss and got permission to pass the assignment to Stephanie. After getting the okay, she called Stephanie to share the news. As she expected, Stephanie was ecstatic. Once she asked Tasia if she was sure nearly a million times, she humbly accepted the opportunity and thanked Tasia for allowing her to go in her place. Tasia assured Stephanie that she was the best person for the job and quickly ended the call so that she could clear her mind.

Tasia wrapped up her work assignments for the day and attempted to take a long, hot bubble bath to ease her mind. As the luscious bubbles surrounded her and caressed her skin, she still couldn't shake the suspicion and concern in her gut. *Why hasn't he said anything? Did something happen? Is he trying to surprise me? Well, why hasn't he given me my money back? Did I do something to make him change his mind?* Tasia let her mind wander until all the bubbles disappeared from the tub. When her bath water became noticeably cold, she climbed out, flipped the drain, and jumped in the shower to rinse off.

Tasia stepped out of the shower feeling physically refreshed, but mentally and emotionally, she was still all over the place. She wrapped up in a big, fluffy white towel and plopped across her bed. While deep in her thoughts, she got a call from Lisa. Tasia had intentionally dodged her cousin's calls since their trip to St. Louis. She still felt some type of way about Lisa cleaning Seth's condo and didn't want to talk about it. However, Tasia knew that if she kept ignoring her calls, Lisa would know something was up.

"Hey, Lisa. Wassup?" Tasia answered casually.

"Hi, T! I haven't talked to you in a minute. What's been up, little cuz!?"

Tasia reluctantly caught Lisa up on everything

happening with her dad, the ordeal with Tracy, and her and Seth's Las Vegas vacation plans.

"*Ooooo! Come through bae-cation!*" Lisa replied authentically excited for Tasia. "So, is Seth paying for the trip?"

"Un-huh." Tasia lied.

"Okayyy! I love that. I hope you guys enjoy every minute of it!" Lisa exclaimed before switching topics. Something about Tasia's response didn't sound so assuring, but Lisa knew better than to pry. So they began gossiping about work and their drama-filled family. As they caught up and reconnected, Tasia put her beef with Lisa behind her. She realized her cousin was just being herself, doing the most like always. So she let the situation go. Despite being annoying, Lisa had always been a solid person in her corner. With all the drama on her plate, Tasia didn't want to push away someone she knew without a doubt had her best interests at heart. After her call with Lisa, her concerns about her trip with Seth flooded her mind again. So, she decided to give him a ring to discuss her worries. "Communication is key in relationships. We will talk this out, and everything will be fine." Tasia told herself as she dialed Seth.

"Hi, you've reached Seth. Sorry, I can't take your call right now, but leave a quick message, and I'll hit you back as soon as possible." Seth's voicemail played after his phone rang a few times.

He should've been home by now, Tasia thought to herself. It was around 11 at night, and he typically left the shop around 9:30, no later than 10 pm. She waited a few minutes to pass and then called Seth again. No answer.

The more she thought about it, she hadn't talked to Seth all day. That was unusual for him, as he typically FaceTimed her during his lunchtime and whenever he had a slow moment at the shop. She knew he wasn't sleeping or busy. Around this time, he was usually sitting in his living room or on his patio, unwinding from the day. Her anxiety got the best of her, and she continued to call Seth back to back until he answered.

"Wassup T? Is there something wrong?" Seth finally picked up, and his tone was aggressive. He had never spoken to her that way, so Tasia was taken aback. However, she refused to flinch or back down. They had two weeks left until the trip, and he still owed her money. She deserved an explanation.

"Naw, wassup with you?! Why haven't you been answering my calls?" Tasia responded back, equally aggressive.

"My bad, bae. I was in the shower. *Uhm.* What you got going on?

"Clearly not a damn thing! We got two weeks until we leave for Vegas. You haven't said anything about the trip or where we will stay. And you still haven't sent me the money for the flights."

"Damn, bae." Seth's aggressive tone softened, and he sounded apologetic. "It really is my bad. I've been so busy with the store that the trip has slipped my mind. I'll look up some spots and send the money for the flights tomorrow. It's just been so hect-- " *Tap, Tap.* Soft, rapid knocks at his door interrupted Seth's sentence.

Tasia listened harder to his background and heard the knocks getting harder. "What you got going on, Seth?"

"Look, T. It's been a hectic day. I'm stressed, and you seem irritated. So, I'll just hit you up in the morning."

Tasia was instantly angry at how Seth tried to turn the situation on her to cover up whatever he had going on. "Oh, word?" Tasia asked with attitude.

"Night, bae," Seth replied, ending the call before Tasia could say another word.

Tasia looked at her phone in disbelief. She knew it was another woman. He had just gotten out of the shower, and now someone was tapping softly at his door. Tasia refused to play stupid. If it was one of his friends, he would have answered the door while on the phone rather than ending their call in a rush. Tasia was perplexed, but she took a deep breath and forced her mind not to jump to any conclusions. She fought to silence her thoughts, so she could fall asleep.

The next morning, Tasia woke up with a major headache and was still as angry as the night before. Her emotions were everywhere, and she couldn't think straight. She wanted to call Seth and go off on him but couldn't. They hadn't made anything official or defined their relationship. Technically, he could be with whomever whenever he wanted. A wave of shame and embarrassment washed over her as Lisa's warnings replayed in her mind. Tasia knew she was the only one to blame. She should have clarified their status before she caught *girlfriend feelings.* She began to spiral until she took a deep breath and pulled herself together. *Regardless of what happened last night, Seth and I are growing something beautiful,* she reminded herself. *We didn't agree to exclusivity, so I have no right to be mad.* She talked herself off the ledge.

The truth is, Tasia had never been with a successful businessman, and she didn't want her emotions to make her lose a good thing. In the past, her strong feelings pushed men away, or so she believed. So she refused to make the same mistake with Seth. She didn't want to pressure him into a relationship with her. Tasia believed Seth when he said he loved her and promised not to do anything to hurt her.

I have to be realistic. It had been months since we last saw each other. I can't be mad if Seth has sex with other women. In reality, he isn't my man. He's free to do whatever he wants. She thought to herself. Tasia worked out, made breakfast before work, and still hadn't gotten a call from Seth. She was determined not to call him. She occupied herself with work and checked her phone occasionally to see if Seth had reached out. His behavior made her fear that their end was around the corner. Even as she worked, her intuition screamed at her. This is over. I know it. I can feel it. The dream is about to become a nightmare. When she visualized her future, Seth was nowhere to be found. "No! Stop that. Don't jump to conclusions. Everything will be fine. He just needs a moment. For all I know, that was one of his neighbors or homeboys at the door." Tasia said aloud before refocusing on the article on her laptop screen.

Despite the emotional roller coaster in her mind, Tasia had a successful day. She finished all of her overdue articles, got a head start on research for upcoming events, checked on her father, and chatted with Stephanie about the fashion event. She was exhausted and decided to call it a night early since she hadn't rested much the night before. After dinner and a shower, she realized that the entire day had passed, and she still hadn't heard from Seth. She shrugged it off and did her nightly skin routine before climbing into bed.

Tasia got comfortable in bed, and just as she started to doze off, her intuition started speaking to her again. Something was off with Seth, and it was getting harder and harder to shake. Curiosity got the best of Tasia, and she pulled her phone off the charger, opened her Instagram app, and went straight to Seth's page. To her surprise, he had been posting in his stories all day. Tasia rolled her eyes and immediately called Seth. He answered the phone on the first ring.

"Wassup, T?"

"Wassup?! Wassup?!? Why haven't you called me today?"

"Been a busy day. But damn. My day has been good. Thanks for asking. How was your day?" Seth replied unbothered.

"Ha. Okay, Seth. I need to ask you something."

"Shoot."

Tasia rolled her eyes. His nonchalant approach to her pushed her to anger, but she did her best to keep her cool for as long as possible. "Are you talking to other people?"

"Naw," Seth replied. "Why you ask that?"

"Well, because last night, I heard a knock on your do...."

"Aye T, let me call you right back. One of the shoe plugs is calling me. I'll hit you right back." Seth said abruptly, cutting her off mid-sentence. That did it for Tasia. She was pissed off and made sure Seth knew it.

As soon as he ended the call, she texted him.

> *Seth, you've been acting real funny lately.*
> *No need to call me back. I'm straight on you!!*

With that, Tasia switched her phone to "Do Not Disturb" mode and went to sleep furiously for the second night in a row. Tasia woke up the next morning to a text message and two missed calls from Seth.

Bae. Stop tripping. I love you.
You're the only woman in my life.
Please answer your phone.
I'm sorry for whatever I did to upset you.

Tasia smiled from ear to ear and instantly put her worries behind her. She figured she was over-exaggerating the situation. She should have known Seth wasn't going anywhere. She washed her face, put on lip gloss, and tossed her hair around to look seductive. She called him but wanted to be prepared if he decided to FaceTime her.

"Morning, bae," Seth answered the phone sweetly.

Tasia pretended to still have an attitude. "Morning." She replied dryly.

"Anastasia, you know I love you, right? I don't ever want to lose you. It's just been mad busy at the store. We decided to expand and add a barbershop. It's going to be mad dope. But I've been dealing with a lot to bring this vision to life. I'm sorry for neglecting you. Imma make it up to you. I promise."

"You better," Tasia replied softly. They talked for a few more minutes before starting their day. Tasia was on Cloud 9 when they ended the call. "He knows just how to calm me down. I love that man." She gushed out loud. Tasia desperately wanted them to work out. She had been giving Seth all her time and energy, and she didn't want to get her heart broken again. She had planned her future, and he was the star of the show. Tasia could see herself moving to St. Louis, getting married, and starting a family with Seth. She couldn't wait to become Mrs. Anastasia Brown and build a legacy with him. She decided to just go with the flow until they eventually became one. *So what if I have to play the long game?* Tasia thought to herself. *Seth was worth the wait.*

Nine

♡♡♡

"Mama, he snapped on me again while you were at your school board meeting." Tasia sobbed. "This time, he got up in my face and yelled at me over two dishes in the sink. I tried to tell him I was running late for basketball practice. He didn't care. He just yelled at me and pushed me against the wall."

"Tae, I'm sorry. You know how Antonio gets about dishes left in the sink. He shouldn't have done that to you. I'm gonna handle it. I promise." Gabrielle replied.

"I just don't understand. Why does Daddy hate me so much? What did I do to make him treat me like this? He doesn't act like this toward you or Antoine." Tasia looked up at her motherly sorrowfully. She hoped she could give her an answer about why her father treated her so horridly.

"Baby, everyone doesn't know how to love. You require a special kind of love. Unfortunately, Antonio doesn't know how to give it to you."

"But why, mama? Why am I so hard to love?"

"Listen. It's not your fault. Antonio lost both his parents when he was young. He really doesn't know any of his family. All he has is us. Like I said, I'm going to talk with him. Don't you worry your pretty little head, okay? Everything will be fine."

"It's not fair, mama. It's just not fair."

"Tae, mama has to go away for a little while. Do you want some shopping money? You want to look cute for your team's trip to see the Hawks, right?"

"Mama, where are you going? Please don't leave."

"I'm sorry, Tae. I've got to go. I'm all out of time. We're all out of time. I've got to go, baby."

Tasia sobbed uncontrollably as her mother faded from view. She was left alone in the living room at her parent's house, crying on the sofa.

"Mama...Mama...Where did you go? Wait. Come back! I need you. Mama...Mama? Mama? Please don't goooooo."

Tasia woke up from her dream crying and calling out for her mother. It took her a while to realize she had been dreaming. She often dreamed about her mother when dealing with emotional drama. During times like this, she missed her mother so much. Just being around her mother, spending time with her shopping, and hanging out in the SWAT's with her mother's family made everything better. Her mother's family didn't have much, but they always made Tasia feel loved and cared for. She hadn't visited them much since her brother was shot and killed. The two would visit their family together after their mother passed away. It was too painful for Tasia to visit without both of them. Outside of Lisa, she didn't talk with her relatives often, but she knew she needed to change that. Too much was going on right now, and she needed her family. So Tasia planned to visit the SWAT's when she returned from her trip to Las Vegas with Seth.

It was a beautiful, early-spring Saturday morning. After starting her day off feeling sad, she decided to shake off her sorrow with a day of shopping and self-care. She needed to get a wax, a fill-in, and buy new clothes for her trip. As she pulled out a comfy and cute outfit for the day, an alarm pinged on her phone, reminding her that this was the day she had planned to visit her dad. *"Fuck!"* Tasia shouted. The last thing she needed right now was to be near him, but she didn't know how much time he had left. She knew she needed to fulfill her obligation and lay her eyes on him. Since it was still early, she decided to visit her father for a few minutes before she began her preparation for Las Vegas.

They would be flying out the following Friday, but Seth still hadn't mentioned anything to her about the trip. She decided not to worry. After the last blow-up, she knew Seth was clear on how she felt, and she trusted he was doing his part behind the scenes to make their trip special. She still hadn't received the money back, but she let it go. Seth had a lot on his mind. Tasia was confident he would more than makeup for her paying for the flights.

During the drive to her father's care facility, concern started to fill her thoughts and mind. *What if this trip really isn't going to happen? What if I'm about to do all this preparing for nothing? We talk every day, and he hasn't said a word. Should I say something? Maybe I should just mention how excited I am about the trip and see what he says.* She pondered. She was in such deep thought she didn't realize she had made it to Garden Manor. The serene view of the nursing facility calmed her thoughts. She took a deep breath, exited the car, and headed to her father's room.

The nursing staff was warm and welcoming, as they always were. Dr. Billups stopped to greet her during his walk-through, checking on patients in the facility. Despite how welcoming everyone was, Tasia was nervous because the one person she was there for wasn't always as welcoming. When she entered her father's room, a nurse stood over his bedside, checking his vitals.

"Hello, An-," the nurse began to greet her but seemed unable to recall her name.

"Anastasia," Tasia assisted her.

"That's right. I'm sorry. Hello Anastasia. I get it mixed up sometimes." The nurse replied.

Who is she mixing me up with? Tasia thought. She quickly assumed she meant another patient's guests because only she visited her father. She shrugged it off and asked the nurse how her father was holding up.

"Today was a rough day for Mr. Ingram. You just missed him more alert. We gave him a sedative to help him rest. He has been in a lot of pain today. He may be out for a few hours. You are more than welcome to hang around until he wakes up."

"No, it's okay," Anastasia replied. "I just wanted to lay my eyes on him. He needs to get his rest. Would you let him know that his daughter stopped by?"

"Sure thing. Anastasia, right?" The nurse double-checked.

"Yes. That's right. Anastasia." Tasia smiled weakly. The nurse nodded and gave Tasia a hopeful smile as Tasia exited the room. She walked out of the facility swiftly and got back in her car.

Visits to her dad always took a toll on her mentally and emotionally, but she was determined to have a beautiful Saturday. She said a quick prayer for her dad, turned on some feel-good music, let her sunroof back, and peeled out of the parking lot to head to her wax appointment and shopping afterwards.

On her way home, she grabbed a quick bite to eat. Shopping was fun, but it was exhausting. She pulled up to her favorite Asian bistro close to her home. When she walked in, the staff instantly recognized her.

"Hello, Anastasia! Dining in or taking home?"

"Take out today, Franklin."

"Very well. Do you need a menu, or will you have the usual?"

"The usual, please."

"Okay, we will have it out for you shortly."

As if they were waiting for her to pull up, Franklin brought Anastasia's order out in less than ten minutes. She paid for her food, gave Franklin a tip, and headed to her car. The aroma of the fresh vegetable tempura and shrimp curry with pineapples filled her car immediately. Tasia couldn't wait to get home, wash off the day, and dig in.

Just as she pulled up to her home, Seth FaceTime called her. *That's strange,* Tasia thought to herself. It's Saturday, the busiest day of the week for the shoe boutique. She thought Seth would be swamped at work.

"Everything okay," she asked when she answered the FaceTime.

"Yea, baby. Everything is good. I left the shop early and thought I would hit you up."

"Oh wow. You're off early, and you're gonna be off next weekend too? You must have done some serious time over the last few weeks."

"Off next weekend?" Seth asked, puzzled.

Tasia took a deep breath. *This nigga gotta be playing. I know this is a joke,* she thought to herself.

"You playing, right?" Tasia asked.

"Baby, what's going on next weekend? When did I say I was off?" Seth asked.

"You know what, *FUCK YOU, SETH!* And I mean that shit!" Tasia glared at the phone with disgust. She was appalled that the vacation was his idea, and now suddenly, he has amnesia. Tasia felt dumb, let down, and embarrassed. She had her hopes up for nothing. She should have known something was up when he said nothing about paying her back for the flights or their room and board arrangements.

"Whoa! T, what's wrong with you?" Seth appeared bewildered and didn't understand where her sudden aggression came from.

Tasia was livid. "Naw, what's wrong with you, homeboy? Who the fuck do you think you're playing with?"

Seth looked at her with confusion and nervously chuckled. "I'm not your homeboy. What did I do wrong, bae?"

"I'm not your fucking bae. Don't ever call me that

again." Tasia replied coldly. "A better question would be: what *HAVEN'T* you done?!" By this point, Tasia was beyond calming down with sweet words. She was irate and yelling at the top of her lungs. "What was the purpose of you purchasing our flights to Las Vegas? You sitting here looking like Boo Boo the Fool when you know damn well we were supposed to go out of town next weekend! I can't believe you're sitting up on this phone tryna play me. I'm not one of those other girls! I'll fuck you up for playing with me like this, Seth! On God!"

"Damn, Tasia. Damn, bae. Fuck! I totally forgot. I know you don't wanna hear this, but I'm so damn sorry. Damn. Imma make it up to you. I swear I will. I'll send your money too. I'll do that shit right now. Since we started working on the barbershop, my mind has been everywhere. Please forgive me, Anastasia. Please, baby. I am so so sorry."

"Seth, fuck you! Fuck that played-out-ass sneaker store and that bullshit-ass barbershop! Fuck all of it! I don't ever want to see your face again! Fuck nigga!" With that, Tasia ended their Facetime call. Within seconds, Seth called her back. She declined the call. He FaceTimed her, and she answered, still fuming.

"Why the fuck you keep calling me, bruh? Did you not hear what I said the first time? I ain't fucking with you NO MORE!" Tasia screamed.

"T, I know you're mad and all, but don't ever talk to me like that," Seth said coolly. "Never disrespect or curse at me. I show you respect. Treat me the same."

"Respect? You want to talk about respect? How is lying to me for six weeks straight about a trip you never planned to take me on showing me respect? Answer that, Seth! You can't! Cause you know that's some bullshit! Respect this. Don't call me. *EVER!*" This time when Tasia ended the call, she also turned off her phone. She didn't want to see his face or hear another word he had to say. She grabbed her food, locked her car door, and headed into her townhome.

Tasia was over Seth and their long-distance dating. He was all talk, and she fell for his game. As she showered, Tasia remembered when she visited him for her birthday. He supposedly had so much planned for her, but all they did was have sex and spend half a day together. She contemplated and concluded that he didn't love or care for her. He was just toying with her emotions, and his intentions were not real. They've been dealing with each other for months, and he still hasn't made it official. Tasia had been loyal to him by default. She felt so stupid that she allowed Seth to play her like a fool. "I should have known this was going to be a fucked up day," Tasia told herself. Rather than jump fresh and hit the club scene with her friends, she allowed herself to wallow in her sadness. She turned on her phone, put it on Do Not Disturb, and scrolled through her Apple Music Playlists until she found her good and faithful "Where Do Broken Hearts Go?" playlist. It was filled with all of her favorite sad R&B love songs. This playlist had gotten Tasia through the worst heartbreaks. By tomorrow, she would be playing her "Fuck That Nigga" playlist, but for the night, she let herself cry and release all her unmet expectations.

Wearing nothing but her panties, Tasia rolled a blunt and poured herself a glass of wine. Tears rolled down her face steadily as she drank and puffed her pain away. She didn't understand why men could never fully love her. No matter the lies she wanted to tell herself, Tasia loved Seth, or, maybe she fell in love with his potential. Now she was sitting on her sofa, nursing her broken heart yet again. Even though Seth was guilty, the true culprit was her father. If he had shown her genuine love, she wouldn't be out here settling for an idea of love from no-good, lying niggas. "I'm damaged goods. I'm cursed. I know it." Tasia sobbed. Relationships never worked out in her favor.

"God, am I destined to be alone? Did you put me on this earth and forget to create my soulmate? You've literally taken away everyone who genuinely loved me… Mama…Antoine. Will I never know love again? Is this your plan for me?!" Tasia screamed at the top of her lungs. Frustration and rage filled her body, and she threw the empty wineglass at the nearest wall. She was so angry and hurt she didn't even budge when the glass splattered against the wall and shards of glass and small droplets of wine shattered all over her hardwood floors. She sobbed some more before standing up and wobbling to her bedroom. She stumbled her way to the bed and buried herself under the sheets.

Her music played throughout the night, and she woke up to someone knocking at her door, nearly drowned out by Mary J. Blige crooning, "I'm Goin' Down" She began to sing along with Mary while throwing on some clothes to answer the door. As Tasia bellowed, the knocks got louder. "Here I come," a hung-over Tasia screamed. "Damn." She looked at her clock, and it was 9:15 on a Sunday morning. She couldn't imagine who would be at her door this early.

She looked through her peephole, and a delivery guy was standing on her porch, looking irritated.

"I didn't order anything!" Tasia shouted to him. The delivery guy looked down at his package.

"Are you Anastasia Ingram?" he asked perturbed.

"Yes," Tasia answered as she slowly cracked open the door.

"I'm with ATL Flowers....got a special delivery for you from Seth Brown." He read from the card. He clearly had better things to do, so Anastasia opened the door to its entirety so he could make his delivery and be on his way. Mr. Grumpy picked up a bouquet of flowers and a teddy bear and handed them to Tasia. "Have a good day." The delivery man huffed as he headed back to his car.

Tasia took the items and set them on the kitchen table. She didn't think anything of it for a moment. She took in the beauty of the two dozen red and white roses. She rubbed her hand across the adorable tan teddy bear and smiled. *Maybe I was overreacting,* she thought to herself. *This man truly does love me. Why would he make such a grand gesture to apologize if he didn't?* Tasia pulled out the card nestled between the roses and read it aloud. "I love you. Please forgive me. Sincerely, Seth." Tasia rolled her eyes and blushed as a slight grin spread across her lips. She planned to thank Seth for the flowers and bear, but not immediately. She was positive he knew they had been delivered, but she would make him sweat a little bit. She went about her normal Sunday routine, cleaned the house, listened to gospel music, washed clothes, and meal-prepped for the week. Once she completed her weekly preparation tasks, she settled down at the computer to take a stab at a gossip article due that week. She had originally planned to turn it in by Wednesday, so she could enjoy the rest of her four-day weekend in Las Vegas with her boo, but since the plans had changed, she decided to get it done before the week began so her schedule would be open for other things. As she worked, her phone pinged with a text message from Seth. Initially, she ignored it but couldn't resist seeing what he said.

Did you get the flowers I sent you?

Tasia opened the message, put her phone down, and continued working on her article. About two hours later, she replied:

Yea. Thanks.

As soon as her message was delivered, Seth called her on FaceTime. She propped the phone up behind her laptop, accepted the call, and looked at the screen behind her laptop but didn't say anything.

He smiled at her. "Hey, bae," Seth said gently.

"Hello, Seth," Anastasia replied dryly before focusing on her laptop screen.

"How is your day going?"

"Good."

"Did you like the flowers?" Seth asked, trying desperately to make conversation with Tasia.

"I did."

"Okay." Defeat covered Seth's face. "I felt bad about yesterday. I had to make it up some way and try to put a smile on your pretty face."

"I appreciate it," Tasia replied without looking away

from her laptop.

"So, what are you doing?"

"Working."

"Forget that job. You should move to St. Louis with me. We can be the next Kim and Ye. Let me take care of us. If you wanna work, you can. It's up to you, bae. But I promise you wouldn't want or need anything. I'm serious, Tasia. I want to be one with you. I don't want to be without you or lose you. It took the thought of me losing you to open my eyes. But Tasia, I'm ready. I want you to be mine. I want to be yours. I'm ready to be all in."

Tasia wanted to jump up and down with excitement. Seth finally said the words she had been waiting to hear him say. Though she was ecstatic on the inside, Tasia decided to play it cool. "That's nice of you. But I love my life here in Atlanta. And you know writing is my passion. So I'll have to think about it."

"Which part? Being official with me or moving to St. Louis?" He asked.

"Both."

"Anastasia, I know I fucked up. I've fucked up a lot, bae. I know that. And I'm sorry. But you are my future. We belong with each other. I hate being away from you. I want to wake up to that pretty face every day. I want to come home to you every evening. I want us to get married. Have children. Build a life together. I want all of that with you, baby."

Tasia blushed but played it cool. "Where is this coming from all of a sudden, Seth? You can't even commit to a vacation with me. How do I know you are serious now?"

"T, I been wanted to make us official. Real talk. It's just

this long-distance thing. It's too much. It would be hard for us to be committed to one another living in different cities. That's why I never asked you to be all mine. It wasn't because I didn't want to. I just didn't know how it would work with us living miles and miles away from each other. Yesterday, when I thought I had lost you, I realized I needed to man up and tell you what I wanted. I want you to move here with me. I want us to be together. More than anything in the world. That's what I want, T."

"Seth, this is a lot to process." Tasia was bubbling over on the inside. It sounded too good to be true, but she wanted to believe him. She didn't want to think that everything they had shared over the last several months was a lie. She wanted to believe he felt the same way she did.

"I know it is a lot to take in. You don't have to rush to make a decision. Just promise me you will think about it?" Seth asked hopefully.

"Okay. I'll think about it."

"Thank you, bae." Seth beamed. "Well, I just wanted to make sure you received the delivery. I love you and I'll hit you up later."

"Love you too. Later." Tasia hung up the phone quickly and screamed like a schoolgirl who had just been asked to prom by her 3-year-long crush. She hugged her phone close to her heart and whimsically spun around in circles. Smiling from ear to ear, she said, "It's like he's in my head." Of course, she wanted to move in with him, but she didn't want him to know it. He was still in the doghouse, technically. She couldn't let him out that easily. Seth kept her on an emotional roller coaster ride. One minute, she was crazy in love, and the next, she was crying her eyes out because her feelings were all over the place. But she loved it. Because she loved Seth.

Though the thought of moving in with Seth was exciting, Tasia had a lot to take in. It would be a big move for her. Atlanta was all she had ever known. She would be leaving her family and friends behind to be with a man she was still getting to know. She knew love made people do crazy things, but this was a risk if there was ever one. Nonetheless, it was a risk she was willing to take. Her intuition rose, and she suddenly became cautious. *Was Seth serious, or was this just a part of a scheme to win her back? Was it possible this was another elaborate lie that would end in disappointment?*

She remembered when her dad had physically abused her for leaving her basketball shoes in the hallway. The next day, he took her shopping to make it up to her. Her dad would always apologize and tell her he didn't mean to hurt her. Less than two days later, when she let her guard down with him again, he was back to mentally, physically, or emotionally abusing her. When she got older, she stopped falling for trips to the mall and apology gifts. Eventually, her father stopped apologizing, making her last few years in the house with him as a teenager a living hell. *Is it possible that Seth was using the same manipulation tactics on her?* Tasia's mind began to mull over the occurrences of their relationship. Right when she began to notice patterns, she shook her head. "No! This is different, Tasia. Seth is not your father. This is different. Don't let what your father did rob you of your shot at true love. Don't let your father win!" She said to herself.

Ten

♡♡♡

Thursday before Memorial Day Weekend, Tasia landed at St. Louis airport, exuding much sex appeal. She had missed her man and wanted to look her absolute best when he picked her up from the airport. Weeks had passed since they discussed making things official, and they had grown closer. Seth purchased her a ticket to visit him for Memorial Day weekend, and Tasia was excited they were spending their first holiday together. Besides, she was long overdue for some TLC and dick.

After grabbing her bags, she headed outside to meet Seth, who pulled up a few minutes after she arrived. She saw his car as clear as day but paused dramatically, threw her hair back, and pretended to be looking for his car. Tasia wanted Seth to get a full view of his beautiful prize. She was looking good, and she knew it. She wore a flowy blue maxi dress that showed off her breasts and legs. Her white-gold accessories brought out the silky-smooth hue of her chocolate complexion. Her hair was in neat box braids, and her make-up was perfect. She rocked her gray Prada purse with the matching sandals Seth had purchased for her a while back. Seth honked his horn and quickly got out of the car to grab Tasia's bag. "Damn." He whispered in her ear when she got close to him. Naturally, impatient drivers began to honk at them, so Tasia got in the passenger seat. Seth passionately kissed her before he closed the driver's door.

"T, I'm so glad you are here. I've missed you, baby."

"I missed you too, boo." Tasia kissed his cheek and flashed him a sexy smile.

Seth drove them to his condo, and once he parked, he stared at Tasia longingly.

"Bae, you look so good. I can't wait to get you out of those clothes." Tasia giggled and blushed.

After Seth grabbed her bags and they took the elevator to his floor. Before Seth opened the door, he turned around to face Tasia. "Bae, please don't be mad at me."

"Why would I be mad at you?" Tasia asked, puzzled.

"Well, I know I said it would just be the two of us this weekend, but my friends were in a bind. I'm letting them stay with me for a few days." Tasia couldn't believe her ears. Before she could give him a tongue lashing, he opened the door to his three friends sitting on the couch.

Tasia was furious but didn't want to make a bad first impression on his friends. She smiled awkwardly and waved at everyone as Seth introduced her as *Anastasia*. Tasia noted that he didn't introduce her as his girl, lady, woman, special friend, or queen. Just simply: *Anastasia*.

After introductions, Tasia whisked around to face him aggressively and demanded that he take her bags into his bedroom.

Tasia, barely into his bedroom, coldly spat, "Seth! What the entire fuck? I could've stayed home if I knew it would be me, you, and the homies."

After completely closing the door, Seth looked at her with big puppy dog eyes. "Bae, I couldn't just leave them out to dry. Please try to understand. What would you have done if it were your friends?"

"My friends would have *NEVER* put me in that predicament! But if they were really in some shit, I would have made other arrangements for them if I had already committed to having my *MAN* over! You planned a weekend just for the two of us! After you reneged on our Las Vegas plans! You telling me you ain't have the balls to tell your friends, no?" Tasia fumed.

"It's not like that, T." Please, just calm down and hear me out," Seth replied calmly.

"I just don't fucking get you. You're always saying one thing and doing the opposite. Like seriously! I can't believe you flew me out here for this shit! As a matter of fact, run me back to the airport!" Tasia snatched up her belongings and headed to the door.

Seth stepped in front of her before she could open the door. "Tasia, wait!" He took her bags and set them aside. Then, he took her by the arms and pulled her into his chest. "Look! I'm sorry! This was never supposed to happen. But I promise…it will never happen again. Please don't leave. We can still have a good time. Just the two of us. Let me show you."

Tasia shook her head in disbelief. They hadn't seen each other in months, and Seth pulled a stunt like this. Tasia was beyond fed up with the excuses. A part of her wanted to fly back to Atlanta, but another part wanted to stay and be with her man. As she contemplated what to do, Seth gently kissed her on the forehead. "Tasia, I'm trying. Please just be patient with me."

Tasia moved her head away from him. She needed some fresh air to calm down, so she grabbed a blunt and lighter off Seth's nightstand, walked to the patio door, stepped outside, and sat in one of the woven black leather patio seats. She adjusted the cushioned ottoman, propped her feet up, and lit the blunt. After inhaling deeply and exhaling slowly, she gazed at the scenery and allowed her mind to clear. Even if Seth was on some BS, she decided she would still have a good time. Her life was so busy in Atlanta with work, dealing with her dad, and everything else. Regardless of Seth breaking another promise, she knew she needed to be away from Atlanta for a little while. She began to think about how she could make the most of this trip with or without Seth.

Tasia began looking at hotels in the city when she remembered that she had connected with Taylor Laflin, the successful attorney, the last time she was there. Though they had only spoken a few times since she was there in October, she knew he was interested in her and would show her a good time in St. Louis. She could book a nice hotel, hang out with Taylor, and enjoy some self-care. The thought of this game plan made her smile. She pulled out her phone and texted Taylor, asking if he was in town for the holiday. To her surprise, he texted back quickly, letting her know he was there and would be hosting a yacht party the next day. The attire was white, gold, or neutral, and he invited Tasia to be his guest. Tasia's spirits perked up, and she told him she would likely take him up on his offer. When he asked what brought her to the city this weekend, she lied and said she was following up on something for work. They texted for about fifteen minutes until Tasia heard the patio door open and close and Seth walking up behind her. At first, she wanted to continue her text conversation with Taylor, hoping that Seth would see it and open his eyes to what he had with her. Instead, she closed the text app and scrolled on Instagram.

"Can I join you?" Seth asked, reaching for the blunt. Tasia silently held the blunt up. Seth took it, put it to his lips, took a deep pull, then handed it back to Tasia as he exhaled. Then, he stood directly behind her and began to seductively massage her shoulders. Instead of brushing him off, Tasia allowed him to serve her. She got comfortable in the patio chair and relaxed. Seth massaged her shoulders for about ten minutes before pulling up a chair and sitting directly in front of Tasia. He took her legs from the ottoman, placed them in his lap, removed her shoes, and began massaging her feet. "It's a pretty day out here, huh?" Seth asked, desperately attempting to start a conversation with Tasia.

"Beautiful," Tasia replied.

"There is so much happening in the city this weekend. I can't wait to hit a few spots with your fine ass on my arm."

Tasia smiled weakly. At this point, she didn't care what he said. She was still going to stick to her plans.

"You know, my friends, they have done a lot for me." Seth began. "When I first came to St. Louis and was finding my place, Chris and them hooked me up with all the right people. They helped me to get on my feet. Sometimes, I feel like I still owe them for everything they did for me. They may never say anything, but as a man, that shit still hangs over my head. Do you know what I mean?"

Tasia looked into Seth's eyes and searched for any sign of sincerity. Honestly, she could understand where Seth was coming from. Even though she made it about good karma, a large part of her only cared for her father because of everything he provided for her as a child. Secretly, she never wanted to feel like she owed him anything for her success. She sympathized with Seth, and her heart softened. Rather than reply, she nodded slowly and continued looking at the scenery.

"They don't live here anymore but came in town for the weekend. Something went left with their hotel room, and they needed a place to crash. Knowing all they have done for me, I couldn't tell them no. The last thing I wanted was for them to throw everything they had done for me in my face. I don't know if they would do that, but I guess my pride wanted to make sure of it. That's why I let them come over. I was afraid to tell you because I still wanted to see you. I didn't want you to change your mind and stay in Atlanta. I missed you, baby. Please tell me you understand." Seth pleaded.

"I understand, Seth."

"Thank you. Baby, I promise to make this up to you. Just be patient with me. Yeah, I could have gotten them a hotel, but that would have taken away from the funds I set aside to spoil you with this weekend. I've been intentional about saving more and thinking about our future. I've put myself on a tight budget so I can set us up for success when you move here. I want to get out of this condo, buy us a home near the water, and begin the rest of our lives together."

Tasia blushed. She was impressed at all that Seth had been doing behind the scenes to prepare for her transition to St. Louis. After hearing him out, she felt bad for how she initially reacted. "Really, Seth? You've been thinking about all of that for us?"

"Yes, Anastasia. I was serious when I told you I wanted you to be here with me. I meant every word, and I've been putting action behind what I said."

Tasia didn't know what to say. She had been looking for jobs in the St. Louis area, but not aggressively because she wasn't sure if Seth was serious. She hadn't even told anyone. However, if this man was already making moves for her, Tasia knew she needed to take things more seriously. "Wow, bae. I didn't know you were serious about me moving here." She replied softly.

"What? Of course, I am, T. I was dead serious. I want you in my arms every day. I'm not perfect, and I know I mess up sometimes. But everything I've been doing, I've been doing for us. I put in the crazy hours with the business because that's a part of our legacy. One day, I won't have to work as hard because I'll have as many employees as I need. Right now, as I am building, I gotta grind, baby. I just want you to always keep in mind that it's all for you. It's all for us. It's all for our future together." He was done massaging both of her feet, so he put her sandals back on, put her feet down, and moved the ottoman out of the way so he could come close and give her a kiss. Tasia kissed him back passionately and smiled.

"What am I gonna do with you, Seth?" She asked as she held his face and looked into his eyes.

"Love me, I hope," Seth grinned.

"I think I can do that," Tasia replied as she kissed him deeply on the lips again. "So, what have you got up your sleeve for us this weekend? It's our first holiday together, bae. Can you believe that?"

"I know! I'm gonna make it really special for us too." Seth began to tell her about his plans for the weekend, and Tasia was giddy, thinking about everything she would wear to each spot. Tasia sat in Seth's lap as they finished the blunt and talked on the balcony. Suddenly, Seth's phone began to ping. He held up his phone to read the message, and his disposition immediately changed. "Damn it." He said under his breath.

"What is it?" Tasia replied. She already had a gut feeling it had something to do with the boutique.

"It's the shop. Bae, I gotta close up for the evening, do the final count, and all of that. Chris took the day off, and the guy we are training as the manager doesn't have the keys to the safe.

Tasia got up from Seth's lap and looked at him with disgust and disappointment.

"I promise I won't be gone long. Just a few hours, and I'll be right back here with you. I'll bring some food, and we will eat in today and get out tomorrow."

Tasia walked back into his bedroom, and he followed behind her.

"Remember, baby. It's just a part of the grind. It won't always be like this. I promise, T." Seth said as he changed his clothes and prepared to go in to work. When he was done, he sprayed some cologne, checked himself in the mirror, and walked over to where Tasia was sitting on his bed. "I love you, baby. I'll be right back."

"Sure," Tasia replied dryly. Seth walked out of the room. When she heard the front door close, she broke down into tears. She was so confused. Tasia was tough, but love always made her lose sight of reality. She was just so fatigued from the back and forth with Seth. He had known for a few weeks that she was coming into town. While she could understand the situation with his friends, she couldn't understand why he hadn't gotten his business affairs in order before she arrived. Yes, he was a business owner, and things were often unpredictable in business, but something as simple as making sure the new trainee had the keys to the safe seemed easy enough.

Why didn't he handle all of this before I got here? Tasia thought as silent tears of frustration rolled down her cheek. We haven't seen each other in months. He should have made sure nothing would interrupt their time together.

Tasia felt a mixture of feelings. Seth said he loved her, always bought her nice things, paid her bills, and made big promises for their future. However, he never proved to be a man of his word. Something always got in the way, and Tasia didn't know if it was a coincidence or if Seth was playing with her emotions. She wanted to stick to the plans she made earlier, but what would Seth think of her? Would he think she wasn't strong enough to handle his business lifestyle? *Is it possible that she could be ruining a good thing because she couldn't be more understanding of his hustle?*

Tasia thought about all the success stories she had heard from power couples. Many of those couples spent a lot of time apart early in their careers. They made a lot of sacrifices so they could have the life they wanted. If she left Seth now, she would never see the other side. Then, she thought about her parents and many other marriages she saw growing up. No one had a perfect marriage. If she wanted to be with Seth, she would have to accept his flaws. She couldn't have one without the other. Even though he wasn't perfect, he did try. After all, this was the second time he flew her out to visit him. Tasia wished she could call one of her friends to discuss everything she was feeling, but she was too ashamed. Everyone knew how excited she was to spend their first holiday together. She was embarrassed to call and tell them it wasn't going as planned. She had even skipped out on a girl's trip with Morgan and some other sorors to be there with Seth. The last thing she wanted was to tell them Seth had left her in the house with The Three Amigos while he went to work.

Tasia wiped away her tears, gave herself a pep talk, and pulled herself together. Then, she took a shower and decided to nap until Seth returned.

Ping! Tasia was awakened from her nap by a text from Seth informing her he was on his way home. It was now 9 pm. It had been almost six hours since he left earlier, promising to return soon. Tasia sucked her teeth and shook her head. She was too emotionally overwhelmed to get upset again. So she scrolled through her phone and replied to a few messages and work emails. Thirty minutes later, Seth still hadn't made it back home. Tasia took a deep breath and decided to move forward with her plan to get a hotel room. Her thoughts were all over the place, and she was hungry. But to her surprise, Seth walked in with plates, cups, a pitcher of ice, pizza, and a black convenience store bag.

"I got food!" He grinned at her as he carefully balanced everything he was carrying. Tasia rolled her eyes and didn't say a word to him. *He looks like a clown,* Tasia thought to herself. "That's it. That nigga is a clown. And I'm sick of his weak ass acts." She said under her breath. She walked into the bathroom and closed the door. She returned to the bedroom and saw that Seth had laid a blanket on the floor with the food he had brought. "Look, bae. I made us a picnic." He grinned at her. Tasia was too overwhelmed with disappointment and frustration to be mad. And she was too hungry to snap at him, so she just stood and looked down at him.

"Have a seat, beautiful." Seth patted the blanket.

Tasia reluctantly sat down, grabbed a plate, and started getting a pizza slice when Seth stopped her. "Let me do that for you." He put two slices of pizza on a plate for her. Then, he pulled bottles of coke and lemonade out of the convenience store bags and made Tasia a drink. He sat everything before Tasia and waited for her to dig in.

"Thanks." Tasia took a bite of the pizza and stirred her drink in the cup.

"No, thank you for being so patient with me. I know you are probably starving. Go ahead and eat. I got something for you."

Tasia gave him a blank stare and continued to eat her

pizza. Seth entered his closet and pulled out three black jewelry boxes. He repositioned himself on the blanket beside Tasia and handed her a napkin before giving her the boxes.

Tasia's eyes lit up. "What's in them?" She asked.

"Take a look and see." Seth grinned.

Each box held a gift more impressive than the next. Seth had gotten her a rose gold Cuban link necklace with exquisite VVS diamonds. In another box was a matching bracelet with rose gold enclosed diamond earrings. The last small box was a 3ct. rose-gold diamond ring.

"Here, let me put it on for you." Seth took the box, removed the ring, and placed it on Tasia's right ring finger. "One day, I'll put an even bigger rock on that other finger. I know I haven't been keeping my word to you. I know I haven't been making good on my promises. But know that none of it was on purpose. No matter how much I get it wrong, I promise to always have your back. I got you, no matter what. No matter what we go through, how mad you get at me, or what happens, I will always have your back. I hope every time you rock this shit, you remember that. I'm sorry for making you wait here so long today. Shit got crazy at the shop, and I had to stay longer than expected. I'm so sorry, baby. But just know, those extra hours I put in were to make sure I can always do stuff like this for you. I want you to have it all. I want to help you start your own business or shit, if you just want to be a housewife, I want you to be able to do that too. Whatever you want, baby. I got you. I promise."

Tasia beamed as she admired her new jewelry. "Seth Brown! You have outdone yourself. I love it. I love it all."

"I told you I would make it up to you, baby. I hope this shows you how much I care about you."

"Seth, it does. It really does."

"I love you, T. Only the best for you."

Tasia's hunger and anger completely subsided as she jumped up and ran to the bathroom with her gifts. She put on her necklace and bracelet and checked her diamonds under the bright lights. Seth watched her from the floor, laughing as she pranced in the mirror.

"So I guess that means I'm forgiven?" He laughed as he took a bite of a slice of pizza.

Tasia flashed him a playful scowl. "Not so fast, mister. You still got a little making up to do." She flashed him a seductive smile. Tasia walked back over to Seth as he packed his mouth with pizza and kissed him on the forehead. "Thank you so much, baby," She purred.

"Girl, you better stop talking to me like that before I devour you next." He replied, chewing on his pizza.

"Finish your pizza. I got dessert for you." Tasia whispered before grabbing a few items from her suitcase and returning to the bathroom. While in the bathroom, Tasia took a deep breath. She knew Seth loved her, and his thoughtfulness and heartfelt apology made her have a change of heart. She realized she could have been more understanding and less of a bitch to him. So tonight, she planned to show Seth how grateful she was and how lucky he was to have a woman like her.

Tasia stepped out of the bathroom just as Seth finished cleaning up their bedroom picnic. He looked up at her and nearly salivated. Tasia was wearing the black and white lingerie set he had gotten her for her birthday, her new jewelry, and a pair of black Christian Louboutin pumps. Her skin and new VVS diamonds glistened as she walked up to him slowly and kissed him. "You ready for me?" Tasia whispered, playfully biting on his earlobe.

"Damn, T. Give me one second," Seth replied as he quickly undressed and went into the bathroom. Tasia sat on the bed and waited patiently for him to finish. When she heard the shower turn off, she leaned against the headboard, bent her knees, and opened her legs wide. Seth stepped out of the shower with his towel wrapped around his waist. Tasia had lit some candles while he was in the shower but had left the lights on so Seth could get a full view of her. Seth flipped off the lights, climbed into the bed in front of her, and dove his face right between her legs. They spent the rest of the night making sweet, passionate love until they were sticky, sweaty, and exhausted. Then, they took a shower together. Once they were all clean, Tasia removed her jewelry and eased into one of Seth's t-shirts. Seth and Tasia cuddled and talked until they finally fell asleep around three in the morning.

Eleven

♡♡♡

The sound of Migos and Lil Uzi Vert's, "Bad and Boujee" and rowdy men playing a video game blared from the other room, awakening Tasia from her sleep.

"*Yeah, Nigga! I just popped yo ass! Stop playing with me!!*"

"*The game ain't over, homeboy!* Keep that same muthafuckin energy until the fourth quarter. Ion wanna hear no bitch ass whining either!"

"Y'all niggas too serious about this 2K shit. *Got damn!* I'm ready to hit these streets and see if these hoes still choosing a nigga!"

The men went on and on about the game and stopped periodically to yell out their favorite Migos lyrics from the song playing at full volume. Tasia tried to cover her ears with a pillow, but the music, game, and yelling were too loud to ignore or sleep through. She groggily turned around to wake Seth and complain about his noisy friends, but Seth was already awake, scrolling on his phone as he smoked a blunt.

Tasia stared at him, but he didn't look her way or seem to notice that she had woken up. "Seth? Seriously? Tell your friends to pipe down."

"Well, good morning, sleeping beauty. Did you rest well?"

Tasia returned his question with a blank stare. "If you don't tell them to turn it down, I will." She began to get out of bed.

"No, no, no, no, no!" Seth laughed nervously as he quickly jumped out of bed and grabbed a shirt. "I got it. You might curse them out, and I want them to still like you after this weekend."

Tasia got back in bed and threw the covers over her head. After a few minutes, the noise from the other room lowered. Even though Seth had fixed the issue, Tasia was still annoyed. *What kind of grown men would make such a fuss early in the day at someone else's home? What kind of friends did Seth really have? Furthermore, what did they think of her? They didn't know her well enough to be using vulgar language around her. Why did it take her to get up for Seth to tell them to cool it? He should have gotten up first, seeing as she was clearly sleeping. Was Seth's friends proof of the type of man Seth really was?* Her intuition spoke loud and clear, giving her the same alarm she had felt since her birthday trip to St. Louis. Again, Tasia brushed it off. Visions of her potential relationship with Seth and their future family played in her mind. *So, what if I have to share space with his rude ass friends this weekend. Pretty soon, it'll be just us.* Tasia thought to herself as she dozed off.

Seth came into the bedroom and woke Tasia to tell her he was leaving for a little while. "Where are you going?" A drowsy Tasia asked.

"I have a business meeting with a major shoe vendor. I'll be back shortly. Love you." Seth said as he kissed her forehead.

"Love you. Good luck with your meeting." Tasia smiled weakly.

"Thank you, bae. Damn! I can't wait to do this with you every day!" Seth exclaimed as he walked out the door. Tasia doubted he would be back soon. She looked over at the clock. It was 9:30 am. Since it was still early, Tasia went back to sleep.

About an hour later, Tasia was awakened by tender kisses on her shoulder. After his meeting, Seth snuggled behind her, holding her around her waist. Tasia opened her eyes and turned to Seth, licking his fingers.

He lowered his hand beneath the cover and put it between Tasia's legs. Using his fingers to move her panties aside, Seth fingered her until he felt her juices dripping. Then, he lifted her leg slightly and entered her without a condom.

Tasia was still half-asleep and couldn't fully grasp what was taking place. They had never discussed having raw sex. She was caught off guard and too deep in thought to object. After a few quick strokes, Seth began to shake and released inside her. Then, he got up and smacked Tasia's ass while cockily proclaiming, "You know this my pussy, right?" He chuckled and strutted to the bathroom to clean himself up. He returned with a warm towel for Tasia and put the towel on her thigh before redressing and going to the living room with his friends, who, from the sound of it, were gearing up for another 2K showdown.

The warm towel landing on her thigh snapped her to her senses, and she quickly rushed to the bathroom to clean herself. She sat on the toilet and prayed Seth's semen would seep out of her before any damage was done. Tasia put her hands over her eyes and shook her head. She couldn't believe what had just occurred. She didn't know how to feel. She didn't know if she felt violated, if Seth might have just potentially trapped her, or both.

Fear and confusion evaded her thoughts. She wasn't 100% sure about Seth, and didn't want to have a child right now. She considered that just because he had nutted in her didn't mean she was pregnant. She checked the Flo app that she used to track her period. As soon as she looked at the date, she realized she was ovulating. The app reminded her that if she had sex during this time, there was a high chance she could conceive. Tasia began to sweat profusely. "What have I done? What did I just let happen? Fuck, Tasia! You can't be this stupid!" Tasia jumped in the shower so she could clear her mind. After her shower, she had calmed down enough to think of a plan, but she wanted to talk to Seth first. "Maybe he did that because he is ready to start our family," Tasia told herself. Tasia didn't think they were at that point yet, but she didn't want to make any decisions before talking to Seth and seeing where his mind was. As she got dressed, Seth stuck his head in the bedroom door.

"Headed to get food for everyone. Be right back." He

announced.

"Bae, can we –" Tasia started. But Seth had already closed the door before she could say anything. Moments later, Tasia realized the house was extremely quiet. For the first time since she arrived, she stepped out of the bedroom and entered the living room. No one was there. She walked down the halls and checked the other rooms and areas. She was the only one in the house. Tasia walked back to the living room and plopped down on the sofa. "No, Seth. I didn't want to ride." She said sarcastically aloud as she used the remote to turn on the TV.

Just when she was getting into a docu-series, she heard laughter at the door. Seth and his friends loudly jostled each other as they came through the door. It was like a bunch of high school buds having the time of their life. Without acknowledging her, they piled the bags of food from Popeyes on the coffee table and rummaged through the kitchen for plates and cups. Then, like ravenous wolves, they dug into the food, dropping clumps of mashed potatoes, red beans and rice, and crumbs everywhere as they fixed their plates. Luckily, Seth had grabbed a plate and put Tasia a few pieces of chicken on it while the wolf gang was scooping sides. When done piling on sides, they dug into the chicken with their hands and layered legs, thighs, and breasts on their plates.

After she finished her food, Tasia walked to the kitchen to put her plate in the sink and was greeted by a mountain of dishes. *Why is Seth's kitchen so messy?* She wondered. She couldn't recall if it was this dirty the last time she was there, but she remembered Lisa's cleaning frenzy during their visit. At first, she told herself that it was Seth's problem and she wouldn't wash a single cup. However, she considered that Seth's busy work schedule had kept him from house chores. He had done some very kind things for her, so Tasia decided to lend him a helping hand. She wanted her future man to know she could be a team player. She took a deep breath, reluctantly grabbed the dish soap and a towel, and washed the dishes. As she washed the last dish, one of Seth's friends came in with more cups and plates and dropped them in the sink abruptly, splashing a few soap suds on Tasia's shirt.

"It's so good to have a woman here to keep everything nice and clean." He said as he went into the refrigerator. Before Tasia could utter a slick remark, Seth rushed over and saved his friend from the tongue-lashing of a lifetime.

"Thanks, bae. I appreciate you for washing the dishes."

"Anything for you, boo." Tasia managed to say sarcastically. As she finished the dishes, his friends gathered around them and asked Seth what he had planned for the rest of the day. He told them that he wanted to take Tasia to a museum. Tasia remained silent. She rinsed the sink, wiped the counters, and returned to the living room. The TV was paused on their video game, so Tasia grabbed the blanket off the ottoman and scrolled through her phone. Later, Seth and his friends returned to the living room, and Seth sat beside her. Tasia placed her feet across his lap while she watched his friends play the video game. She realized that, at some point, Seth had started to move away from her. She didn't jump to conclusions, but her suspicion proved true after a while because her feet were no longer in his lap but on the sofa.

I know this nigga ain't trying to act funny in front

of his homeboys, Tasia thought. She looked at him with annoyance. *"What? You don't like feet all of a sudden?"* Tasia snapped as she recalled one night when Seth couldn't resist putting her feet in his mouth.

"Nah, T. It's not like that." Seth laughed nervously.

"Well, what's the problem?" She inquired.

"Chill out. We good, T," Seth uttered under his breath.

"Chill out? Chill out? Seriously, Seth?"

Seth's friends looked goofily between each other, eyes stretched, anticipating Seth's response.

Suddenly, they were interrupted by an incoming call on Seth's phone. He answered, and Tasia attempted to hear what the caller was saying. Seth told the caller that he had already discussed that he had other plans for the weekend, and Tasia knew where the conversation was headed...*Seth would be leaving soon.* Tasia went into the bedroom and put her phone on the charger.

A few minutes later, Seth entered the room and informed Tasia that he had to go to the shop and would return shortly. "Do you have to leave right this minute?" Tasia asked, trying her best to hide her anger. She could tell he was already frustrated from his demeanor, but she really wanted to talk.

"Yes, T. I gotta go now." He said as he rushed to gather a few things.

"But we really need to talk." Tasia sulked.

"Cool. I'll holla at you when I get back." Seth replied. "I'll be back soon. We're closing at 4 pm today." He closed the door before Tasia could object.

The entire day had passed, and there was no word from Seth. She sat on his bed, staring at her phone, waiting for him to call. It was 6 pm, and Tasia knew the shop had been closed for a couple of hours. She called Seth's phone twice, but he didn't answer.

"Fuck!" Tasia cursed as she tossed her phone across the room with frustration. She had had enough of Seth's foolishness. "Who the hell does this nigga think I am?" She asked herself. Tasia was done feeling neglected. She had done enough talking. It was time for action. "I've got two more days left in St. Louis. I'll be damned if I spend it confined to this condo, waiting on Seth's ass to spend some quality time with me." Tasia decided to pack her things and go to a hotel. Instead of discussing their potential pregnancy, she decided to grab a Plan B pill on the way to a hotel and terminate any opportunity for her to be carrying his child. When she made it back to Atlanta, she would forget Seth ever existed and move forward with her life. Just as she stood to pack her things, her phone rang. Assuming it was Seth, she marched over to where her phone had landed on the floor, picked it up, and prepared to answer aggressively before she realized it wasn't Seth calling. It was Taylor Laflin. Tasia took a deep breath and answered, trying to sound calm and unbothered. "Well, hello. What a pleasant, *uh,* surprise. How are you?"

"Ms. Ingram, I am well. I must admit I am delighted to hear your voice." Taylor said smoothly.

"We're back to surnames, huh?" Tasia replied.

"Well, I haven't gotten to know you more personally, so yes, Ms. Ingram. We are." Taylor quipped.

"How unfortunate," Tasia agreed with the slightest bit of sarcasm.

"An unfortunate dilemma, indeed. Nevertheless, one

you can rectify if you so desire." Taylor offered.

"Why, what did you have in mind, Mr. Laflin?" Anastasia probed.

"The yacht party tonight. Join me. It begins at 9 pm. You're painstakingly gorgeous already, so I imagine you wouldn't need more than an hour and a half to prepare. My driver and I can pick you up at 8:45. Depending on where you are in the city, we could arrive on time or be fashionably late."

Anastasia blushed at the notion. "I'd love to join you, but I have a lot going on with, *uhm*, work." Tasia was careful not to make the slightest hint about what she was currently dealing with. If she had left Thursday evening, she would have been in a better mind space to attend the yacht party. But staring in the face of a potential pregnancy, dealing with Seth's childish homeboys, and Seth's work bullshit, she wasn't okay. However, talking to Taylor put a smile on her face and took her mind off things, so she decided to continue the conversation. "So, what will you be dazzling the people with tonight?"

Completely ignoring her attempt to decline his invite and move forward in the conversation, Taylor persisted, "What's your boss's name? I'll give them a call myself. From the sounds of it, you would be able to deal with your "*uhm work*" better if you stepped away for a moment."

A small smile crept across Tasia's face. She definitely liked men who didn't give up easily. Taylor's determination to get her out for the evening made her feel valued. She couldn't say that for Seth at the moment. "I didn't even bring anything to wear. I had no plans on attending such an extravagant affair during my visit."

"I considered you might offer that excuse," Taylor began. "It's just my luck that my sister, a superb fashion designer, happens to be in town for an exhibit. She has a gorgeous white piece I'm sure would look marvelous on you. You'd be the talk of the evening. Look at your phone." Taylor sent Tasia a photo of the most striking cocktail dress she had ever seen. Tasia loved exclusive, high-end fashion pieces, and everything about the dress screamed elegance and class. It was a short, form-fitting number with a revealing split on the left thigh and a modest v-cut. The dress had astonishing details. The bottom half was solid white with a lace overlay, but the top portion was only lace. Skin-toned padding covered the breast area. The lace that covered the entire dress was woven with small delicate white leaf patterns, and the tips of the leaves lifted off the dress, giving the ensemble a 3-D look. The lace was lightly embellished with lovely Swarovski crystals and small white-pink pearls. Tasia knew the dress would look beautiful against her chocolate skin.

"Oh, Taylor. It is breathtaking." Tasia was at a loss for words. "I would love to wear it. But how do you know it's my size? And what will I do about shoes? Accessories? Taylor, there's no way I can pull this off in an hour and a half. I'm so sorry. But maybe another time."

"You can't be more than a size six, and my sister says the dress gives in all the right places. You'll be fine. Also, a dear friend owns a shoe boutique here in town. She has closed for the evening, but she owes me a favor. I can have her pick out a pair of shoes for you. Tell me your size."

"I don't know, Taylor." Anastasia wondered aloud.

"I'll tell you what. I have a suite on the yacht for the

evening. Host perks. Gather your items, and my driver will pick you up. Everything you need will be here when you arrive."

"Taylor, look. I really wish I could. I'm not in the headspace for fun. I-I-I, I really need to take care of this work stuff. I just don't know —" Tasia explained, nearly breaking down in tears. Even though she tried hard to mask her feelings from Taylor, the more she talked, the more she neared an emotional breakdown. Something about his soothing tone, persistence, and willingness to make the evening so easy for her made her even more sorrowful about her situation with Seth.

"Ms. Ingram, I don't know you well, at no fault of my own, however, I know human beings," Taylor interjected. "Today, you sound nothing like the vibrant, sassy, life-loving woman I met many months ago. Let me give you a little bit of advice, in fact, it's the secret to my success. Sometimes, we must step away from what's draining the life out of us. In our time away, we can gather the strength and strategy to maneuver through life's challenges. Tonight, that's all I'm offering you. A moment to step away and get some fresh air. Catch your breath. Remember who you are. No commitments. No responsibilities. When you've got all the fresh air you can handle, my driver will take you home."

"You're right, Taylor. It's just that...it's so much going on. With work, my dad, m-m-my –. Yeah. It's a lot, Taylor." Tasia stopped abruptly. She was too embarrassed to let anyone in on her relationship issues.

"No need to explain. I'm sure you had no intention of sharing the details of your trouble with me. We're not there, so I don't require it. Just text me your address and your shoe size. I will handle the rest." Taylor assured her.

"Okay." Tasia reluctantly gave in.

"My driver's name is Victor. He will be there shortly. See you soon, Ms. Ingram."

When they ended the call, Tasia texted Taylor her address and shoe size before she changed her mind. Taylor was right. If she was going to get her mind together to deal with Seth, she needed to step out of his element and into an atmosphere that could feed her. She loved fancy parties and being around successful people. Taylor didn't know her well and could tell she wasn't herself. The more Tasia thought about it, attending the yacht party was just what she needed to shake free from her emotional roller coaster with Seth. When she returned, they would have a serious conversation and let the chips fall where they may. Also, she didn't want her Memorial Day trip to St. Louis to be marked by drama with Seth and sharing the condo with his homeboys.

She quickly slipped on a simple but cute long black maxi dress she had packed for a quick lunch date with Seth and paired it with her gray Prada sandals. She didn't have much time to get dressed and pack her bag, but she didn't want to look like she had been crying all day. She ran to the mirror, washed her face, and put on a little make-up since she would give herself a full beat for the yacht party later. She threw her make-up case, undergarments, perfume, lotions, and oils in her carry-on bag. Tasia packed a pair of silver YSL strap-up heels and threw them in the bag, just in case Taylor's friend couldn't find anything her size. She also packed some sexy sleepwear. Tasia had no plans on spending the night with Taylor, but she wanted to be prepared in case she didn't have a choice. The way she felt about Seth at that moment, she had no clue how the night would end.

Moments after Tasia double-checked her bag to ensure everything was there, she got a text from an unknown number. Victor, Taylor's driver, told her he was downstairs. Tasia grabbed her bags and left the condo. When the elevator reached the top floor for her to get on, Tasia heard laughter behind the doors and knew it was Seth's friends.

"*Yo, what's up, T!* I can call you T, right? Can't remember your name." One of his friends said to her. Tasia rolled her eyes and stepped aside to give them space to exit the elevator, ignoring his childish comment.

"Aye, is Seth in the condo?" The other friend asked.

"No," Tasia replied shortly. Once they were off, she stepped on and pressed 1. As the elevator closed, she could hear Seth's friends talking.

"Dang, she looks pissed. Seth in trrrooubble." One of them laughed.

"Where that nigga at anyway? He ain't answered my calls. I know he off work."

Their conversation faded away as the elevator slowly declined to the first floor. Tasia shook off her encounter with the Three Musketeers and decided she wouldn't think about them or Seth for the rest of the night. When she stepped out of the condo's front entrance, a black Chevrolet Tahoe LT, with heavily tinted windows and black-on-black trimming and rims, awaited her arrival. A handsome, middle-aged white man dressed in a gray, tailored suit stepped out and opened the back passenger door.

"Good Evening, Ms. Ingram. I am Victor. May I?" Victor motioned to take Tasia's bag. Tasia gave him her bag, and he took her hand to assist her into the vehicle. Once she was in, Victor closed her door and swiftly walked to the driver's side.

"Please make yourself comfortable. There are chilled bottles of water and champagne to your left and an assorted snack tray above it. Please help yourself to whatever you would like. We will be at our destination shortly." Victor replied before letting up the partition with a pleasant smile.

The interior of the vehicle was astonishing. It had been customized with a mini buffet table, and the seats had been turned inward, facing the adjacent window, like in a limo. The leather seats were big, plush, and comfortable. White LED lights trimmed the roof and the floors. On the buffet were bottles of Fiji and Moet, glass champagne flutes, and a bucket of ice in the middle. High-end brand snacks ranging from baked chips, nuts, and cookies were stacked neatly on a tray above the beverages. Tasia sat back, took a deep breath, and exhaled. She grabbed a snack and a bottle of water and gazed out the window for the rest of the ride.

"Ms. Ingram, we have arrived," Victor announced. After a smooth 25 minute drive, they reached the Gateway Arch, where the yacht was docked before taking off North of the Mississippi River for the party on deck. Victor escorted Tasia through the building to the docking area. Tasia could not believe how huge the yacht was.

Standing about three stories high, the beautiful white yacht glowed with lights pouring in from every window. Each floor had an open patio, and a DJ was finishing up his setup on the main patio floor. Smaller patios on the sides led to rooms with double doors. White and black patio furniture complimented each outdoor area. Large, split-leaf, Monstera plants were situated in corners of the patios, giving the yacht a relaxing, upscale, tropical vibe. Bartenders and servers were walking in and out of the yacht, carrying glasses, trays of food, and bottles of different drinks.

A red carpet had been rolled down the dock's pathway, leading to the front door of the yacht. Victor helped her onto the boat, and Tasia was instantly drawn to the polished, black stone flooring. It was the most exquisite stone flooring she had ever seen. Color-changing LED lights trimmed the baseboards to lead guests throughout the dimly lit watercraft. Large LED blocks were beside each door, illuminating each room's doorknob and landing area. From the front door, Tasia could see the main meeting room that led to the patio where the DJ was setting up.

The room had been furnished with black, armless leather chairs, small circular tables, white table clothes, and green and silver décor. There were also tall tables with similar décor and tall bar stools with black leather cushions. All the tables and chairs were positioned loosely around the dance floor, with a microphone stand in its center. As Tasia admired the layout of the first floor, a familiar voice entered the yacht's foyer behind her.

"Ah, Ms. Ingram. What a lovely surprise. I almost thought Victor would return empty-handed." Taylor chuckled.

"Cut it out, Taylor. You were not taking no for an answer!" Tasia excitedly replied. Seeing Taylor and the yacht was indeed a fresh breath of air.

"Right you are, Anastasia. What can I say? Blame it on my occupation." Taylor joked. "Well, I am anxious to see you in that dress. Guests will be arriving shortly. Victor will escort you to your room for the evening on the third floor."

"My room for the evening?" Tasia questioned.

"Why, yes. I pulled a few strings and arranged for you to have a room. I want you to be completely comfortable and relaxed. If you choose not to stay the night, it's totally fine." Taylor offered.

Tasia didn't respond. She simply smiled and followed Victor to her room to get dressed.

Twelve

♡♡♡

The inside of Tasia's room was just as exquisite as the rest of the yacht. The room was lightly decorated to not take away from the well-crafted furniture. The floors were deep brown hardwood, and all the furniture had a similar wood finishing. The right side of the suite had an 82-inch flat screen, sofa, coffee table, king-size bed, and a mini kitchen, complete with a refrigerator, microwave, and small stove top. A vase overflowing with red roses was on the coffee table in front of the sofa. Next to the flowers was a bucket of ice, chilling a bottle of Moet. There was a card with Anastasia written in cursive on the front. Tasia smiled and opened the note from Taylor.

Thank you for coming. Before you rush downstairs, enjoy a glass of champagne, and take a moment to remember who you are. Text me when you're ready.

Taylor

The dress, a shoe box, and dark green jewelry boxes from Simons, a high-end jeweler in St. Louis, sat on the bed. Tasia opened the shoe box and was amazed at how beautiful they were. Taylor's friend had picked out a pair of nude pink Valentino strappy heels that went perfectly with the light pink pearl embellishment of the dress. In another bag was a matching clutch. "These people have good taste!" Tasia exclaimed as she hurried to check out the jewelry Taylor had selected for her. Seeing the jewelry boxes made her think of Seth and the jewelry he had given her the day before. *He can be so sweet sometimes,* Tasia thought to herself. Just as her mind began plummeting into thoughts about her situation-ship with Seth, her phone rang.

"I trust everything is to your liking," Taylor asked when she answered the phone.

"Taylor...yes. It's all gorgeous. Thank you. Thank you so much." Tasia replied gratefully.

"Don't mention it. Just wanted to check on you. See you soon." Taylor hung up the phone.

"Okay, Tasia. Get your ass in gear! It's time to step out and have a good time. You can worry about Seth and his bullshit later!" Tasia gave herself a pep talk as she slid out of her dress. She played her "Get It Girl!" playlist on Apple Music and walked around the room in her underwear, pulling out everything she needed to shower and do her make-up. Once everything was set up, she stepped into the shower and allowed the hot water to wash her worries and concerns down the drain. When she was done showering, she oiled and lotioned her body, pulled a chair to the large bathroom vanity mirror, did her make-up, and pinned a few of her braids away from her face. Then, realizing she hadn't opened the jewelry boxes, she tiptoed to the bed, grabbed them, and headed back to the mirror to check them out and put them on. In one box was a pair of dainty diamond stud earrings. In another was a sleek white-gold necklace with a simple string of diamonds. It was gorgeous but not too overpowering that it would clash with the dress. In the last box was a matching bracelet. Tasia was impressed with how well every piece went together but wasn't shocked. Taylor was a man with good taste, and he clearly had a circle of people around him who knew a thing or two about fashion.

Tasia looked at herself in the mirror and was astonished. She had always believed she was beautiful, despite how her bad luck with the opposite sex sometimes made her feel otherwise. "Why in the hell do these men try to play me?" She asked herself out loud. *A better question is, why do you allow these men to play you?* Her intuition kicked in. Tasia brushed off the question, knowing it would probably lead her to tears. She refused to mess up her perfectly beat face.

Out of the corner of her eye, she caught a sparkle from the dress lying on the bed and immediately perked up. Not only was she attending a yacht party, but she would be wearing a custom cocktail dress. She jumped up, put on the Valentino heels, and put her items in the clutch purse. She looked longingly at the dress but waited to put it on. It was so beautiful, and she didn't want to mess it up in any way. She decided to put it on before she walked out the door.

She walked around and tidied up the room to break in her new heels. Peeking through the curtains covering the patio door, she saw a line of people walking down the dock and onto the yacht. Excitement filled her heart, and she couldn't wait to turn heads and have a good time with Taylor.

She poured a glass of Moet and sat on the couch with her phone. She subconsciously checked her phone for a message from Seth, and after realizing he still hadn't texted or called, she decided to scroll through her social media page. Seth had posted in his stories earlier that day, showcasing new shoes and apparel and showing off the packed boutique. Tasia rolled her eyes and went back to scrolling through her timeline. One of her favorite influencers had posted a picture with the words: *Girl, you bad!* Tasia liked the post and reshared it to her own story. The post reminded Tasia of Taylor's instructions.

She put her phone down, relaxed into the sofa's back cushion, and deeply breathed. "Who am I?" she asked herself. Rather than think about all the negative circumstances she had dealt with, Tasia thought about everything she had accomplished. She was a well-sought-after writer in Atlanta. She had been to events most young writers only dreamed of covering. She knew people from all walks of life all over the world. She had graduated top of her class in high school and college. She had friends who loved her. She was part of an amazing sorority. Her list of accomplishments rattled through her mind. "I really got it going on!" Tasia said out loud to herself. Despite everything she had gone through, Tasia had a beautiful heart and had accomplished a lot in a short period of time. "I deserve the best." She whispered to herself. She decided right then and there that she wouldn't accept less than she deserved from Seth or any other man.

After finishing her glass of Moet, she stood up, walked over to the bed, and carefully removed the dress from its protective covering. She walked to the mirror and slid the dress over her head and body. Gazing at herself in the mirror, Tasia adjusted the dress, turning her body to different angles to ensure every piece was situated properly. Taylor's sister didn't lie. The dress stretched in all the right places. Tasia couldn't believe how good she looked. She gave herself one more look over, then grabbed her phone to call Taylor. She was ready to have a good time.

Tasia exited her suite and walked toward the end of the hall where Taylor was waiting for her.

"Anastasia Ingram." Taylor breathed when he saw her.

Tasia laughed and did a seductive spin so Taylor could get a full view of her look.

"It's probably best we have separate rooms. You look enticing." Taylor said, still staring her up and down.

"I'm the dessert on the menu you want but know you don't need!" Tasia joked, snapping her fingers. Taylor laughed at Tasia's joke, stepped back, and smiled.

"Now, here's the feisty woman I met last October."

Tasia threw her arms around Taylor and gave him a tight hug. "Thank you," she whispered in his ear. "It is my pleasure," Taylor whispered back, returning her tight hug.

"Get a room, would you?" A familiar voice teased them. Tasia spun around to see Christian Turner, Taylor's business partner grinning at them.

"Hello, Christian!" Tasia exclaimed.

"It's good to see you again, Anastasia. Sad your partner

in crime didn't take this trip with you." Christian replied, referring to Morgan.

"I know," Tasia replied sadly, thinking of her friend. "Maybe next time."

"Give her my regards, and take plenty of pictures so she can see what a good time she missed!" Christian laughed. "I'll see you chaps downstairs. I think I hear the DJ playing my song."

Taylor and Tasia laughed and shook their heads as Christian smoothly cascaded down the stairs toward the main floor. "Shall we?" Taylor asked as he held out his arm for Tasia to take it.

"We shall!" Tasia smiled as she took Taylor's arm. They walked down the stairs, and to Tasia's surprise, the foyer and hallway areas were clear.

"It appears all of our guests have made it to the party area," Taylor informed her. "Are you ready to make an entrance?"

"Always!" Tasia replied back quickly.

"Well, let's do it. One second." Taylor told Victor to inform the DJ he was ready to begin. Suddenly the music lowered, and the DJ's voice boomed through the yacht as Tasia and Taylor made their way down the hallway to the main party area.

"Ladies and gentlemen, put those glasses in the air and welcome our host for the evening, Mr. Taylor Laflin!"

Everyone cheered and clapped as Tasia and Taylor walked through the crowd.

"Join me for a second," Taylor whispered to her as he smiled and waved at everyone. Tasia nodded and allowed Taylor to escort her alongside him to the microphone in the middle of the dancefloor. Once he grabbed the microphone, he smiled at her and addressed the audience.

"Well, don't you all look different tonight? I barely recognized some of you without your Starbucks cup." Taylor joked. The crowd laughed.

"Yes, tonight is all about networking and connecting with other business owners and professionals here in the city, but I want you all to take a moment and breathe. Everyone in this room wakes up each day and decides to make a difference in this city. That's hard work. You deserve a day to relax, have fun, and cut a rug or two."

"I know that's right!" Someone in the crowd yelled back at Taylor. The crowd laughed in agreement.

"Servers, watch that one." Taylor teased the party attendee.

"Before I release this microphone and have some fun of my own, I want to introduce you all to a special friend of mine, visiting us from Atlanta, Georgia, Ms. Anastasia Ingram."

Anastasia waved delicately at the crowd as everyone cheered and clapped for her.

"Come on, I know you all can do better than that. Isn't this woman wearing this dress? Goodness!" Taylor flashed a big smile at Tasia, and Tasia blushed. The crowd's cheers got even louder, some men whistled, and women shouted variations of "Yaaassss ma'am!" and "You better wear that dress, girl!" A few women even snapped their fingers in the air.

Taylor stepped aside and beckoned for Tasia to step to the mic. At first, Tasia hesitated but then pushed her nerves to the side and greeted the audience.

"You all are too kind. I am elated to be here today amongst such inspiring individuals. Taylor, thank you for the invite. I look forward to connecting with you all, and who knows, maybe even cutting a rug or two." Tasia shuffled her shoulders and chuckled as she stepped away from the microphone. The crowd clapped, and Taylor resumed his opening speech.

"Well, you all heard the lady. Let's connect and cut up some rugs! DJ, give us something good to jam to!"

The DJ quickly obliged and hit the audience with an oldie, but goodie, Rick Ross's Aston Martin Music remix with Drake.

Taylor escorted Tasia from the center of the dance floor to a table where his closest friends were sitting. Tasia recognized a few from her birthday visit to St. Louis and greeted everyone before taking her seat. They all chatted and caught up. Tasia was so busy laughing and talking to others she didn't feel alone as Taylor walked around the room and greeted guests. Periodically, he checked in on her to make sure she was okay.

A few of the ladies at the table invited Tasia to venture throughout the yacht with them, and Tasia obliged. She had so much fun chatting about men, business, and fashion with her new connections. Everyone inquired about her dress and her writing career in Atlanta. They seemed thoroughly impressed by her. Even though she was new to the circle, they included her in their laughs and conversation all night. There wasn't a moment during the party where Tasia felt like an outsider or a sore thumb. Whenever thoughts of Seth would drift through her mind, Taylor would appear from nowhere with a drink or whisk her away to the nearest dance floor to dance. Tasia had so much fun she lost track of time. As the night progressed, her concerns about Seth melted away.

Around 2 am, the DJ announced that the boat was about to return to the mainland. Tasia wanted to take in the view, so she stepped away from Taylor and his friends, walked out on the deck, and sat at a table near the edge of the yacht. She took a deep swig of her drink, exhaled slowly, and gazed out into the water, taking in all the fun of the evening. A part of her still couldn't believe she was sitting on a yacht floating down the Mississippi River with many people she barely knew. As if they knew every burden she was carrying on her shoulders, everyone welcomed her with open arms and made her feel included. She was so grateful Taylor didn't accept her decline. She knew she would have been at Seth's condo, pouting and infuriated, waiting for him to get home. Getting out of that condo was the best decision she had made since she landed in St. Louis.

Taylor, Chrisitan, and some friends walked over to where Tasia sat and asked if they could join her. Flashing the biggest smile, Tasia nodded, and everyone took a seat and joined her in watching the yacht cruise back to the mainland. Some people chatted, while others laughed and finished their drinks. Tasia watched everyone interact as she and Taylor laughed and talked.

"You have no idea how much fun I've had!" Tasia exclaimed.

"Everyone has been buzzing about you, Tasia. You sure do know how to work a crowd."

"What can I say?" Tasia joked confidently.

"You can say you promise to do stuff like this more often." Taylor quipped back.

"I promise," Tasia replied. Suddenly, sleepiness took over her, and her eyelids grew heavy. "I am going to head to my suite and call it a night," Tasia informed Taylor.

"Very well. I'll have Victor escort you to your room. I will bid the guests goodnight, and if you aren't asleep when I'm done, I'll stop by to check on you."

"I would love that."

Victor appeared and gently took Tasia by the arm.

"Did you enjoy yourself tonight, Ms. Ingram?" Victor asked as they walked up the stairs to Tasia's suite.

"Oh, Victor. It was everything."

Victor grinned. "Well, it certainly made Mr. Laflin's evening to have you accompany him."

"He made my night. The last few months have been a lot. Tonight I got to disappear from it all. It felt really good."

"I am happy to hear that. However, Ms. Ingram, can I give you a little advice?"

"Of course."

"Build a life that you don't have to disappear from."

Tasia took a deep breath, looked at Victor, and nodded sincerely.

"You can do it. I'm rooting for you. Have a goodnight." They had made it to Tasia's room. After ensuring she made it inside her room, Victor returned to the main room.

Once she entered the room, Tasia slowly removed her dress, took off her shoes, and plopped backward on the bed. She had been having such a good time she didn't check her phone all night. She pulled her phone out of her clutch and was alarmed to see 16 missed calls and 10 texts. Seth had been calling her nonstop since around 1 am. In his texts, he inquired about her location, stating that he didn't have time to deal with her shit. She laughed. "Pressed, much?" She said out loud as she read his back-to-back messages. He had just sent a message ten minutes ago, and she decided to reply in the morning. Scrolling through her missed call log, she didn't recognize the other number that had called her twice. She was nervous that it may have been someone with information about her dad, so she called it back.

"Hello," the caller answered.

"Did someone call this number?"

"Yo, T."

"Who is this?"

"Look, I ain't tryna get in y'all business or anything, but Seth ain't alright right now. He needs you bad."

"Who is this?"

"It's Rick, Seth's homeboy. We met here at the condo."

"What you mean Seth ain't alright?"

"A shooting happened at the boutique. Chris is in the ICU."

Tasia was stunned. Without thinking, she grabbed her carry-on bag, slipped on the black maxi dress and sandals she had on earlier, and headed downstairs.

Victor was by the door with Taylor, saying goodbye to the last stragglers. They looked at her with concern, and

Victor hurried to her. Tasia quickly explained that she had a family emergency and had to return to her condo. Victor nodded, motioned to Taylor that he was leaving, and whisked Tasia to the SUV.

Thirteen

♡♡♡

Tasia entered Seth's bedroom slowly. The lights were dim, and the air smelled like weed and Hennessy. Seth was sitting on the edge of the bed. Even with the lights lowered, Tasia could tell that Seth was still wearing the clothes he had on when he left for work. As she walked closer to him, she realized his shirt had blood spattered all over it, and there were dried traces of blood on his neck and ears. Tasia didn't know what to say. Her anger had subsided, and her heart welled with sympathy and compassion for Seth. Whatever had taken place at the boutique had shaken him to his core. She stood directly in front of him, held his face in her hands, and lifted his face to her. He looked at her, and his eyes were bloodshot red. His facial expression was emotionless. Tasia saw the fear in his eyes. The beef she had with him earlier no longer mattered. He needed her. Though he didn't have the words to express that, she knew he needed her. Guilt gripped her stomach so bad she winced at the pain. She couldn't imagine how Seth felt walking into an empty condo after witnessing whatever he saw that evening.

Tasia gently released Seth's face and walked to the bathroom. Without turning on the light, she turned on the shower. Once the water was hot, she adjusted it to make it more comfortable. She entered Seth's closet and pulled out a towel and fresh clothes for him. Once everything was ready, she gently took Seth by the hand and guided him to the bathroom, where she removed his shirt. She threw her arms around him and hugged him tightly. "Shower." She motioned him to the water. He nodded slowly, and Tasia exited the bathroom to give him some privacy.

After an hour, the shower turned off, and Seth entered the bedroom wearing the clothes Tasia had put out for him. Tasia rose from the bed and approached him as he left the bathroom. She hugged him again and held him as he broke into tears. "They fucking shot him, T," Seth whispered as his tears soaked Tasia's dress. "They shot him."

"I'm so sorry, Seth," Tasia whispered, soothingly rubbing his back. "Come sit down. I know you're hurting right now. Do you need me to get you anything?"

Seth shook his head and allowed Tasia to guide him by the hand to the bed. They sat in silence for a few moments. "What happened?" Tasia asked softly.

"Chris got into it with a customer. He was trying to steal a pair of shoes. We caught him on camera. Dude damn near tore up the store when security escorted him out. I thought it was over. I thought that was the end of it. But dude and his friend were waiting on us outside after we closed up for the evening. His friend ambushed me, then ol' dude pulled out his gun and shot Chris."

"How is Chris?"

"I did everything I could to keep him alive. He passed out from losing so much blood. The ambulance arrived in time. He's going to pull through. He is going to make it."

"I'm glad to hear that, Seth. I know how much your business partner means to you. I know today was a lot. How are you feeling at this very moment?"

"I don't know how I feel. I feel a lot of things. I am angry because there was nothing I could do to stop it. I am frustrated because I know this is going to fire back on the store in a negative way. I am afraid because that could have been me. One wrong move. I could have been the one shot. I am all over the place. I-I-I I just don't know anymore, T. Is this really worth it?" Seth heaved forward, placed his face in his hands, and cries rippled from his throat.

Tasia threw her arm around his shoulder and squeezed him tightly. She rubbed his back to console him. "Seth, do you want to pray?"

He didn't respond, only nodded. Tasia took the lead and began to pray for Seth and Chris.

They asked for guidance, strength, understanding, and healing for Chris and his family. After they prayed together, Tasia pulled back the covers on Seth's side of the bed and guided him into bed. Once he got in the bed, she pulled the covers over him and kissed him on the cheek. "Get some rest," she said. "I'm right here. I'm not going anywhere. I'll be right here." She kept an eye on him throughout the night, and when he dozed off, she went into the bathroom to shower and prepare for bed herself. It was close to 5 am, so she knew they would sleep in late.

As she got in the shower, she began to think about when her brother got shot. It was such a painful season for her. Even though they were five years apart, she and Antoine were extremely close. Good or bad, he had her back. He had taught her everything she knew about basketball. When they were children, he always took the blame for anything she did wrong. Her brother knew how their dad mistreated her and tried his best to stand up for her. Losing Antoine broke her to her core. It was more hurtful that he was unfairly taken away from her. Tasia remembered how she felt when she got the call that her brother had been shot. She couldn't imagine if she were there to witness it. She knew Seth would need help and support to recover from seeing Chris come within an inch of his life. Tasia finished her shower and got in bed next to Seth.

Periodically, Seth would awake, and Tasia could hear him sobbing. She would wake up, hug him, and rub his back each time until he fell asleep. The entire experience was new for Tasia. She had never seen a man vulnerable. She didn't know if she was doing the right thing, so Tasia asked God to help her be there for Seth. He was traumatized, and he would never be the same. Tasia didn't know what that meant for their relationship, but she was determined to be there and support him the best way she knew how.

The next morning, Tasia woke up around 11 am and prepared breakfast for Seth. Once everything was ready, she fixed him a plate, poured a glass of orange juice, put everything on a tray, and took it to Seth in bed. "I need you to try to eat, okay?" Seth slowly sat up, grabbed the fork, and poked around at his food.

"I don't have much of an appetite."

"I know. But you need to get something on your stomach."

"Okay." Seth slowly began to eat the food. "This tastes really good, Tasia. Thank you for taking care of me."

"I got you, Seth."

"Bae, I don't want you to leave. I need you here with me."

"Seth, you know I have to work.

"Fuck that job, Anastasia!"

Tasia scrunched up her face and prepared to give a rebuttal.

"T, I didn't mean it like that. I know you love writing. What I mean is, you can write anywhere. I want you here with me. I told you I got you, bae. At least stay with me for a few more days. I don't want to be alone. My friends leave later this afternoon, and then you're right behind them. I mentally can't handle all of this alone right now."

Tasia was silent as she considered staying with Seth a little longer. Her issues with Seth may have taken a backseat to his current situation, but it was still an issue. At first, she wanted to keep her current travel plans and leave the next day. However, she realized that this situation allowed them to connect more emotionally. Even though it was a devastating situation, it allowed her to get to know Seth deeper, beyond the sex, gifts, and hanging out. Besides, she knew better than anyone that Seth would need her support. He didn't need to be left alone. Not now. She pulled out her phone and rescheduled her flight for the next weekend.

For the entire week, Tasia juggled caring for and catering to Seth and taking care of work responsibilities. She didn't bring up any of their previous issues during her time with him. Instead, she focused on nurturing and loving Seth. As the week progressed, Seth got stronger, and the light was slowly coming back into his eyes.

When the weekend approached, and it was time for Tasia to depart, Seth looked much better than he looked the week before. She hated leaving him, but Tasia knew she had to return to her place and life in Atlanta. She hadn't seen her father in almost two weeks and needed to check on him. Seth was sad to see her go, but Tasia promised she would return soon. She felt okay leaving since Seth appeared to be getting back to his normal self and would be returning to work the following week.

Ding Dong. Ding Dong. "T, open this door, woman!" Kyle shouted.

Tasia laughed as she put down the clothes she was unpacking from her suitcase and walked to the front door to let Kyle in. The constant doorbell pinging soon turned into heavy knocks. Tasia walked quickly to answer the door before Kyle kicked it in. "Damn, nigga. You do know this ain't the projects. I heard you when you rang the doorbell."

"Ion give a damn about your bougie lil neighborhood. You know a nigga don't like to be standing outside the door waiting too long." Kyle joked as he hugged Tasia. "It's been too long since I've seen you. What you got going on? Where you been? I wanna hear everything." Kyle walked into Tasia's living room and went straight to her cocktail buffet, pulling out glasses and preparing drinks for them as Tasia began to brief him on her entire trip to St. Louis. They took the drinks to Tasia's room so that Tasia could finish unpacking as she caught Kyle up on everything. Midway in the conversation, Kyle pulled out a sack of weed, rolled two blunts, and lit one of them. After taking two deep pulls, he passed the blunt to Tasia, who was still mid-conversation.

Tasia talked Kyle's ears off, giving him details about her interactions with Seth and his homeboys, Taylor's yacht party, helping Seth through the trauma of the shooting, and potentially moving to St. Louis to live with Seth. Tasia had a lot on her mind and was grateful to have Kyle's listening ear. Her lease was ending in a few months, and she needed to decide whether to renew her lease or pack up her life and move to St. Louis. She wasn't one hundred percent sure about anything with Seth.

Before the shooting, she was sure she wouldn't move in with him. After all, right before the shooting, she was on a yacht, forgetting about Seth and planning to wipe him away from her life as soon as she returned to Atlanta. Spending a week with him, helping him navigate his emotions, and supporting him as he processed everything that happened softened her heart toward him. Now, she was torn between her heart and her brain. Her brain kept reminding her of the many red flags Seth had displayed. However, her heart pushed her to move and see the potential of her life with Seth in St. Louis. After sharing all the details with Kyle, she sat on the bed, leaned against her headboard, and took a deep breath. "Okay. Keep it a hundred with me, Kyle. What do you think? What should I do?"

Kyle was at a loss for words. "Tasia, you know I will always keep it a hunnid with you. That was a whole lot in less than two weeks." Kyle reached for the blunt, took a deep pull, and exhaled real slow. "Look, I know he says he love you, and everything, but his actions are not adding up to his words. Do you really want to move all the way to the Lou and be with a man like that? I'm not gonna play you. I real deal believe he got love for you. But homie just ain't that into you. Not on no moving-in type shit. At the end of the day, he a nigga. And niggas gone make time for what they want. It seems like every time you visit him, he gives you a few good gifts, a couple of pumps, and then sends you on your way."

"Well, we got to spend a lot of quality time together this week. I feel like we really connected on a deeper level." Tasia rebutted.

"T, you way smarter than that. The only reason y'all had quality time was because his friend got shot, and the shop was closed for the week. If his friend didn't get hit, do you really think he would have made time for you? Be real with me? Based on his patterns, do you think y'all would have connected so deeply if his friend was never shot?"

Tasia knew Kyle was right. She took a swig of her wine and slowly shook her head no.

"Tasia, you're my friend, and I want what's best for you.

If you believe that's with him, I can respect your decision. You've been through a lot, and I just want you to be happy. I know you want a fairy tale ending and a family. And ain't nothing wrong with that. I just don't know if this Seth guy is your Prince Charming."

"It's just so confusing sometimes, Kyle. He's no Prince Charming, but I'd be lying if I said he was all bad. I can see him making an effort to be more intentional. Sometimes, I don't think he's trying to play me. I know he is just starting his business, and it takes a front seat in our relationship. On the other hand, he makes moves sometimes that give me a feeling he's hiding something. I want to listen to my intuition, but I'm afraid that's just fear trying to keep me from being patient and allowing our situation-ship to evolve into something beautiful. Know what I mean?"

"Yea. I get that T. I promise I do. At the end of the day, you have to do what's going to make you happy. No matter your decision, know I got you one hunnid percent. Just because you change zip codes don't mean shit. I'm always just one call away. I got you forever."

"I know. I appreciate you, man. When you get so damn wise?" Tasia joked, attempting to lighten the mood.

"I meannn, you know a nigga be on his Dr. Phil shit from time to time."

Tasia burst out into laughter. "Dr. Phil, my boy? Hell naw!"

"Hell yeah!" Kyle joined her in laughing. "I clearly need to sit on my own couch sometimes. I keep finding myself in the craziest situations."

"Aw, hell. What did you do, Kyle?"

"So check this out. You remember the Asian chick

from like a year ago?"

Tasia nodded her head. "Yeah, I remember her. I thought you were done fooling with her?"

"Well, I went back for a little more. But that's beside the point! Tell me why I caught the bitch on my ring cam keying my car?"

Tasia didn't know if it was the weed or how Kyle's voice kept changing from low to high-pitched, but she could not stop laughing. "What you do to make her act crazy?" Women don't act like that for nothing!"

Kyle shook his head. "Shawty talking bout I didn't hit her up after we had sex. Hell, I didn't think I had to! I made it CRYSTAL clear that I didn't see her like that." He continued to go into detail about his crazy week, and Tasia gleefully indulged in Kyle's hilarious commentary.

Fourteen

♡♡♡

.

uck!" Tasia shouted in distress. Her period was supposed to come on days ago, according to her period tracker app. With everything going on, she had forgotten to grab a Plan B pill, and by the time she thought about it, it was too late. She hadn't seen any early symptoms of pregnancy, so she brushed it off. However, as the days drifted by and there was no sign of her period, she began to worry.

A few weeks had passed since her Memorial Day Weekend in St. Louis, but she still hadn't shared the pregnancy concern with Seth. They picked up right where they left off with their long-distance communication. Seth seemed to be bouncing back pretty well, but she could still tell he was struggling. So, Tasia decided not to alarm him until she had news to share.

As she took a break from work and snacked on a bag of her favorite chips, she got a call from a St. Louis area code. Tasia accepted the call hesitantly and listened to the background noise of the caller before saying anything. The office sounds in the background put Tasia at ease, and she politely said hello.

"Hi! May I speak with Anastasia Ingram?" The gentleman on the other line requested.

"This is Anastasia. Who am I speaking with?"

"Hi, Ms. Ingram. My name is Jim Elks, and I'm with STL New Age Blog. I obtained your number from Mr. Seth Brown. He informed me that you were moving to St. Louis and were interested in a position. We have a Freelancing opportunity for our lifestyle and celebrity gossip section, and I wanted to schedule a time to go over your resume and what our company has to offer you. I was impressed by some of your articles with your current employer. Are you still looking for new opportunities?"

Tasia grinned from ear to ear. "Yes, I'm interested. I can email my resume, and we can schedule a time to discuss the position."

"Wonderful!" Jim exclaimed. They scheduled a meeting to further discuss her future with the company and ended the call.

Tasia was shocked. After hanging up with Jim, she walked out of her office, into her living room, and sank into the sofa. She took a deep breath and prayed to God. She asked for his guidance and signs to determine whether she should move.

Later that day, Tasia called to tell Seth about her conversation with Jim. "*Bae!* You're not gonna believe what happened to me today?"

"Oh yeah? What?"

"*I got a call from Jim at STL New Age Blog, the company you referred me to!*"

"That's what's up. Today has been pretty crazy for me. We got these dope kicks that everybody in the city has been looking for. *NOBODY* was able to cop them but us, so I know it's about to be crazy over the weekend. I can't wait. Things are really starting to look up for the store. Which is shocking because you know, after everything with the shooting, I didn't think........"

Seth's voice faded into the background of Tasia's mind. She was excited to give him the good news, and before she could go into detail, he cut her off and began telling her about his day. *How selfish,* she thought to herself. She was so taken aback she didn't want to listen to anything he had to say. So she mindlessly said, "Wow!" "That's awesome." "Yeah." Every few seconds, to give Seth the illusion that she was listening. He was so wrapped up in himself that he didn't even realize she wasn't listening to him. Tasia thought about interrupting him to express her feelings, but Seth had been kind of snappy and selfish since his friend was shot. He made every conversation about him, or he would interject when she talked, sharing some deep sadness that made her forget all about what she was trying to communicate. While Tasia understood that the last few weeks had been hectic for him, she didn't like walking on eggshells with him. Daily, Seth had started to remind her of her dad. It was like she was afraid to get on his bad side.

After sharing a few more details about his day, Seth abruptly ended the call, saying he had to return to work. Tasia didn't object. She was feeling ill and wanted to take a quick nap. Unfortunately, the nap didn't work. She woke up later that day feeling worse than when lying down. Tasia had a horrible headache and was extremely nauseated. As a person who didn't get sick often, her symptoms caused a lot of concern. Tasia began to panic. *Could I really be pregnant?* She wondered. *Could there really be a little Seth or Tasia growing inside of me?* At a different time in her life, the thought might have brought a smile to her face. However, at that moment, being pregnant would bring about drastic changes that she wasn't ready for. Tasia wanted children, but the timing was wrong. And there was a strong possibility that Seth was also the wrong man.

Rather than continue agonizing herself with *what ifs,* Tasia decided to get a pregnancy test. She couldn't do anything or make any decisions until she knew the truth. She also needed to do some grocery shopping. It had been a few days since she left the house, so getting some fresh air would help ease her mind. The thought of getting some fresh air stopped her dead in her tracks. *Taylor......* Her mind raced back to the phenomenal yacht party, her gorgeous dress, the shoes, and the jewelry. She was so shocked that she had left everything behind on the yacht...even the memories and the promises she had made herself. So much had been going on that she hadn't called Taylor to thank him for showing her a good time. After she jumped out of the shower and dressed, she pulled out her phone and called Taylor.

"Anastasia, I'd hope to hear from you soon."

"Hey, Taylor. How are you?"

"I'm doing fairly well. The question is, how are you, Cinderella?"

"Man, I left my shoes and dress at the ball, huh?" Tasia

joked.

"Certainly an ending I wasn't expecting. Maybe we should call Disney and tell them we've got a spin-off for them." Taylor and Tasia laughed. "Seriously. How are you?"

"Taylor, I'm so sorry. A friend of mine had a very traumatic incident at work, and I had to be there for him."

"I understand. But you still haven't answered my question. How are you?"

"Honestly, I don't know."

"And that's okay," Taylor assured her.

They spoke briefly, sharing work updates and discussing the yacht party. Before they ended the call, Tasia thanked Taylor again for an amazing evening, and Taylor requested an address where he could send the items to her. Tasia was so happy that Taylor hadn't gotten rid of her gifts. She was also relieved he didn't write her off after the disappearing act she pulled. Taylor was a good person, and Tasia knew she would connect with him more if she moved to St. Louis.

Rather than go to her usual grocer, she went to a store further away from her house. The last thing she needed was for one of the cashiers she often saw, seeing her purchase a pregnancy test. The pregnancy test was the last item she got off the shelf before heading to checkout. After the cashier rang it up, she put it in her purse for safekeeping.

She wanted to open the test immediately when she got home but decided to put away her groceries and settle in for the night first. Just as she was heading into the bathroom to learn her fate, she got a FaceTime call from Seth. She answered before she could wipe away the worriedness from her face, and Seth immediately saw that something was wrong.

"What's going on, bae? Are you okay?"

"Yea, umm. I'm okay. I just don't feel good." Tasia said nervously. She wanted to tell him, but fear of his response made her hesitate.

"Anastasia, what's going on? Talk to me. I can clearly see that something isn't right. Don't block me out like that." Seth replied, slightly agitated.

"I-I-I...I might be pregnant, Seth." She looked at him fretfully, waiting for his response.

"Oh, word?" Seth chuckled anxiously. "Well, congrats."

"Excuse me?" Tasia peered at him, confused by his distant response.

"Look, T. We'll have to talk about this later. I'm at the shop right now."

"You know what. Go to hell fuck nigga!" Tasia hung up the phone and burst into tears.

She stormed to the bathroom to take the pregnancy test. "I can't keep doing this shit with him!" She shouted in frustration. After seeing just how much Seth really didn't give a damn, she prayed relentlessly that the results were negative. She couldn't imagine dealing with Seth for the rest of her life. She understood that he couldn't talk much at work but still felt he could have been more supportive. *How could he congratulate her as if the child she might be carrying was hers alone?* Anger and disbelief coursed through her veins as she paced back and forth, waiting for the results that would determine the rest of her life.

Her phone timer went off, letting her know it was time

to look at the test she had turned face down on the counter. Her fingers trembled as she reached for the white and blue stick. When she flipped it over and saw the negative "NOT PREGNANT" results, the relief she thought would rush over her body failed her. She had mixed feelings. The truth is, a part of her actually wished she was pregnant. She didn't know why.

For the rest of the evening, Tasia sulked around the house. Seth never called back, and she didn't bother to call him. She thought about Kyle's words. If Seth really cared, he would make time to call me. Rather than force herself to make any quick and rash decisions, she allowed herself the rest of the evening to feel what she needed to feel. She cried, journaled, and spent time unpacking the different emotions going through her body. By the end of the night, she didn't have a resolution, but she felt a lot better after confronting the different emotions she was feeling. She had a busy day the next day, so she decided to get into bed early.

Sunlight peered through the curtains, gently waking Tasia alongside her alarm clock. At first, she was startled that she had left her curtains open overnight. Then, she was happy her first interaction of the day was with the sun that poured into her bedroom, warming her face and exposed skin. Despite what she had gone through the day before, she was determined to have a great day. Today was her company's quarterly meeting, and the entire staff would be in the office for the meeting. The quarterly meetings were always refreshing, and Tasia couldn't wait to see everyone. After considering what she would wear, Tasia decided to dress business chic and do a little color-blocking. She wore a pink, tailored, high-waisted skirt suit that was form-fitting. Her skirt fell right below her knees. She pulled out a light pink chiffon blouse to wear underneath her suit blazer, a hot pink YSL purse, and high heels the color of her blouse. She put on a dainty diamond necklace with the bracelet and earrings to match. She did her makeup perfectly and wore her hair bone straight with a part in the middle. She misted a few sprays of her Prada perfume and prepared to walk out the door.

Even though her morning had begun without a hitch, she was running late for the meeting. She looked at the clock on her truck's dashboard and realized she had less than forty minutes to make it through Atlanta traffic and get to the office on time. She turned up her music and sped off to the office.

Passing through Buckhead, an officer was posted up on the side of the interstate. Tasia knew without a doubt that he had clocked her and was headed her way. She looked at her speedometer and saw she was going 85 mph. *"Shit!"* She shouted. Tasia pumped the brakes and tried to slow down, but it was too late. The police officer pulled out behind her and flipped the sirens on. Tasia hit the steering wheel aggressively. "Damn! Mr. Officer, please don't give me a ticket." She whispered as she put on her signal light and pulled over on the side of the road. She put her car in park and turned the engine off. To be safe, she pulled her phone out of her purse, placed it on the car phone mount, and hit the record button. She rolled down her windows and placed both her hands on the steering wheel just as the cop was walking up to her window.

"License and registration." A fat older pale white man with a gray buzz cut peered at her while resting his hand on his gun holster.

"The requested items are in my purse," Tasia stated loud and clear. "With your permission, I will go into my purse and get them."

"Go ahead." He replied dryly, still not removing his hand from his gun holster. Tasia found the items quickly, handed them to the officer and put her hands back on the steering wheel.

"Do you know how fast you were going?" He asked.

"No, sir. I am running late for a work meeting. I lost sight of my speed, and I am very sorry."

"Late for a work meeting, huh? Well, where do you work at? Can't be anywhere too serious. You're all dolled up like a Black barbie doll." The officer smirked at Tasia as he rested his arms on the window.

Tasia bit her tongue and took a deep breath. She didn't take kindly to comments like that, especially as a black professional. However, with the Philando Castile case still fresh, she knew better than to retaliate. "I work for a magazine. My attire is completely acceptable for my line of work." She answered dryly. Her hands were planted firmly on the steering wheel, and she looked straight ahead.

"What's a pretty girl like you doing with such a big-time job around these parts?"

"I'm sorry, sir. I don't understand how your question relates to this traffic stop. If you don't mind, I would like to stick to the reason you pulled me over, receive any reprimand for my actions, and proceed with my day."

"Oh, so you do have brains?" The officer laughed. "Are you saying I'm holding you up and wasting your time?"

"Sir, I really want to get to work," Tasia replied. She could feel herself growing angrier and angrier. However, she kept her cool.

"You know what, bitch. Get out of the got damn car!" The officer suddenly became irate.

"Why am I getting out of the car? You haven't ran my license and registration! Like seriously?! Why do I have to get out of the car?"

"Get out of the car now!"

Tasia looked at him in disgust. "I do not feel safe. I will not get out of the car."

He reached inside the open window and yanked her door open from the inside handle. "We can do this the easy way or the hard way. It's your decision!" He shouted.

"I'm not getting out. I didn't do anything!"

The officer yanked her out of the seat by her arm and turned her around to face the open door.

"Are you serious? Please stop! You are hurting me!"

The police officer looked around for any onlookers, and there were only cars driving by. He pressed himself against her back and whispered in Tasia's ear. "Look, black bitch. Put your hands up and spread your legs. Maybe, just maybe, I won't report your little mishap today. You can go to work without a ticket or any repercussions."

"Get off of me. This is not right. Get the hell away from me!" Tasia shouted. He pushed himself up against Tasia even more and put his nose on her neck, inhaling her fragrance.

"Ooo, pretty lady. You smell like flowers." He chuckled.

Tasia knew what this could possibly lead to. The officer was so close to her that she could feel his erect penis on her behind. Tears rolled down Tasia's face as she prayed that someone would pass by, see what was happening, and put it to an end. She knew there was no way she could push the officer off of her. He was huge and much stronger.

"*Oh shit.*" The officer suddenly said under his breath. He had discovered the phone on Tasia's dashboard, recording the entire ordeal. He removed his badge, moved from behind Tasia, and turned her around.

"I'm going to let you go with a warning, ma'am." He informed her.

Tasia rolled her eyes. "I bet you are, you fat piece of shit! I hope you rot in hell!" Tasia quickly hopped in her truck and sped off. She drove to the next exit, pulled into a convenience store, and cried. "I just can't catch a damn break." She sobbed. Even though he was an ass to her yesterday and still hadn't called her back, she wanted to call Seth. She thought it was possible that with everything he had going on, Seth didn't know how to respond to potentially having a baby. So she put the previous day's interaction behind her and called him on FaceTime. She needed him.

"Wassup T?" Seth took one look at her and instantly became annoyed.

With tears still dripping, she attempted to tell him what had happened. "He sexually assaulted me, Seth. That big, fat officer put his hands on me, and I ---"

"I'm in a meeting, T. I'll call you back." Seth cut her off and ended the call before Tasia could speak. After how much she had been there for him, she couldn't believe he was being so cold to her. Tasia looked at the clock on her dashboard and realized she didn't have another second to sit around and mope. She was ten minutes late at this point. Her survival mode kicked in, and Tasia pulled herself together, fixed her makeup, and drove to work.

Fifteen

♡♡♡

Tasia arrived at the office late and was still in a daze. Luckily, everyone was still mingling and eating refreshments, so Tasia hadn't missed anything important. She spoke to her colleagues and grabbed a few things to snack on during the meeting.

One of her closest colleagues sat at the glass boardroom table across the room. They locked eyes, and Josiah pointed to a seat next to him, motioning Tasia to sit with him. Tasia considered Josiah her work boyfriend. He wasn't the typical corny-looking work boyfriend most women claimed. Josiah was fine enough to be her real boyfriend, and even though he was the perfect gentleman to everyone, Tasia knew he was especially sweet on her and would jump at the opportunity to date her. Josiah was a fit, tall, caramel man in his early thirties. He was very attractive, kept his curly hair neat, and was always well-dressed. Whenever they worked together, Josiah would cater to all her needs. He often brought her flowers, snacks, and lunch and would help her with her research if she ever needed it. Josiah was a good catch, but they worked together, and Tasia didn't want to cross those lines. She only entertained him at work, but there was always romantic tension between them. Tasia always did her best to keep that at bay.

Before sitting beside Josiah, she saw her boss, Mrs. Julie, and walked over to greet her before the meeting began. Mrs. Julie was a poised, older black woman in her late fifties, but she was walking proof that black never cracks. With her short, slim stature, and smooth dark chocolate skin, Mrs. Julie could pass for a thirty-year-old any day of the week. She wore her natural hair in twist outs, buns, and sometimes a curly afro. Mrs. Julie was warm, pleasant, wise, fashionable, and soft-spoken, and her employees knew her for always keeping it real. Tasia was honored to work for her and confided in Mrs. Julie about her personal life occasionally. When Mrs. Julie saw Tasia approaching, she stretched her arms out for a hug. They embraced each other, and Tasia took a deep breath. Mrs. Julie always smelled like sweet lavender and cocoa butter.

"Hi, Mrs. Julie." Tasia managed to say without breaking down into tears. Mrs. Julie's hugs were known to bring you to your knees if you weren't okay. However, she knew she had to hold it together while they were in front of the entire staff.

Mrs. Julie instantly knew something was wrong and began to softly and unnoticeably rub Tasia's back. After a moment, she released Tasia and looked at her with concern. "I know something is wrong with my baby girl. Come to my office after the meeting."

"Yes, ma'am." Tasia nodded. Then she walked away to take her seat next to Josiah.

When Josiah noticed Tasia was a few steps away, he stood up, pulled out the seat for her, and greeted her. "Good morning, beautiful."

Tasia smiled bashfully. "Good morning, Josiah."

"I got something for you." Josiah grinned. "It's your favorite." He reached into a bag beside him and pulled out an acai bowl and silverware from their favorite breakfast spot up the street." I know you didn't eat anything this morning, so I got this for you."

"Josiah, you're so thoughtful. Thank you. You're too good to me."

"I could be more," Josiah whispered back to her. "You should allow me to take you out sometime."

Tasia felt vulnerable and considered that a date with Josiah might be just what the doctor ordered to cheer her up. "I may take you up on that offer. I'll let you know."

Josiah beamed and turned his attention to Mrs. Julie's secretary, Carmen, who had stood up to call the meeting to order.

After Carmen greeted everyone and discussed the day's agenda, Mrs. Julie shared the quarterly stats, facilitated a few team-building exercises, and discussed quarter expectations. Everyone loved the quarterly meetings. They were always right to the point, fun, interactive, and over quickly. They were done within an hour.

Tasia greeted a few colleagues but didn't stay around for small talk. She desperately needed some motherly advice, so she darted to Mrs. Julie's office as fast as she could. Her corner office in the building was extravagant. Her wall-to-floor windows provided Mrs. Julie with Atlanta's most beautiful skyline view. Pictures of famous black writers, like Langston Hughes, Zora Neal Hurston, and Amiri Baraka, hung from the wall alongside black and white abstract artwork. Her furniture was lavish, including deep hues of burgundy with gold highlights. A lovely vase with fresh white flowers was in the corner of her large L-shaped desk. Tasia loved visiting Mrs. Julie's office. Even though it was the epitome of black excellence, which Tasia loved, her favorite part was the calming vibe. It felt like the perfect place to lay your burdens down. After leaving Mrs. Julie's office, you felt like you could take over the world.

When Tasia walked in, Mrs. Julie was finishing a phone call but motioned for her to come in and sit. Mrs. Julie and Tasia had always had a beautiful bond. Their relationship blossomed when Tasia had a mental breakdown at work after arguing over the phone with her father. That day, Tasia thought she was in the restroom alone when she had the quarrel, but she wasn't; Mrs. Julie was in one of the stalls. After the call ended, Tasia stood in front of one of the sinks and began to break down. Mrs. Julie emerged from the stall and comforted her. At the time, Tasia was a new writer and just getting her feet wet in the field. Mrs. Julie took her under her wing that day and began mentoring her.

Mrs. Julie ended her phone call, stood to close her door, sat down, and took a deep breath. For a few moments, she just looked at Tasia sincerely. "Talk to me." She finally said calmly. Holding back tears, Tasia shared everything in her life with her father, Seth, and her encounter with the police officer earlier that morning.

Mrs. Julie listened intently without interrupting her. When Tasia was done, Mrs. Julie took a deep breath. "Wow. That's a lot to take in, Tasia. First things first, I know people down at the precinct. We're going to take action and get that officer terminated. He's going to pay for what he did to you."

Tasia nodded in agreement.

"Now, about Seth. Tasia, you're a smart girl. All the signs are there. His words and actions don't line up. You have to judge him by his actions. Not his words. Now, if you want to move, that's understandable. But with him? That's questionable. If he doesn't make time for you when you visit, what makes you think he'll make time for you once you move there? Baby girl, don't let him keep running game on you. His intentions aren't genuine. Let this situation go. He doesn't deserve you."

Tasia sulked. "Honestly, Mrs. Julie, I've been holding on to him because after I asked God to send me someone to love me, I met Seth soon after. If it doesn't work out, I feel like I would be the one to blame. I just don't know why it's so hard for someone to love me." The tears Tasia had been holding back erupted. Mrs. Julie moved from behind her desk, sat on the loveseat next to Tasia, and held Tasia in her arms as she shook uncontrollably.

"Anastasia, listen to me. Excuse my language, but fuck him. Do you hear me?" She pulled Tasia upright to face her. "Fuck him. You deserve better. God is testing you. Everybody that comes into your life isn't meant to stay.

Fuck somebody loving you. Find that love within yourself. Once you find that, everything else will fall into place. Take some time to yourself to learn your worth. Never be anyone's fool again. Learn your lesson and move on."

Mrs. Julie confirmed everything Tasia's intuition told her since meeting Seth. She couldn't trust her intuition because she had been wrong many times. Mrs. Julie was right. Tasia knew she needed to move on. God had been giving her signs that Seth was not the one, and she ignored them.

Mrs. Julie handed her some tissues. After Tasia dried her tears, they talked more about work, her dad, and other life updates for about an hour. Tasia knew Mrs. Julie was a busy woman, so she thanked her for being there for her, gave her a hug, and left her office so she could work. After all, Mrs. Julie had given her a lot to think about, and she needed to set a few things in motion.

Tasia headed back to her desk and began working on an article on the new trends for home décor. When she was in the middle of doing research, Josiah stopped by her desk to check on her. "Hey, pretty lady." He said, flashing his gorgeous perfect smile. "Did you think about what I asked earlier?" Honestly, Tasia hadn't given it a second thought. However, she had such an awful morning and desperately needed a pick-me-up, so Tasia decided to take him up on his offer.

"You know what, Josiah? I did." Tasia smiled back. "I'm free tomorrow."

"Whaaattt? Say that again. I can't believe my ears." Josiah raised his eyebrows and leaned back, acting dramatically shocked. "About damn time, shawty."

Tasia rolled her eyes playfully. "Stop it. You know why we haven't been on a date. But I guess I'm open to new things now."

"Well, I'm glad you have had a change of heart. I'll plan something nice for us and send you the details tomorrow." Josiah winked his eye at her.

"Cool. I'm working from home tomorrow, so I'll see you later that night."

Josiah left her desk, and Tasia distracted herself with work for the rest of the day.

The next morning, she got a good morning text from Josiah, along with the details for their date. He had secured an eight o'clock reservation at an upscale steakhouse downtown. Tasia thought the best way to get Seth out of her system was to welcome new energy into her life. "The best way to get over one man is to get under another." She said out loud as she replied to Josiah's message with her address. She was excited to go on a date with a real gentleman.

Later that day, she got a call from Seth. She hit the decline button and continued researching for her article without flinching. Tasia decided to keep Seth off her mind and think about her date with Josiah. Even though she was excited to take her first step away from Seth, she hoped things would go well between her and Josiah. If not, things would be awkward between them at work. She hoped for the best, but with her luck with men, she couldn't be sure how things would turn out. *I can't dwell on what ifs*, Tasia thought. *I won't know unless I try. And Josiah is definitely worth it.*

After a successful day of work, Tasia pushed away from

her desk and jumped in the shower. She took her time in the shower, then sat on her bed to moisturize her skin. She had been so busy with work that she hadn't considered what she would wear on her first date with Josiah. He had always seen her looking her best, but tonight, she wanted to show him a different, sexy, all-fun, no-business side of her. Tasia walked into her closet and shifted things around in search of the perfect look for the night.

Ring. Ring. Her intuition told her it was Seth, and it was right. Tasia looked at her phone in annoyance. At first, she considered sending him to voicemail again. Then, Tasia decided to test her theory once again. She had all the proof she needed that Seth was playing games with her, but a part of her wanted to be sure before she stepped out with Josiah.

"Sup?" Tasia answered unenthused.

"Hey T. Are you doing okay from whatever happened yesterday?"

"Why does it matter? I was literally crying my eyes out, and you rushed me off the phone."

"Tasia, I was busy. Baby, I'm so s---"

"Sorry. Yea, yea, yea. You're always so sorry. Save it, Seth."

Seth was taken aback but tried to lighten the mood by making a joke. Tasia wasn't having it. She didn't laugh. Tasia answered the phone for one reason: to prove to herself that she wasn't delusional and that Seth had been gaslighting her. *He can miss me with the pleasantries,* she thought to herself. Why would he go so far as to make her fall in love with him and not have any intentions of catching her? The entire situation was confusing. To see where Seth's head was, Tasia attempted to bring up her move to St. Louis at least three times. Seth dodged her questions or switched the topic each time. Tasia could see clear as day that Seth was all talk and game. She couldn't believe it, but Tasia knew she would end things fairly soon with Seth. Tasia was done being toyed with. At this point, if she continued on the same path with Seth, she would only have herself to blame for the heartbreak.

While Tasia was deep in thought, Seth was doing the usual, talking about himself. He was so consumed that he didn't even realize Tasia hadn't responded. "Hey, homeboy. I'm gone hit you back later." Tasia cut him off abruptly.

"Homeboy?" Seth asked, confused. "I don't know what all that's about, but I'm your man."

Tasia chuckled. "Sure, Seth."

"Well, before you go, did you find out if we're expecting?" Seth asked.

"We?" Tasia quipped back. "Oh, you speak French now? Congrats, Seth. You're not a father." She disconnected the call before Seth could say another word. She connected her phone to her bedroom's Bluetooth speaker and played her "Fuck Boy" playlist. The first song that played was "Don't Trust No Nigga" by Khia. Tasia turned the volume to the max and sang along to the top of her lungs. The song was just what she needed to get back focused on the task at hand and find the perfect outfit to wow Josiah.

She chose a black body con dress, red strappy YSL heels, and a red Gucci clutch. She laid her outfit on the bed, did her make-up, and styled her hair with voluptuous curls. Tasia looked in the mirror and admired her work. She took a selfie and uploaded it to her social media. Seth was in her DM within seconds, asking where she was going. She opened the message so that he could see it was read but refused to give him a reply.

She heard a knock at her door and knew it was Josiah. There wasn't a doubt in her mind that he would be punctual. She sprayed her Marc Jacobs perfume, grabbed her clutch, and slowly headed to the front door. Tasia took a deep breath in and then exhaled deeply. "Be open to new things and experiences. Bitch, enjoy yourself." Tasia said aloud. She took one last look at herself in her large living room mirror before she opened the door. When she finally opened the door, she was greeted by Josiah, looking more handsome than usual, holding a bouquet of fresh red roses. Tasia blushed. As if he had been looking through her window the entire time she got dressed, Josiah matched her perfectly. He wore a tailored black suit, a red pocket handkerchief, a white silk button-down shirt, and black Louboutins. Tasia wasn't shocked because he always dressed nice, but tonight, he had a sex appeal she hadn't seen in the office. It appeared the two of them had the same idea for the night. Josiah took one look at Tasia and shook his head with amazement. "Anastasia, I always knew you were fine, but damn."

Tasia blushed. "Well, I see you didn't come to play tonight either."

"Oh, no. I'm definitely not trying to play with you." Josiah replied, giving her a playful look up and down. "Come now. Your chariot awaits, my lady." Josiah extended his hand, and Tasia took it. He escorted her to the front passenger side of his white G-Wagon and opened the door for her. Once he closed her door and got on the driver's side, he started the car and turned the volume low on the smooth R&B tunes on his car stereo. On the ride to the restaurant, they shared a little about who they were outside the office. Josiah laughed extremely hard as Tasia shared that she had a little ratchet to her and revealed that he did as well. They were shocked to learn they had so many things in common such as favorite bars in the city, music, food, and even TV shows. Their night was off to a pleasant start, and Tasia was hopeful about the rest of their evening.

They arrived at the restaurant and were guided to their table. Tasia was truly enjoying herself and didn't have to force herself not to think about Seth. He drifted to the farthest part of her mind naturally. She hated that she hadn't given Josiah a chance sooner. He was handsome, entertaining, well-spoken, romantic, and an overall gentleman. After they had ordered their food, Josiah took a deep breath and stared at Tasia.

"What?" Tasia inquired.

"Anastasia, I'm really enjoying myself. I'm glad you finally gave me a chance outside of the office."

"You know something? I was just asking myself why we didn't do this sooner." Tasia replied. "To be honest, I just loved our bond and didn't want a failed date to ruin that and make things awkward, ya know?"

"Yea, I definitely get that. But I'm glad we were able to make this happen."

Tasia agreed and smiled softly. "I'm enjoying your company, Josiah."

"We never talk about our love lives, but I assume you're single since we're on a date. Am I right?" Tasia hesitated to answer, and Josiah could tell she was stalling, so he said, "Well, I'm single if you were wondering. I ended a two-year relationship about six months ago. I'm finally out of my feelings and ready to get to know someone on a deeper level."

"Thanks for sharing that with me, Josiah. I'm happy you didn't let the last situation keep you from pursuing love."

"Yeah. I know there is someone out there for me. I learned a lot in my last relationship, and I think I'm a better man because of it." Josiah said. He paused and looked at Tasia, hopeful she would share her current status. Tasia picked up the hint and decided to be completely honest with Josiah.

"Well, it's a bit more complicated on my end." Tasia began. "I'm dating someone, but we're not in a relationship. A situation-ship perhaps. It's long-distance, and I'm concluding that we are not meant to be. So, I'm now open to dating." Tasia was careful not to overshare. The last thing she wanted was for the night to become a deep conversation about Seth.

"I can't say that I'm surprised. You are quite the catch. I would have thought you were lying if you told me you were completely single and ready to mingle." Josiah laughed to lighten the mood.

"What are you looking for right now?" Tasia asked.

"You mean relationship-wise or the type of woman I'm looking for?" Josiah asked for clarity.

"Relationship wise. What do you want? A situation-ship, casual dating, a cut buddy? What?" Tasia replied.

"I'm thirty- two years old. At this point in my life, I'm

ready to settle down, get married, and have a family. I've had fun playing the field. I don't regret it because I learned the type of woman I want and need in my life. And, like I said before, I've learned and matured in a lot of areas. I'm far from perfect, but I believe I'm on the right track. So, I'm ready to be some lucky woman's husband."

"That's what's up," Tasia said. She wasn't shocked at all. Josiah never came off as the type of man who wanted to play and toy with women's hearts. However, she had heard those lines before. Only time would tell if that's what Josiah wanted, and furthermore, if he wanted that with her.

"What about you? I know you are wrapping up a situation-ship, but what do you want?"

Tasia took a deep breath and realized that no man had ever asked her that. Most of the time, men made lofty promises about the type of man they could be to her and what they wanted to do for her, but no one had ever asked her what she wanted. She was almost nervous to say it aloud, but something about Josiah made her feel comfortable being honest and baring her heart about her desires for her romantic life.

"Josiah, I want it all. I want to be somebody's wife, homie, lover, and best friend. I want to be a mother and have a huge family. Big house. Family vacations. All of it. I've had my share of dating experiences as well. But I'm tired of the games. I'm ready for a space where I can be safe to love and be loved."

"Damn. I can feel that, Anastasia. For real. I literally felt your heart as you shared. I'm on the same thing. All that other stuff is for the birds! I'm ready to take my kids to soccer practice and hear my wife fuss because I forgot to take out the trash!" Josiah and Tasia laughed. She loved his sense of humor. Laughing with him was healing to her soul.

"Josiah, you are crazy! But I'm with you one hundred percent."

They talked about their hobbies, goals, aspirations, and career paths for the rest of the night. Their evening ended just as beautifully as it began. In the car on the way back to Tasia's place, they agreed to date more, take their time, and really get to know each other. Tasia was nervous, but she had nothing to lose. She decided right then and there to kick Seth to the curb and give herself a real chance to get to know Josiah. When they arrived at her home, Josiah walked her to her front door and thanked her for a lovely night. She thanked him with a kiss on the cheek and smiled to herself when Josiah blushed.

Once inside, Tasia sunk into her living room sofa, kicked off her shoes, and grinned so hard her cheeks hurt. She spent the evening reminiscing about her night with Josiah. She was on such a high cloud she didn't notice the eight missed calls from Seth until the next morning. Even then, she refused to call him back. Seth was her past. Josiah could possibly be her future. She had already given Seth enough of her time and energy.

Sixteen

♡♡♡

After two weeks of ignoring Seth's calls and texts, Tasia was slowly getting over him. As the days went by, she thought about him even less. Having Josiah's company certainly made the process easier. They kept their word and took things slow. Tasia enjoyed allowing Josiah to court her. Since their first date, they had a lot of great experiences with each other. They had a picnic at Piedmont Park, visited the aquarium, went to the museum, went hiking, attended a poetry night, and had brunch one Sunday. Tasia loved how Josiah made time for her, gave her attention, and romanced her.

Kyle's approval gave Tasia more hope that Josiah could be good for her. Tasia didn't know they knew each other until the week before. Josiah had invited Tasia to watch him play intramural basketball at a gym near their job. While sitting in the stands, Tasia thought she saw a familiar face near the entrance, but she wasn't sure. After the game, she went down to congratulate Josiah on the win. That's when Kyle walked up and asked her what she was doing there. Josiah joked and said Tasia had come to see him beat Kyle. That's when they all discovered that they knew each other. Kyle called her the next day and requested all the details. He assured Tasia that Josiah was a good guy and he was happy they were dating. He was even happier to hear that she was done being played to the left by Seth. Kyle was the only consistent male figure in her life, so his approval of Josiah made Tasia feel more at ease.

One Saturday, Tasia realized she hadn't visited her dad in weeks, so she decided to check on him. Rather than her usual dark clothing, she was feeling good and wanted to wear something bright and cheery. Besides, it was a hot July summer day, and she was sure she and Josiah would do something later.

Even though she was nervous about seeing her dad because she never knew what to expect, potentially seeing Josiah later gave her something to smile about. Josiah felt like the fresh breath of air she got on at the yacht party with Taylor. He made her feel genuinely sought after, respected, and considered. She floated around her room, smiling at thoughts of things Josiah had said to her.

After ironing a yellow and blue sundress for the day, she got dressed. At first, she decided on silver accessories, but she didn't like how they looked, so she rummaged through her jewelry case for something gold instead. As she searched for the perfect pieces to complete her look, her phone rang. It was Seth. Tasia was feeling pretty confident that she wouldn't get sucked in by his antics, so she decided to answer.

"Wassup." She answered nonchalantly.

"Woman, don't wassup me. What the hell I do to make you not talk to me for weeks?"

"I was busy with stuff at work," Tasia replied sarcastically, using one of Seth's favorite lines. "Anywho, how are you? What have you been up to?"

Her sarcasm and dryness made Seth furious. "Anastasia, you better stop fucking playing games with me!" He shouted.

"I'm not playing. I was busy. You do need to check your tone though before this conversation goes sideways."

"Do I need to take a trip to the A for you to act right? Cause you clearly think this is a mutha fucking game, T!" Seth fumed.

"Boy, pipe down." Tasia chuckled. "Besides, you're probably too busy to fuck with ya girl."

"What the hell has gotten into you?!" Seth continued to yell.

"Some sense, Seth! Some damn common sense!"

"The fuck is that supposed to mean?" Seth's voice was getting louder and louder, but Tasia remained unbothered.

"Seth, you're not a man of your word. You could give a rat's ass about me. You're all talk, no walk. Nigga, you don't love me, and you never did."

"Man, look! I don't give a fuck about what you're talking about. I don't wanna hear this bullshit. Someone must've gotten into your head. I do love you, Tasia. You know that. Name another nigga that flies you out first-class and pays your bills! Iced you out with VVS jewels? Decked you out in the finest? Put some real heat on your feet? Not one of them! I did that shit! Fuck you mean I don't love you?"

"Fuck all of that, Seth. I could have bought that shit myself, and you know that. Spending money isn't all it takes to satisfy a woman. At least not me. I need genuine love, affection, and intentional time. I gotta have someone who acknowledges my feelings. And I've realized that I can't force you to treat me how I want to be treated. You're a grown-ass man, and you're going to make time for what you wanna make time for. I'm just not on your list of priorities, and I'm cool with that. So I'm giving my time to someone who will."

"Oh, so you out here cooling it with some other nigga?" Seth replied angrily, completely ignoring everything Tasia said.

"What I do and who I do it with is my business. We never made things official. Did you forget?" Tasia replied, still remaining calm and collected.

"Oh, you funny! You got real fucking jokes. Check you out. T the fucking comedian!" Seth shouted.

"Yep. And you're the funniest joke I've ever told. Clown ass nigga." Tasia laughed cooly.

"*Yo, Fuck you, T! And I mean that shit! Fuck you!*" Seth yelled aggressively and disconnected the call.

"No, the fuck he did not," Tasia said to herself. She called him back several times, and Seth ignored every call. This made Tasia livid, so she texted him instead.

> *Nigga! Don't you ever in your raggedy ass life talk to me like that again. Stupid ass bitch!*

Seth replied back quickly.
Anastasia! Fuck you! You're the dummy.

Tasia was ready to destroy Seth, but she decided to calm down before she took things too far. Besides, it was a beautiful day, and she refused to allow Seth to waste any more of her time. She was already dealing with anxiety about seeing her dad. So, she took a few deep breaths and exhaled slowly. Once calm, Tasia jumped in the car and headed to Garden Manor.

Garden Manor had changed the guest sign-in process since her last visit, and now, each patient had their own visitor log. When she found her father's log, she was surprised that Angelique Jenson had visited her dad often. In fact, she had just left a few hours before Tasia arrived. Tasia had no clue who she could be. To her knowledge, she was the only one who visited her father. She shrugged it off. It was good to know that somebody else was visiting the old man, especially with his track record. She took a deep breath and walked slowly to her father's room. Even though she visited often, she never knew what to expect. He appeared to be getting worse with every visit.

Tasia entered her father's room and instantly noticed that he had lost more weight. She walked closer to him, and she stood by him. "Daddy?" she whispered. He was so still it looked like he was dead. However, he was only resting peacefully. He fluttered his eyes open at the sound of her voice.

"Is that my favorite girl?" He said sweetly.

Tasia scrunched up her face. She didn't know who he was referring to, but Tasia knew he wasn't talking about her.

"It's me, Anastasia."

"I know," he replied softly. "I'd know your voice from

anywhere." Tasia raised her eyebrows and chalked it up to dementia. There was no way he was being this kind and sweet to her. He had to believe she was her mother again.

Tasia shrugged it off and proceeded with her routine questions. "How are you doing?"

"Well, my body has really been hurting. The medicine doesn't take the pain away anymore." He replied feebly.

"I'm so sorry to hear that." Seeing how illness could humble people made Tasia feel sorry for her dad. She rubbed his hand gently to comfort him. As if her touch set off an alarm, he looked up at her in confusion and snatched his hand aggressively.

"Who are you?" He shouted weakly.

"Daddy, it's me. Anastasia. Your daughter."

He shook his head violently! *"Where is my son? I want my son!"*

Tasia's heart dropped. "Daddy, Antoine passed away a few years ago."

Her father began rambling about something that she couldn't make out. Tasia tried to console him and wipe away his tears, but he shifted away from her.

"Daddy, if you remember Antoine, I know you remember me."

"I want my son. Where is he?" her father continued to sob. "He doesn't visit me at all. Is he still mad at me? Tell him I'm so sorry for hitting his sister. He loved his sister. But what Gabrielle did was wrong. So wrong. I could never love..." he stopped abruptly.

Tears fell down Tasia's face. Her father went on and on, rambling about something that she couldn't make out. It sounded like her dad was referring to when Antoine fought him for roughing her up. His dementia was getting worse, so she knew she couldn't get upset. It hurt her so much that he didn't recognize her. Tasia couldn't handle staying in the room with her father for another second. She knew that if she didn't leave soon, she would break completely down in front of him. Tasia grabbed some tissues and headed to the door.

"I love you, Dad. I'll see you soon." Tasia said to him. He didn't reply to her. He was still sobbing about Antoine. He turned his back to her and continued to cry his eyes out.

Before leaving, Tasia stopped at the nurses' station and asked one of the nurses if they knew the Angelique Jenson woman that had been visiting her dad. Unfortunately, it was the nurse's first week at the location, and she was still learning about the residents and their frequent visitors. Tasia thanked the nurse, and before she could walk away, the nurse said to her, "Baby, I see the distress on your face. I know it's hard seeing him like that. Pray for peace and understanding. God got you, baby. He's watching over you and will guide you through this."

Tasia let out a sigh of relief. "Thank you. I really appreciate that." Then, she powerwalked to her car to let out her emotions. Before she could get inside, she got a call from Josiah. She answered the phone holding back tears. Josiah sensed something was wrong and asked for her location. Tasia shared it with him, and he told her to sit tight until he arrived. Tasia screamed and cried uncontrollably as she waited for Josiah to arrive. She didn't know she had so much emotion inside her. It was settling in that her dad would pass soon, and she would be the last one alive from her immediate family. Her mom and brother were gone, and her dad would soon join them on the other side. She felt alone and like an orphan. It felt like everything in her world was crashing down, and no one was willing to save her.

Josiah arrived, parked behind Tasia's Jeep, and rushed to her driver's side door, where he found Tasia with her head against the steering wheel, balling her eyes out. He knocked on her window, and she turned to look at him. Her eyes were bloodshot red. He asked her to open the door, and she unlocked it. Josiah immediately opened the door and embraced her. He calmed her down and told her that everything would be okay. Then, he helped her out of her Jeep, got her belongings, and escorted her to his whip. Josiah told her that he would take her to his crib and take care of her until she was ready to go home.

Josiah lived in a stylish loft in Midtown Atlanta. He had decorated his loft in black and gold, the same colors as his beloved fraternity. He sat Tasia on his plush black velvet couch and brought her a glass of water. Josiah sat beside her and asked if she was ready to discuss what had happened earlier. Tasia took a deep breath and mustered the courage to tell him no. He understood and didn't pressure her to talk. He turned on his flat-screen TV and gave her the remote. "I'll make you some tea. Go ahead and get comfortable."

Later, Josiah came back from the kitchen with a hot cup of chamomile tea and aspirin. He was startled to find Tasia sitting in a daze. He had never seen her like this and wanted to be there for her. He planned to do whatever it took to help her to feel better. Josiah called her name, and she snapped out of her daze. He told her to take the aspirin and to be careful drinking the tea. He sat back next to her and pulled her into his arms. Tasia nestled up to him, resting her head on his shoulder.

Tasia was exhausted from crying and dozed off almost immediately. Josiah gently kissed her forehead and laid her down on the couch. He pulled out a warm throw, laid it across her, and removed her shoes. He wanted her to feel like she was at home. While Tasia was asleep, Josiah ran out to grab her food, wine, toiletries, and clothes. After taking everything back to his loft in case she awoke sooner than he expected, he called an Uber to take him to get Tasia's Jeep from Garden Manor. When he returned, Tasia was still asleep.

A few hours later, Tasia awoke to Josiah sweeping and tidying up his place. Tasia sat up and smiled at him.

"Thank you for coming to get me," Tasia said softly, startling Josiah, who didn't know she had awakened.

"Don't mention it, beautiful. That's what friends do."

Tasia looked at his kitchen island, and there was a plethora of shopping bags. Tasia, being inquisitive, asked what was in the bags.

"I wanted to make you feel comfortable and at home, so I stopped at Pink to get you some night clothes and underwear. I also got food, snacks, wine, and a bubble bath. I'm going to run you a bath after you eat." Josiah informed her.

"Josiah, you didn't have to do all of this." Tasia sighed.

"You're right. I didn't, but I wanted to. You needed me. I told you I got you." Josiah said gently as he continued to clean.

Tasia took a long bath. As the water and bubbles floated around her, she tried to make sense of her reality. Dealing with Seth and her dad was affecting her mental health. She knew she would fall into a deep depression again soon if she didn't change something. When she was in that state of mind, she often made decisions she later regretted. She shuddered at the thought of what she did after her mother and brother passed away. Before getting out of the tub, she decided to take some time off work and away from everything to take care of her mental health. After her bath, she dressed and reentered the living room, where Josiah had dinner waiting for her. They ate and had minimal conversation. As the night winded down, Tasia told Josiah she was ready to talk. He turned off the TV and gave her his undivided attention. She was in tears yet again, talking about her life. She apologized for being a wreck, and Josiah wiped her tears away and held her until they both fell asleep.

The next morning, Tasia woke up to flowers, a handwritten card, and a homemade breakfast that Josiah had prepared. Tasia was appreciative and couldn't thank him enough. They spent most of the day together, and that evening, Tasia went home to reflect.

Once she arrived home, she received a call from Lisa.

"Damn, Tasia. Where have you been? Haven't heard from you." said Lisa.

"My days have been hectic, and I've been dealing with a lot." Tasia updated Lisa. The two caught up, and Lisa reminded Tasia that she needed to schedule an appointment with her therapist before she had another episode. Lisa tried to cheer her up by letting her know that gray skies eventually turn to sunshine over time and that Tasia would get through it all.

Lisa then said, "I can't believe Seth. The audacity! What was the reason? Why is he out here lying and giving out false hope? What type of bullshit is that? I look at him totally differently now."

"Girl! Fuck him." Tasia agreed.

"The nerve of that nigga!" Lisa continued to fume. "How can he ask you to move in with him when he's late on all his bills and was damn near about to be evicted from his condo."

Tasia's eyes grew wide. "Lisa, what the hell are you talking about?"

"When I was cleaning up while we were there for your birthday, I found an Adidas shoe box under his couch stuffed with documents. You know I'm nosey, so I went through it. There were handwritten credit card numbers on small pieces of paper, bank statements with luxury purchases, cards in other people's names, and his personal accounts were in the negative."

"What?? Lisa! Why the fuck didn't you tell me this?"

"Tasia, I didn't know that man was asking you to move in with him until now. I didn't want to be the bearer of bad news on your birthday. I figured you would eventually find out."

"Shawty, damn my birthday. You could've told me this." Tasia was utterly dumbfounded and suddenly remembered that he still owed her money for the tickets for the vacation they never went on.

"Gah damn! I've been hoodwinked!" Tasia exclaimed. "I ain't never been played like this before. Ain't this bout a

bitch? Lisa, let me call you back."

Tasia was furious. She paced back and forth through her living room. "Why would he offer her security and a new life when he couldn't provide for himself? She fell in love with his potential and ignored all the red flags and inconsistencies. Tasia was appalled that she even considered settling for Seth. The real question she wanted to be answered was how could the owner of a seemingly lucrative business be broke? Tasia threw on her detective hat, pulled out her laptop, and googled information about the shoe store. She found a government website that provided information on active businesses and Viola. She located the business details of the shoe boutique, Opulent Kicks STL, and searched for Seth's name under ownership, and his name was nowhere in sight. Chris was the sole owner of the boutique. Tasia was stunned. She took a screenshot of her findings and sent it to Lisa. Lisa was in disbelief as well. Seth had been lying for years. He wasn't a CEO. He just worked at the boutique. Tasia didn't stop there. She sent the photos to Seth and confronted him about being a liar. She texted him back to back, infuriated and demanding an explanation.

> *What was the reason for lying?!*
> *You ain't no boss! You're just a worker! Nigga run me*
> *my money for them flights! I didn't forget!*
> *You're such a fuck boy! You're too old to be lying.*
> *Oh, so your weak ass can't even respond?*
> *You ain't no real man!*
> *You scammed me out my panties.*
> *Liar, liar, liar pants on fire.*

Moments later, Tasia's phone began to ring; Seth, of course.

Tasia answered immediately. "What do you have to say for yourself?"

"Look, bitch! Stop texting me!"

"Seth, I could literally have someone come to St. Louis and straight beat your ass. I ain't gone be too many more bitches."

"Anastasia, you're dumb to think I would ever want to be with your damaged ass! I had a craving and you filled it!"

"Seth, be real with yourself. If that was the case, you wouldn't have done half the shit you did!"

"Oh, those lil bills and gifts weren't nothing. To be honest, I kept you around because I was bored. Tasia, if I wanted you, I would have been made it official with you. You're so gullible. That's why I kept fucking with you."

"Seth, I really had love for you, but you disgust me. You have one evil soul. You probably don't know what love is. I know your mom died when you were young, so you prob--"

"Aye, bitch! Leave my mom out of this before I start on yo dying ass daddy."

"Wow, you're really showing your true colors. Don't be upset because I found out you're not the boss that you say you are! Pipe down before I put that ass on blast!"

"You ain't gone do shit!

"I really can't believe we are going back and forth like this. Why would you lie? Why would you go out your way to get me an interview for a writing gig? Tell me so I can at least have closure!"

"Tasia, I never wanted you to move here. I just wanted you on demand. I'm shocked you even got the interview. Your writing is trash. Also, if you did move here, you wasn't gone be shit without me! You would only have connections because of me!"

Tasia let out an evil cackle. "Seth, you're talking out the side of your neck! If I would've moved to St. Louis, I would've been that bitch. I'm that bitch in my own city! What makes you think I wouldn't be able to make a name for myself in small ass St. Louis."

"Sweetheart, you mentally and emotionally unstable! You fucked up in the head! You wouldn't be shit without me if you lived here. I'm that nigga and will always be that nigga."

"Seth, don't fuck with me. I would move there just to shit on your entire existence and bring my ass back to Atlanta like nothing happened. You fucking with the right one."

"Bitch, bye. You ain't tight like that!" Seth laughed.

"Seth Brown. I'm about to make your life a living hell. You will regret the day you ever played with me."

Tasia ended the call, and her mind began to overflow with irrational ideas. "Oh, Imma show him why I'm that bitch!" She shouted to herself. Hell has no fury like a woman scorned.

Tasia sat at her desk and began looking up apartments in St. Louis. Her lease was up in two months, and Tasia decided right then and there that she was moving to St. Louis. She checked her savings and had more than enough money to move and maintain her lifestyle. She emailed her boss and asked her boss if she could work remotely out of state. She refused to work for a company Seth referred her to. Tasia stayed up for hours, planning her move and making to-do lists of things to handle before she left Atlanta. Not once did Tasia second guess her decision. She felt it was her duty to make a fool out of Seth. She sent Seth one last text message:

You played the wrong bitch.
Keep your head on a swivel, hoe.

Tasia was on a rampage to get her affairs in order in the following days. She located a townhome in Creve Coure and began the application process. Mrs. Julie accepted her request to work out of state, and the company would fly her in for the quarterly meetings. Tasia was a valuable part of the team, and Mrs. Julie did not want to lose her. Tasia knew she was moving illogically, but she couldn't stop herself. She had a point to prove and was determined to show Seth who she was.

Next on Tasia's list was getting rid of things she didn't need. All the jewelry Seth got her would be the first to go. She decided to pawn it and use the money towards her move. She didn't want anything that reminded her of him. Moving to his city was bad enough.

Tasia drove to a pawn shop on the south side and was greeted by an older black man dressed as a black cowboy. She placed her items on the counter, and he grabbed his magnifying glass to examine the pieces.

"Miss, I've been in the business for a long time, and this is what we call diamond simulants." He informed

Tasia.

"Say what now?" Tasia asked him to explain.

"These are diamond imitations."

Tasia couldn't believe it. "Wow! This is embarrassing. These were gifts."

"Cupcake, if your man got you this fake jewelry, kick his ass to the curb. "

"I'm sorry for wasting your time." Tasia gathered her things and darted to the exit. Knowing that he wouldn't respond, she texted Seth.

> *Seth, you're such a fraud.*
> *Even the jewelry you got me was fake.*
> *Fake, just like your ass.*
> *Count your days, buddy.*

Later that evening, Tasia was at home, sulking, drinking wine, smoking weed, and listening to sad R&B songs. After rolling up another blunt, she lit it, and a lightbulb went off in her head. She rushed upstairs to get everything Seth bought her, ran to her backyard, and began placing items on her barbeque grill. She poured lighter fluid on the items and then lit everything on fire. She sat in her patio chair and watched everything go up into flames while smoking her blunt.

She thought since God wanted to take everyone away from her, this would be Seth's funeral. He was dead to her. She would never look at him the same again. She felt the tension release from her body as the flames began to settle. Tasia self-medicated the rest of the night and ordered takeout. The next morning, she woke up with a major headache and was still high from the night before.

She moped around the house until she got tired of feeling sorry for herself and decided to go to Piedmont Park for a run. She needed to release the negativity that was built up inside of her. While out for her run, she got an email notifying her that she got approved for the townhome in St. Louis. It was official. Tasia was moving.

Seventeen

♡♡♡

Tasia announced to her close friends that she was moving to St. Louis. They didn't understand but respected her decision. Tasia had a point to prove and was standing her ground. Pride was one hell of a drug. She was a grown woman and made her own choices, and they couldn't stop her. Despite her dad's illnesses, he wouldn't stop her either. She planned to come back to visit him as often as she could. Tasia concluded that she was going to a new city not just to get back at Seth but so she could start over and create something of her own. She decided that she was finally going to start a social blog.

The following week, Josiah invited her to a wine tasting at a winery in Talking Rock, GA. They both were dressed nicely. Tasia wore a pastel flowery, flowy dress with sandals and Josiah wore a white polo Versace shirt, white linen pants, and loafers. While at the winery, they took a tour of the property and purchased a few of their favorite wines. The winery had an outdoor sitting area, and they sat outside to enjoy the scenery. Josiah noticed something was off with Tasia. She had been daydreaming for most of their lunch.

Josiah called her name, and she didn't respond. He poked her arm, which startled her. She quickly apologized for not being present. He looked at her inquisitively and asked what was bothering her. Tasia told him it was nothing. He pulled Tasia close to him and turned her to face him. Josiah gently caressed her hands and asked Tasia to talk to him.

Their friendship had grown, so Tasia was slightly nervous about telling him she was moving. She took a deep breath and mumbled, "I'm moving."

Josiah looked at her in disbelief. "Why?"

"I need to get away from Atlanta. I need something new. So, I'm moving to St. Louis to start my blog.

"You can't do that here?"

Tasia shook her head no. "Josiah, the time is now. I need a fresh start."

"Damn. Well, when are you leaving me?"

"I have a month or so left before I leave." Tasia could see the disappointment on his face. "I'm sorry, Josiah. I have to do this for me. Please don't be mad."

"No. I get it." Josiah said compassionately. "You've been through a lot. But what about your dad?" Tasia took a long deep breath. "Josiah, I can't keep putting my life on hold while my dad is in hospice. I can't help him. There's no coming back from his illnesses. I do plan to come back to visit him, but nothing can stop me from leaving."

Josiah looked at her, and sadness filled his eyes. "Tasia,

I'm not judging you. It's your choice. I hate that you're leaving. I'm happy for you, though. You're one courageous woman."

Tasia kissed him on the cheek and they gazed into one another's eyes for what felt like hours.

"I appreciate you," Tasia whispered.

Josiah moved her face closer to his and kissed her passionately. "Do you know how long I've wanted to do that?"

Tasia blushed. "How long?"

"Since the day I met you."

Tasia kissed him again. They were in bliss for the rest of their time together.

The following weeks were a blur for Tasia. She was consumed with packing, visiting her dad, and spending most of her time with her friends and Josiah. On Tasia's last weekend in Atlanta, Kyle invited her to their favorite lounge for one last drink in the city. He also told her that they would stop by his homeboy's birthday party before they hit the lounge and instructed her to dress in all black. Kyle told her they would mingle for a few minutes and then head to the lounge. Tasia opted to wear a black silk knee-length dress, black Louboutins, and a black clutch. She did her makeup perfectly and wore her hair in a sleek high bun. Kyle picked her up, and he was dressed nicer than usual. Before pulling off, he said, "Let's fuck the city up one last time."

"Oh, let's do it!" Tasia replied enthusiastically.

They arrived at one of the nicest restaurants in Downtown Atlanta that had the best skyline view.

"Oohhhh, your friend is fancy," Tasia exclaimed when they pulled up.

Kyle chuckled. "We're only staying for a few minutes. Then, we gone head out for the real turn up."

"Sounds like a plan!" Tasia was excited to spend her last Saturday in the A with Kyle. She knew out of everyone, he would send her off right. They entered the restaurant and were greeted by the hostess, who asked if they had reservations. Kyle rushed to the woman's podium, leaving Tasia at the door. Kyle and the hostess whispered back and forth for a few moments. Tasia looked at them both strangely. Finally, the hostess escorted Kyle and Tasia to the back of the restaurant, where they served large groups.

Tasia stepped into a dimly lit, decorated room and was shocked to see many familiar faces. She saw Brittany, Lisa and her parents, Mrs. Julie, Josiah, her close co-workers, and influencer friends. Tasia was baffled for a moment until she realized...she was at her own surprise dinner.

Tasia was so joyful that she couldn't hold back her tears. Kyle hugged her tightly. "I love you, best friend. I'm really going to miss you," said a heartfelt Kyle. They embraced until everyone came up one by one to greet her. Tasia was amazed that Kyle and her friends had pulled a surprise like this off without her knowing.

"Girl! I'm so glad this day has finally come." Lisa laughed. "I don't think I could've held this in much longer."

"Oh, I'm sure you could have. You love to hang onto secrets." Tasia assured her with a sarcastic smile.

Lisa rolled her eyes. "Drop it. I apologized, didn't I?"

Tasia smirked. "Okay. Okay. The past is the past."

"Excuse me?" A familiar voice interrupted their playful banter. Tasia turned around and saw a smiling Josiah. Tasia playfully hit him on his arm.

"Josiah! Why didn't you tell me?"

"I couldn't be the one to ruin the surprise. Have you met Kyle?"

They both laughed. "You know what, you're right. I don't blame you." Tasia agreed. She knew Kyle had a little bit of crazy in him. There's no telling what he would have done if Josiah had ruined the surprise he had worked so hard on.

Lisa cleared her throat, and Tasia cut her eyes to her. Lisa put her hands on her hips, insinuating she was ready to be introduced to Tasia's new beau.

"Oh, please forgive me. Josiah, this is my cousin, Lisa. Lisa, this is Josiah." Tasia introduced them.

"It is nice to finally meet you," Josiah said as he shook her hand.

"Likewise, Josiah. I have heard nothing but great things about you. Keep up the good work." Lisa winked at Josiah.

Tasia grabbed him. "Come on, Josiah. Let's go before my cousin says something to embarrass me." Lisa laughed as they walked off. Tasia took Josiah to an empty, quiet corner of the room.

"Thank you for coming," Tasia said softly.

"Of course. I couldn't miss seeing off my favorite girl." Josiah replied, looking deeply into her eyes.

"I've really enjoyed my time with you. I don't deserve a friend like you, but I'm so grateful to have gotten to know you. Choosing to date you has been the best decision I've made in a while. You have brought so much joy and healing to my life. Thank you."

"Stop acting like I'm never going to see you again. I value our friendship. I promise to visit you in the Lou. This isn't a goodbye. Long distance won't stop me from coming to see your fine ass." Josiah smiled.

Tasia wrapped her arms around him slowly, and they embraced until Kyle interrupted them. "Excuse me, lovebirds. Can I steal Tasia for a sec?"

Tasia rolled her eyes at Kyle and excused herself from Josiah. She followed Kyle to their table. Before they sat down, Tasia grabbed his hand and pulled him away. "I really love you, best friend. I'm going to miss the hell out of you. Thank you. For everything." Tearing up, Tasia stopped talking and hugged Kyle.

"T, you talking like you're dying or some shit. You'll just be a few hundred miles up the road. Don't worry. I'll be in the Lou so much you gone think I moved too. Ain't shit changed. We locked in for life. Now sit your sensitive ass down so we can eat." Kyle had tears in his eyes, and Tasia knew her moving away touched him more than he wanted to let on. Kyle had always been tough, so she smiled at him and shook her head before taking a seat.

Tasia and her guests were served a five-course meal. After dinner, everyone gave a speech where they wished Tasia success in her new endeavors and gave her gifts. During Kyle's lengthy speech, he announced that he had reserved a VIP section at one of the hottest clubs in Atlanta and invited everyone to celebrate. At the end of the dinner, Tasia gave her speech, expressing her gratitude for everyone's support. At that moment, Tasia realized how blessed she was. She held back tears as she looked around at all the smiling faces looking back at her.

After dinner, everyone mingled around the room and chatted. Some people left after a few minutes, and others stayed behind to join her at the club. Before the group left the restaurant, Kyle ordered a round of shots for everyone. *"Tonight, we're going to get fucked up!"* Kyle shouted with his shot in the air. "Let's head out!" Everyone cheered as they took their shots.

The crew pulled up to the club, parked in valet, and hostesses met them at the door to escort them to their section. Saturday night was the club's busiest night, and it was packed from wall to wall. The hottest songs of the summer were blasting, and waiters with drinks and bottles were delivering beverages nonstop. Once Tasia and her crew got situated in their booth, the bottle girls came out with sparklers and bottles of Patrón, D'Ussé, and Ace of Spade.

Tasia and her friends took shot after shot. Kyle got so drunk that he began throwing money into the crowd. Tasia laughed and shouted, *"Turn up, best friend! Throw that shit!"* Kyle laughed and drunkenly dapped her up as he threw more money into the crowd.

Tasia wasn't a heavy drinker but she took shots way past her limit. She knew she needed to stop, but it was her last weekend in the A for a while, and she didn't want the fun to end. Josiah had been watching her all night, so he noticed when she started to look off.

"Are you okay?" Josiah pulled Tasia to the side to check on her.

"I don't know, T. You don't look too good. I'm going to get you some water. Sit tight."

Tasia nodded her head, sat down, and danced to the music. She shakingly picked up a blunt Kyle had rolled and exhaled it deeply. The blunt made Tasia sweat profusely. Kyle looked over and saw sweat dripping into Tasia's eyes and down her face. Tasia was too drunk to notice. Kyle grabbed a napkin to wipe her face.

"Damn, am I sweating that bad?" Tasia asked Kyle.

"Nigga, you're soaking," Kyle replied, looking at her with concern.

Josiah returned with water and sat it in front of Tasia. "Drink up," Josiah instructed her. After taking in the water, she put the cup down and began to gag as if she was about to throw up. Josiah noticed and put the cup back in her hand so she could puke in it. He gave her the cup right on time. Josiah handed her a napkin to wipe her mouth.

Tasia looked at Josiah, her face sour from the taste in her mouth. "I think I did too much," Tasia said groggily.

"You think?" Josiah replied.

Brittany rushed over, apologized to Josiah for Tasia's episode, and whisked Tasia to the ladies' room to get herself together. There was a line for the women's restroom, and Tasia grew impatient. She gagged several times and prayed that a stall would open before she puked all over herself in public. When one became available, Tasia rushed inside and threw up again. She couldn't believe she had drunk so much. Once she was done, she stumbled out of the stall, and Brittany was waiting to help her pull herself together. Brittany helped her fix her hair. Tasia rinsed her mouth in the sink, patted the sweat away from her face, and freshened up her makeup and lip gloss. Brittany handed her an aspirin and a piece of gum. Afterward, they headed back to the booth.

They returned to their section to see Lisa passed out asleep. Tasia looked at Lisa and laughed. *"Damn, shawty tore up!"* She shouted before leaving to dance with her co-workers. Brittany tried to stop Tasia and make her sit down, but there was no stopping her. Brittany shook her head and turned to Lisa, who was now throwing up on herself. Brittany immediately rushed Lisa to the restroom as she had done Tasia.

When Brittany and Lisa returned to the section, Lisa crashed into the booth and laid her head on the table. She was not okay, so Brittany found Josiah. They were the only sober ones and both of them agreed it was time to go.

"I'll take you ladies and Kyle home and will call an Uber for the rest." Josiah offered.

"Sounds like a plan." Brittany agreed before heading into the crowd to find everyone. She was able to pinpoint everyone except Kyle. She walked back and forth through the crowd on the dance floor. Out of the corner of her eye, she spotted Kyle in a section with a group of middle-aged women. One of the women was twerking on him as he threw dollars all over her. The other women watched and cheered their friend on, smacking her butt and shouting, "Get it, biiihhh!" Brittany shook her head in disbelief and went to retrieve Kyle. While removing Kyle from the section, one of the women began cursing Brittany out.

Brittany was short, but she was just as feisty as Tasia. "Look bitch, you don't want no problems with me." She told the woman sternly. "My friend is drunk, and it's time for us to go. You better turn the fuck down."

The woman saw the look in Brittany's eyes and decided to stand down.

Kyle, amused by the entire ordeal, screamed over the music to the woman, "It's okay, baby. Hit me up on IG! @ KyletheGreat!"

Brittany yanked Kyle by his arm. *"Bring your ass on!"*

"You want to give me some ass, don't you, Britt?" He played with her drunkenly. "Gone tell the truth. You been wanting me to bend that yellow ass over for a while, huh, shawty!"

Brittany rolled her eyes and continued to drag him out of the club.

Kyle, Brittany, Lisa, and Tasia piled into Josiah's G- Wagon. Josiah and Tasia sat in the front, while Kyle, Brittany, and Lisa sat in the back. They all decided it was best to crash at Tasia's house so Josiah wouldn't have to drive around Atlanta so late at night.

The ride to Tasia's house was just as eventful as the club. Out of nowhere, Kyle blurted out, "Brittany wants to give me some ass!"

Brittany reached around Lisa's head and popped Kyle on the back of his neck with her open hand. "Stop lying before I beat your drunk ass!"

Everyone burst out into laughter. Tasia, still very much drunk, said, "Well, I know who I want to give some ass to." Josiah turned his head toward her and raised his eyebrow.

"Tasia, shut up!" Brittany told her before she could utter another word. Brittany knew Tasia would regret saying that when she sobered up. She knew Tasia was trying to take things slow with Josiah.

Tasia turned her entire body around to face Brittany in the back seat. "Damn, bitch. "Don't be telling me to shut up."

"Anastasia, turn your drunk ass around." Brittany snapped back.

Tasia followed her instructions. "Dang, who made you the mama?" She pouted.

The yelling woke Lisa up. "Y'all need to be quiet. Y'all too damn loud." She shouted groggily.

"Shawty, take yo tore up ass back to sleep. Ain't nobody talking to you!" Kyle looked at her and said.

"That's right. Don't nobody care that you tryna sleep. It's still my party, bitch!" Tasia said as she twerked in the front seat.

"You need to take your ass to sleep too!" Brittany said to Tasia.

"Hold on, lil red. Don't be telling my best friend what to do!" Kyle defended Tasia.

"That's right! Get her ass, Kyle!" Tasia piped.

They continued to bicker back and forth like children. Josiah, annoyed, shouted to get everyone's attention. "Yo! Everybody shut the hell up! Y'all are arguing just to argue. Sit back, buckle up, and the only thing I want to hear is someone asking me to pull over to puke. I don't want a drop of vomit in my damn truck. Everybody understand?"

Drunk murmurs came from the backseat, and Tasia saluted Josiah, saying, "Sir, yes, Sir!" Josiah couldn't help but laugh at Tasia's silliness.

Eighteen

♡♡♡

"A re you feeling better, party girl?" Josiah asked from behind Tasia.

Tasia was still hung over but had mustered up the strength to cook everyone breakfast. Kyle, Lisa, and Brittany were still asleep.

"I have a massive headache, but I'm okay. How did you sleep?" Tasia asked as she checked on the biscuits rising in the oven.

"I slept pretty well. I would have loved to sleep next to you, but your bed was already pretty full. Your sofa was pretty comfy, though." Josiah joked. The girls had slept in Tasia's bed while Josiah and Kyle slept in the living room.

"It's probably a good thing that you didn't sleep in my bed. We probably wouldn't have done too much sleeping." Tasia replied.

"That's true. Would you have regretted it the next morning?" Josiah asked.

Tasia thought for a moment, then shook her head no. "I'm feeling you, Josiah. If we had taken it there, I wouldn't have felt bad. What about you?"

"Well, I wouldn't have taken advantage of you being drunk, first of all. But if we ever went there, I wouldn't feel bad about it either. If that's what you wanted to hear. And based on what you said last night, it's clearly been on your mind." Josiah chuckled, reminding Tasia of her drunk confessions.

Tasia shook her head. "I'm so sorry, Josiah. I know I probably got on your nerves real bad last night."

"Yeah, you did. But I was more concerned about you than anything. You went kinda heavy on the drinks. Once I knew you were okay, I was fine. You were actually quite hilarious drunk."

Josiah walked closer and hugged her from behind as she scrambled eggs. "I'm really going to miss you."

"I'm going to miss you too," Tasia replied, facing him.

"Damn, y'all stay hugging on each other," Kyle shouted from behind them.

"Shut up, Kyle!" Tasia laughed. "You stay popping up on us! When you wake up anyway?"

"Shidd, I just got up. That floor hard as hell. You know a nigga couldn't sleep down there forever. I was about to get in your bed until I saw Brittany and Lisa asses in there knocked out."

"Dang, I'm sorry, friend. I'm just about done with breakfast, though."

"Aiight, bet. I'm finna wash my face and shit. Towels in the same place?"

"Yeah, Kyle. And it's some toothbrushes under the

sink."

Josiah and Tasia laughed as Kyle walked towards the guest bathroom to freshen up.

"Don't worry. I'll make sure we get some alone time before I leave," Tasia whispered to Josiah.

"I can't wait." Josiah kissed her, then left to straighten the living room as she finished breakfast.

After everyone had eaten breakfast, they sat around the house, talking and laughing about how much fun they had at the club the night before. Once everyone gained enough energy to function for the day, Josiah offered to take everyone to their cars. Tasia and her friends hugged and said their final goodbyes since Tasia was leaving for St. Louis in the next few days. Josiah was the last one out of the house; everyone else had already piled in his car. Tasia kissed him on the cheek and thanked him for giving her friends a ride.

"Come on, lover boy! We ready to go!" Kyle yelled from the passenger side window.

Tasia and Josiah laughed.

"Aye, you and your friends are something else." Josiah shook his head and chuckled.

Tasia giggled. She knew he wasn't lying. "Sorry, we can get wild at times."

Before Josiah's G-Wagon drove off, Tasia's friends let down their windows and yelled goodbye again.

"I love y'all! Be safe!" Tasia shouted back. "Call me when y'all make it home."

"We love you too, but go back inside before you get to crying," Lisa yelled. Tasia laughed and flicked her off. Her chest tightened as she watched them drive off. It was a bittersweet moment for Tasia. She couldn't believe she only had three days left in the city. She had to finish packing so she could spend time with her dad and Josiah before her departure.

The next day, Tasia thought more and more about her and Josiah's conversation as she wrapped up packing. She decided to spend the rest of the evening underneath Josiah, so Tasia texted him to see if he was available. "Why not go out with a bang?" Tasia said aloud. "Pun intended." She giggled, thinking about how she would let Josiah have his way with her. He deserved it, and so did she. Tasia was moving and didn't know the next time she would have sex. Josiah replied that he was available and that she could come over whenever she got ready. Tasia finished packing the remaining items, took a shower, slipped into something sexy, and headed to Josiah's loft.

Knock. Knock. Knock. Tasia knocked gently.

"Be right there!" She heard Josiah yell. Tasia stood outside his door anxiously. She took a deep breath and exhaled slowly, trying to calm her nerves. She was excited to start the party, but was extremely nervous. This would be their first time having sex. Even though they had shared intimate moments, had a lot of chemistry, and discussed their sexual needs, there was no way to tell if they were sexually compatible until they were in the act.

After a few deep breaths, Josiah finally opened the door. "Tasia, I'm sorry I had you waiting. I was clean---. Whoa!" Josiah noticed Tasia was wearing a black trench coat and strappy red heels. He knew the night was about to get interesting. "Damn, ma! What you got up under that trench?"

Tasia walked past him and stood in the middle of his living room floor. "Come take a look for yourself." She told him sultrily.

He looked at her with excitement and bit his bottom lip. "Damn, it's like that?"

Tasia nodded slowly. "Yea, it's like that, baby. It's only right I give you a parting gift. A little something to remember me."

Josiah rubbed his hands together smoothly and walked toward her. He softly grabbed her face with both his hands and kissed her passionately. He grabbed her butt and pulled her closer to him. Looking deeply into her eyes, he asked, "Shall we begin?"

Tasia nodded without saying a word. Josiah grabbed her hand, and she followed him to his bedroom. Josiah sat on the bed, and Tasia stood before him as he untied her coat and slid it off her arms. Once her coat fell to the ground and revealed her red silk lingerie, Tasia pushed Josiah's hands away and pushed him onto the bed. Josiah groaned, letting Tasia know he was ready for her. Tasia seductively looked him up and down. Making sure he got a full view of her attire, she slowly spun around in a full circle. Then, she walked toward Josiah and unbuckled his belt and pants. After slowly pulling his shirt over his head, Tasia motioned for him to come to the end of the bed. She removed Josiah's pants and underwear and came eye-to-eye with Josiah's massive package.

"Oh, my," Tasia whispered as she stroked Josiah up

and down with her right hand. She looked up and locked eyes with him while slowly licking his shaft up and down until it was completely wet. Josiah leaned his head back in ecstasy. Tasia took every inch of him in her mouth, leaving no parts of him exposed. Josiah squirmed and panted Tasia's name in pleasure. As she continued to please him, he grabbed Tasia's head. Josiah began to shake uncontrollably, but Tasia continued until he released in her mouth, and she swallowed every drop. After catching his breath, Josiah pulled Tasia up by her hand and positioned her in front of him. He pulled her panties down and rubbed her to feel her moisture.

Josiah massaged Tasia's clitoris with his thumb as he kissed up and down her stomach. Tasia zoned out and almost lost herself until Josiah grabbed her leg, put it over his shoulder, and dove face-first between her legs. Tasia moaned with satisfaction, grabbing his head to push his tongue deeper inside her. In one swift move, Josiah was able to keep them in the same position and lay her on the bed. Josiah had his way with Tasia until she released all over his face. Josiah came up for air and told her to lie still. He went into his closet and returned with two silk, black and red ties. Josiah removed Tasia's bra, grabbed her arms, pulled them over her head, and tied her wrists together.

"You gone let daddy take control?" Josiah asked.

"Yes," Tasia responded, already turned on. Josiah grabbed the other tie and used it to blindfold her eyes. Then, he softly kissed her from head to toe. He pulled a condom from his nightstand, pulled Tasia to the end of the bed, and positioned himself in the middle of her. After securing the condom, Josiah spread Tasia's legs and slowly inserted himself inside her. Tasia gasped as Josiah inched himself deeper and deeper inside of her. Josiah flipped Tasia around and positioned her knees for doggy style. He arched her back and positioned Tasia just how he wanted her. He slapped her ass, spread her cheeks, and licked her from back to front. Catching her completely off guard, he entered her again and swiftly dove deeply into her. He gave her long hard strokes, causing her to orgasm. She tried to escape his strokes, but Josiah gently pulled her back.

"Stop running and take this dick," Josiah whispered provocatively. He continued to stroke her slowly and deeply. Tasia climaxed once again. Only then did Josiah pull out to lick up her juices, then slapped her ass. Get up and ride me." Josiah instructed her. He laid down and guided Tasia on top of him and inserted himself inside of her. He held onto her waist while she slow-grinded and bounced up and down on his dick. Tasia made his toes curl. Josiah then lifted her up and sat her on his face. He sucked on her clitoris, again bringing Tasia to ecstasy. She lost count of how many times she orgasmed. Josiah laid her down on her back, held her constricted wrists above her head, and gave her fast and hard strokes until he shook with pleasure.

After a few moments, he removed the tie from her eyes. Tasia looked at him, bewildered yet smiling from ear to ear. Josiah had blown her mind, and she was at a loss for words. Josiah grinned proudly, then kissed her as he untied her hands. Next, he guided her to the bathroom, turned on the shower, and told her to step in. He followed behind her and bathed her entire body. It was the best sex

Tasia ever had. She was pissed that she had waited this long to have sex with Josiah. They snuggled under the covers for the rest of the night, watching TV and talking. Later that night, they explored each other more until they fell asleep.

The next morning, Tasia woke up to the smell of breakfast. Josiah had cooked for her. "Good morning, beautiful. How did you sleep?" Josiah asked as he watched her sit up in the bed. He grabbed his robe from the back of the door and passed it to her.

Tasia giggled. "I slept like a baby."

Josiah kissed her forehead. "Come eat. I made you some breakfast and there are a few things in the bathroom for you to freshen up."

Tasia blushed. "You're so thoughtful. Thank you." Tasia got up from the bed and got herself together. After her shower, she put on Josiah's robe, walked out of his bedroom, and was greeted with flowers. Tasia was swooning.

Josiah kissed her as he handed her the flowers." I wish I was moving with you."

"Me too," Tasia whispered. She really meant it. Josiah gave her everything she wanted, but the timing was wrong. If they were meant to be, time would tell. So she decided to keep in touch with him, visit often, and see where things went. They both enjoyed breakfast and had sex one last time before she left. Tasia had one more stop to make before she left, and there was no way she could pop up in a trench coat. So, she left Josiah's loft, went home to change, and headed out again for Garden Manor.

Signing into the visitor log, she noticed Angelique had

just left. She was still curious about the mystery woman but had too much on her mind to play inspector gadget. She entered her father's room and saw the nurse checking his temperature.

"Wow, the entire family looks alike." The nurse said when she noticed Tasia had walked in. "Let me guess, you're his daughter?"

Tasia grinned slightly. "Yep." People often said she looked like her father, but Tasia never saw it. She was the spitting image of her mother, and there was no denying that.

"He was in a lot of pain earlier, so he is heavily sedated. We are doing our best to keep him comfortable." The nurse informed her.

Tasia nodded. "Thank you for taking good care of him."

"No worries." The nurse assured her. "I would want someone to do the same for my dad. I'm headed to the front. Give me a buzz if you need anything." The nurse gently patted Tasia's arm as she left the room to give them privacy.

Tasia took a deep breath and walked over to her father. Like every time, she searched deep within herself for some sentimental emotion, something a daughter should feel for her dying father, but she felt nothing. However, something felt different about this visit. She didn't know if it was because she was moving or that his condition was worsening by the day, but something felt final. She held back tears as she looked over his body, dying before her eyes. He was leaving this world, and they never had the chance to repair their broken relationship. She couldn't understand why she even desired anything from him when he didn't have an ounce of love for her. Tasia knew her dad wouldn't be alive much longer and figured this was the perfect time to talk to him since he couldn't give a rebuttal.

Tasia grabbed his hand. "Daddy....thank you for helping to bring me into this world. Without you, there would be no me. Thank you for providing for me and for the few good times we shared with one another. I don't hate you, but I can't say I fully love you. I appreciate the things you did for me, but I don't know why you were so cruel to me. I guess I'll never know why. Anyway, I'm moving to St. Louis." Tasia chuckled to herself. "My dumb ass is really moving to prove a point to a man that doesn't want anything to do with me. It's kinda crazy when I think about it, but hell, I've made my choice. It's too late to change my mind. I somewhat blame you for this stupidity. If you had loved me properly, I wouldn't be in this predicament. I wish you treated me better. I wish we had a better relationship. I just wish you loved me, Daddy. But I love you and hope God has mercy on your soul." Tasia hugged her father and left the nursing home.

Tasia was content with her visit for the first time in a while. She was glad she got everything off her chest. But her intuition told her that would be the last time she saw her father alive. She left the parking lot without a tear in sight.

That night, Tasia decided to write in her journal. The more she wrote out her thoughts, she began to second-guess her move. *Why do I seek vengeance against Seth?* She wondered. I could let this go and move on. But her heart wouldn't let him go. Seth was a wolf in sheep's clothing who broke her heart. Tasia was a hopeless romantic and was ashamed of how everything played out. Seth gave her false hope. He promised a family she could call her own and genuine love from a man she could grow old with. And every single word was a lie. Anger began to surge through her veins again, and she was sure she had to move to St. Louis. Seth deserved to pay for what he had done, and Tasia would make sure he did. She finished her journal entry and called it a night. Her new life started the next day, and despite her hatred for Seth, she was excited to begin a new chapter in her life.

The movers arrived bright and early the next morning. Tasia waited as they packed her entire house in their truck. Before Tasia hopped on the road, she took one last look at her empty townhome and remembered all the good times and accomplishments she had achieved over the years. She knew everything would be okay. If she could make it in Atlanta, she could make it anywhere in the world.

Nineteen

♡♡♡

Tasia had been in St. Louis for a few weeks but was still working hard to adjust to her new city. For the first few days, she cried her heart out. Even though Seth had broken her heart, she still grieved all the plans they had made. He was supposed to be the one. She was ashamed, and on many days, she blamed herself for how things turned out between her and Seth. Her mind constantly replayed his last hurtful words, *"You are mentally and emotionally unstable. I never wanted you! I had a craving and you filled it.....you're a dummy."* In many ways, she felt like Seth was right. She spent a lot of days feeling worthless and dwelling on the past. She had thought about hitting up Taylor to let him know she was in the city, but she was too embarrassed to tell him why. Josiah called her often but due to her many mood swings, she rarely answered. So, she worked for the first few weeks, only went out for necessities, and moped around the house.

One Thursday evening, Tasia decided to shake her blues and take advantage of the new opportunities around her. She didn't know anyone in the city, so she decided to join a dating app to meet new guys and get herself back out there. Tasia didn't want anything too serious, just companionship with someone who could show her around the city. She closed her laptop early for the day and got comfortable on her couch while creating her dating profile. Tasia made her bio short and sweet and selected five of her best photos. She used a fake name and number to protect herself from craziness. Once she was done setting up her page, she dived into the sea of potential suitors. After scrolling for a few minutes, she was ready to delete the app and try another company. The app was filled with freaks and weirdos.

Before deleting her page, Tasia got a notification. It was a private message that simply said, "Nicole?" The person's profile name was Mr. C. His photo was a quote that said, "If it doesn't challenge you, it won't change you." Tasia rolled her eyes at the thought of someone using a meme as their profile picture on a dating site. She went to the profile and surprisingly saw a familiar face. Reluctantly, she replied to the message. "Wade?"

He sent two eye emojis, and Tasia laughed out loud as she replied, "Yes, Mr. Canton. It's me, Anastasia." Wade sent his number and told Tasia to call him.

Wade answered the phone, chuckling. "Well, well, well. Anastasia Ingram. Shawty, wassup?"

"Hey, Wade!" Tasia exclaimed. "It's been a very long time. I don't think I've seen you since high school."

"I know. It's been a while. I almost reported your page. Thought you were a catfish." Wade laughed.

Wade was six feet and three inches tall, slim muscular built, dark chocolate, and wore a Caesar fade. Tasia secretly had a crush on him back in high school. He was a bookworm, and she thought his intelligence was so sexy.

"Are you in the Lou or the A? What you got going on?" Wade inquired. Tasia told him she had just moved to St. Louis and was on the site to meet new people. He welcomed her to the city and told her to lock in his number. He promised to get in touch with her to make plans to see her over the weekend. They ended the call, and Tasia sank back into her sofa, satisfied with her day's work. "Okay, bitch. You still got it!" She said aloud. Tasia didn't think too much about meeting Wade. It was just something to get her feet wet in the city. She figured meeting up with Wade would be harmless. They were just old friends wanting to reconnect and catch up.

The following day, Wade texted her the details for Saturday night. They planned to meet at a lounge downtown. Since Tasia hadn't seen him in years, she wanted to look her best. She decided to get her nails done at the salon near her home. At the salon, she sat next to a woman that looked close to her age. The woman was beautiful and petite in stature. Her silky hair was sleeked back into a low ponytail. She wore a cute two-piece Adidas tracksuit that matched perfectly with her shoes and Gucci purse. Tasia overheard her on the phone and noticed she had a thick northerner accent. While Tasia picked out the nail color for her toes, the woman beside her noticed her purse and complimented her style. Then, she asked Tasia where she got her clothes from and if she was a stripper. Tasia rolled her eyes and looked at her in annoyance. "What makes you think I'm a stripper?" She snapped.

"Well, I can just tell you're not from here. I peeped your swag and demeanor. You giving real boss bitch vibes."

"Thanks, I guess," Tasia replied.

"I'm Fallon, by the way." The woman extended her hand, and Tasia shook it hesitantly.

"I'm T." Tasia decided to entertain Fallon and her questions.

"You visiting from out of town?"

"Nope. I just moved here from Atlanta."

"Well, welcome to the Show Me State. I'm not from here either. I'm from Philly. I like it here. My man and I moved down here last year. My man is a rapper. He does performances throughout the city. He has a show this weekend. You should come out and see him. You seem pretty cool. We should hang out." Fallon said as she handed Tasia a flyer. Tasia knew instantly she was not going to see him perform. They exchanged social media information, and Tasia planned to block her once she got home. Tasia thought Fallon was too friendly and didn't know if she was setting her up or trying to hang with her.

After their nails were finished, Fallon and Tasia left the nail salon simultaneously. When departing to their cars, Fallon yelled, "Bye, friend, see you soon."

Tasia waved with a fake smile. "Bitch I am not your friend," Tasia said to herself as soon as she closed her Jeep door. The following evening, Tasia prepared for her night out with Wade. She decided to wear her hair in a messy bun. She slipped into a sleeveless black bodysuit, skintight jeans, Louboutin black booties, and a Chanel purse and belt. She accessorized with gold jewelry and painted her face flawlessly. She didn't want to do too much because she didn't know Wade's motives. After getting dressed, she texted him that she was on the way.

Tasia drove to the lounge with an open mind. When she pulled up, Wade was outside waiting for her. He paid for her valet, opened her door, and grabbed her hand to assist her out of her whip. Wade pulled her in for a hug. Tasia's insides tingled from the scent of his cologne. He was wearing Bond No.9, one of her favorite men's scents. Wade released her and looked her up and down. "Damn, Anastasia! You're aging like fine wine. Looking good, girl."

Tasia blushed. "Thank you. You don't look too bad yourself, old friend." That was an understatement. Mr. Wade Canton stood before her as a grown man and was fine as hell in Tasia's eyes. He was rocking True Religion jeans, exclusive Retro 1's, and a fitted button down. He was a long way from that cute young boy from high school.

After they caught up briefly, Wade escorted her inside. "I'm here with a few of my pals. We have a table upstairs."

The lounge was an upscale establishment with top-tier décor and ambiance. Tasia complimented Wade for choosing a nice location. He told her that it was one of his go-to spots. I have a couple more spots I would like to show you. I would love to show you around the city whenever you have time."

Tasia smiled, "I think I would enjoy touring the city with you." They took the elevator upstairs and stood on opposite sides. To avoid the silent awkwardness, Tasia pretended to be on her phone. Out of her peripheral, she could see Wade seductively looking her up and down.

Ding! The elevator sounded, letting them know they had made it upstairs. Tasia followed Wade to the table where his two friends were sitting. "Mel and Isaiah, this is Anastasia." Wade introduced them and shared a little about everyone, just enough to open the door for friendly conversation. Then, Wade pulled a seat out for Tasia and sat beside her. Tasia greeted Wade's friends and gave them a sweet hello.

"Anastasia, you are too fine to be with Wade." Mel joked.

Wade chuckled. "Chill, Mel. Anastasia is my friend from high school. I haven't seen her in years. Don't scare her away."

Mel laughed. "Aiight, aiight. I won't ruin it for you, big dog.

Isaiah joined in the conversation, "We apologize for Mel in advance. He doesn't know how to control himself in front of pretty women." They all laughed.

"Yo, a pool table just opened up. You tryna lose some money?" Isaiah invited Mel to play a few rounds with him.

"I don't know about losing no money, but I can take yours if that's what you tryna do." Mel laughed, and they dismissed themselves.

Wade turned to Tasia with a grin on his face. "Well, Ms. Anastasia Ingram, what brings you to the Lou?"

"Writing opportunities," Tasia replied shortly.

"That's dope. I knew you would always become a professional writer. I still remember your articles from the school newsletters."

Tasia's cheeks grew warm, and she smiled shyly. "What

about you? What made you move to St. Louis?

"I'm an engineer. I've been working for an airline in the city. The job opportunity was better than what they were offering me in Atlanta.

"Wow, Wade. That's dope. I can't say I'm surprised. You were always so intelligent."

It was Wade's turn to blush. "I appreciate that." He chuckled nervously. "So, tell me this...Did you meet anyone on the dating site?"

Tasia giggled. "Oh, heaven's no. It was a lot of characters on that site, and I did not want any parts of it. I deleted my profile the same day. I figured I would meet people the old-fashioned way. You know, like in person at the grocery store or something." They both laughed.

A waiter came by, and Tasia and Wade ordered drinks and hookah. They enjoyed each other's company and conversation until Tasia heard someone yell, "*T! HEY T! T!*"

Tasia swiveled her head and cursed under her breath when she realized it was Fallon from the nail shop. Fallon didn't wait for Tasia to invite her over. Instead, she walked over quickly with her head in the sky.

Wade looked at Tasia with confusion. "You know her?"

Tasia shook her head. "I will explain later." She told him as Fallon wildly bombarded their table.

"Hey, girl!" Fallon shouted as if she was greeting an old friend.

Tasia's face was flushed with embarrassment. "Hey, Fallon. What are the odds of me seeing you here?"

"I know, right!" Fallon exclaimed as she placed a hand on Tasia's shoulder. "We are clearly meant to be friends!"

Tasia laughed and gave Wade a look to help her.

"Ana—uhm, T. You still tryna head over and play a game with Mel?" Wade attempted to rescue Tasia.

"Absolut—" Tasia began.

"Girl! Is this yo man?" Fallon cut her off, curving Wade's attempt.

Tasia tilted her head sideways and decided to directly tell Fallon to fuck off. "Fallon, this is my friend from high school, Wade. We haven't seen each other in a while, and we're here catching up. If you don—"

Fallon interrupted her. "Awww! Girl, y'all so cute together. You should make him your man!" She said. "Baby, he is fiiinnnee," Fallon loudly whispered to her.

"You should listen to your friend. I like her." Wade decided to join Fallon's foolishness. He secretly got a kick from watching Tasia interact with her new ghetto acquaintance. Tasia scolded him and mouthed that she was going to get him back. Wade laughed and patted her knee under the table.

"I ain't gone hold you and your boo thang up! My man is waiting on me outside. I just came through to drop these flyers off to the DJ. Let's exchange numbers. I didn't get it earlier. Imma hit you up so we can hang sometime next week."

Tasia reluctantly gave her number to Fallon to rush her along.

"Okay, boo. I got you locked in." Fallon said as she saved Tasia's number. "It was good seeing you again. Nice to meet you, Wade." As she walked away she mouthed to Tasia, "Keep him!"

Tasia was relieved that Fallon had finally removed

herself from the table. She was humiliated, but Wade was clearly amused. "Well, she seems fun." He joked.

Tasia rolled her eyes. "I met ol' girl earlier today at the nail shop, and she just befriended me." "Be open-minded." Wade chuckled. "She might be a good person to know here in the city. Go out with her. If y'all vibe, cool. If not, block her. Anastasia, it's not bad a thing to make new friends that are, um, different from you."

"Ugh, okay. You might be right. I just typically wouldn't hang out with someone like her. I guess I'll give her a chance. I might go have drinks or something with her."

The waiter came back with another round of drinks, and Wade and Tasia began to get comfortable with one another. Wade pulled Tasia closer to him and put his arm around her shoulder. "So why did you really meet me here, Tasia? A birdie told me you had a crush on me in high school. Trying to make up for lost time?" Wade licked his lips while staring into her eyes.

Tasia raised an eyebrow at Wade's directness. "Oh really? Well, that may be true. However, I just got out of a situation-ship. I'm not looking for anything too serious right now. I want to have fun, see the city, try nice restaurants, and explore new things and people. That type of vibe. What about you?

"I'm on whatever you on," Wade said as he continued to eye her seductively.

Tasia quivered internally at the look he was giving her but decided to play it smoothly. She knew she would eventually give in to him, but for now, she wanted to play hard to get. "Whatever I'm on, huh?"

"Yes, ma'am."

"Cool. I'll keep that in mind."

For the rest of the night, they flirted, talked about the past, and caught up on mutual friends. Before going their separate ways for the evening, they promised to reconnect soon.

A few days later, Tasia took Wade's advice and agreed to grab food and drinks at a restaurant in University City with Fallon. They arrived seconds after one another, and Tasia pulled into a parking spot next to Fallon's Infinity. Tasia's windows were rolled down and she could hear Fallon screaming at someone through her car speaker. Tasia rolled her eyes and said out loud, "This bitch is too ghetto for me to be open-minded." She had second thoughts and began to reverse out of her parking spot to head back home.

Fallon caught her trying to leave, rolled down her window, and yelled to get Tasia's attention. *"T! T! Girl, where are you going?"*

"Oh, nowhere, girl!" Tasia lied. "I thought I parked crooked. Just straightening up." Tasia parked took a deep breath, and mentally prepared herself for an eventful day." Fallon met Tasia at her driver's door and hugged her once she stepped out.

Fallon's phone rang, and she answered, yelling at the top of her lungs. *"Yo! Stop fucking calling me. I told you where I was."*

Other people in the parking lot began to stare at them. Tasia stared at Fallon in disbelief. "Aye, I can head back home if you want to have a yelling match on the phone in public," Tasia said, annoyed.

"Girl, my bad. My man brings the hood side outta me sometimes. We both be trippin'." Fallon apologized.

"So, your man don't let you out the house or something?" Tasia inquired.

"T, he is so controlling. But, he's alright for the most part."

"Ohhhh, okay. But, aye, check this out. Don't be doing all that yelling and screaming in public. If you gone argue, finish that shit at home. I don't get down like that."

"Girl, I got you. I'm good. Fuck him! I'm out with my new friend, and he gone have to deal with it. Come on, girl. Let's go in. I know the owner, and he has a table waiting for us." Fallon assured her she wouldn't get into any more yelling matches and that they would have a good time together. Tasia wasn't sure about that, but she decided to give Fallon a chance. They walked into the restaurant, and the hostess greeted them, acknowledged Fallon by name, and escorted them to a booth.

"You're going to like this place, T. All the socialites of St. Louis frequent here. I will introduce you to a few people you need to know." Fallon introduced Tasia to business owners, social media influencers, up-and-coming artists, fashionistas, and even a few scammers and drug dealers. After watching her move through the crowd, Tasia saw Fallon in a different light. She conducted herself with class and grace and was totally different from the ghetto girl she had portrayed to be beforehand. Tasia was impressed and decided she could actually hang around the tamed version of Fallon. Tasia felt bad for judging her too soon. *I guess Wade was right,* she thought to herself.

Tasia was excited to finally be meeting new people and

networking. She also ran into a few people she had met with Taylor previously and made a mental note to call him as soon as she got home. She would hate for him to find out she had moved through a mutual connection. Taylor had been a lifesaver the last time she was in St. Louis, and she definitely wanted to maintain the connection. Taylor was a good person.

Tasia told everyone she met that she was a writer working on a new blog. They were impressed by her demeanor and instantly wanted to collaborate with her. After networking at the restaurant, the ladies chatted outside before departing.

"Fallon, thank you for inviting me out. I didn't expect to have such a good time."

"You are welcome! When I saw you, I just knew we would click. You're so pretty and classy. Off the bat, I could just tell you was a real ass bitch, and you got a little hood in you. Real recognize real." Fallon said.

"I ain't gone lie. I thought you were ghetto as hell, but you did your thing by suggesting this restaurant. I really enjoyed myself. I didn't think we would vibe, but you are alright in my book. You've just been here a year and already got some dope connections. That's what's up. You clearly been on your shit since you touched down, girl."

Fallon giggled. "Well, you know, you know." Fallon strutted a boss chick pose and laughed. "It's crazy how many people I've met. Like I told you, my man is a rapper. That's how I made so many connections. We are always at the hottest spots getting the DJs to play his music to get his name out in the streets. It's been working for us."

"I can dig it. That's wassup, girl."

"Girl, you have got to tell me more about your blog. You literally had everyone eating out the palm of your hands. Very impressive. T, you're new to the city, but I can already tell things are most definitely going to work out in your favor."

"I hope so. Meeting those people definitely struck a fire under my ass. I need to get to work asap. I'm going to aim to have the biggest blog in the city. I want to post and promote black entrepreneurs, creatives, restaurants, the flyest boutiques, beauty and clothing brands, local and celebrity gossip, breaking news, and so much more. I really want to create a following and make a name for myself here."

Fallon was excited about Tasia's aspirations. "Everyone will flock to you. The more you go out and meet new people, the more your following will grow. You're passionate about your goals, so everything else will fall into place for you."

"I appreciate that, Fallon. I'm on it!"

"This was hella fun. If you're free next week, let's do this again."

"Let's do it!" Tasia agreed. They said their goodbyes and headed to their cars. Tasia couldn't wait to get home. She stayed up all night, writing her goals and mapping out the steps to release her new blog.

Twenty

♡♡♡

Tasia and Wade had been hanging out heavily, and Tasia enjoyed exploring the city with him. She also continued hanging out with Fallon. Going out weekly with Fallon and Wade widened her list of contacts. Tasia was ecstatic that her social life was growing within the city. Every day, she committed to doing something for her blog. Within two months, she had decided on a name *The Realness*, created a website, and built social media pages for her brand where she posted consistently. She and Josiah had begun to talk more consistently again, and he supported her every step of the way. Despite their spicy rendezvous before she left, they decided to continue to take things slow. Tasia was on a mission and didn't want to get too distracted. She missed being near Josiah, but she was grateful he understood where she was at in life.

Within a few months, her blog and social media pages gained over thousands of followers and subscribers.

She even secured paid promotions and modeling gigs with different boutiques throughout the city. She was so focused on the success of her blog that she had pushed Seth to the back of her mind. He was still on the top of her shit list, but she knew she had to focus on building her platform and connections if she would hurt him as much as he had hurt her.

One day, while Tasia was out running errands, she received a phone call from Wade. He was proud of the strides she had made in the city and wanted to take her out to celebrate. It was brisk, and fall was almost over, so Tasia knew exactly what she would wear for the night.

She rushed home after running errands to rummage through her closet to find her outfit. She pulled out a nude brown dress that hugged her body like a glove. Her choice of shoes were a pair of silver diamond studded stiletto heels, with her silver Prada clutch and diamond accessories to match. Tasia straightened her 30-inch sew-in bone straight and did her makeup.

Wade picked her up from home and looked quite dapper himself. He wore a black and brown Fendi shirt, black tailored pants, and black Fendi loafers. Together, they looked like a million bucks. The two were headed to one of the most exclusive clubs in the city. Wade paid for valet and knew the owner, who escorted them to the club's VIP section. The bottle girls came to their section with signs that read, "Congrats!" As the bottle girls sat three bottles of liquor on the table, a waitress took their food order. Tasia turned to Wade and asked, "What are we going to do with all of this liquor?"

"Drink it!" Wade exclaimed. "We can call an Uber

if we need to." As always, Tasia and Wade enjoyed each other's company and had a good time. They took photos, ate good food, drank until they couldn't take another sip, and danced with one another all night long. After a while, Tasia could feel the effects of the liquor taking over her body. She knew she was treading on thin ice dancing so provocatively with Wade. They had only been hanging out as friends, but how they carried on could lead to more. They had never been sexually intimate, but Tasia started having visions of herself riding Wade's face. Daydreaming about sexing, Wade turned Tasia on, and she began biting her bottom lip. Suddenly, Wade nudged her, interrupting her daydream.

"Did you hear me?" he asked.

She shook her head no. "Sorry, what did you---"

"Stop daydreaming about me!" He cut her off mid-speech.

Tasia laughed awkwardly and rolled her eyes. "Boy, whatever."

"Don't act like that. I see you eyeing the kid." Wade laughed as he stood up. "I'll be right back. I have to run to the restroom."

Tasia poured herself a glass of champagne and gulped it down in seconds as she watched Wade go to the bathroom. That last dose of liquid courage would push her to go ahead and take things to the next level with Wade. She briefly thought about Josiah but reminded herself that he was not her man. She was done putting all her eggs in one basket. Tasia only had lustful feelings for Wade. He was cool, but she didn't want to be anything more than friends with benefits. While stuck in her drunken thoughts, a woman sitting nearby at the bar with her friends approached Tasia's section.

"Can I ask you a question?" She said to Tasia as she took a seat next to her.

Tasia was drunk and prepared for the bullshit. She looked the woman up and down. She was average height, had a dark complexion, and wore a big curly wig. She had on a red spaghetti strap dress with red heels to match.

"Yea, what's up?" Tasia said aggressively.

"First of all, you are absolutely beautiful." The woman gushed.

"Thank you so much. You are gorgeous as well. I love that hairstyle on you." Tasia genuinely thought the woman was pretty.

"That man you were with, is he your man? Y'all look good together." The woman smiled.

"Why do you ask?" Tasia inquired.

"Well, I'm from out of town and here with some friends. But I'd rather party with y'all...specifically you. I could do some things to you that your man can't do." She said seductively as she scooted closer to Tasia.

Tasia scooted back from her and giggled nervously. "You're absolutely beautiful. I'm flattered, but I'm not interested, and neither is my man. This ain't that type of party. It was nice meeting you. I hope you enjoy the city, though." The woman accepted Tasia's rejection gracefully but still handed Tasia her business card, just in case she had a change of mind.

Tasia couldn't believe how bold the women were in St. Louis. Tasia was drunk but not drunk enough to bump vaginas. Finally, Wade came back, and Tasia told him what had happened.

"Hell, I don't blame her. She liked what she saw and went after it. I need to take note." He grinned slyly as he inched closer to Tasia and began twirling her hair.

Before Tasia could say something clever, she saw a familiar face near the bar. It was Seth and his friends, and they were headed to a section near her and Wade. Apparently, Seth saw Tasia well before she saw him. His eyes were glued on her, watching her and Wade's every move. Since he's looking so hard, I might as well give him a show, Tasia thought. She leaned over and seductively whispered in Wade's ear. "If I let you, what would you do to me?"

Completely unaware that he was being watched, Wade perked up at the opportunity to talk dirty to Tasia. "I would taste you. Explore every part of your sexy body. I wouldn't take my hands off you." Wade rubbed her waistline, pulling her closer.

Tasia looked deeply into his eyes. "And what else?"

"How about you let me show you?" Wade replied as he gently held her chin, pulled her face closer, and passionately kissed her. Tasia returned his kiss and moaned as his hands moved from her waist to her thigh.

After their intense tongue war, they came up for air and stared hungrily at each other. Tasia was lost for words because she wanted to fuck him right then and there in their section. Meanwhile, Seth watched their entire interaction, just as Tasia knew he would. For the remainder of the night, he scolded her. When Tasia's phone pinged with a text message, she instantly knew it was from Seth.

So this is what we're doing?
    Tasia replied:

                                                              ???

So that clown is your new nigga?

            You're the only clown I see in here, sweetheart.
        Did you stop scamming? You're looking kinda bummy.

Fuck you, T! You ain't nothing but a hoe anyway.

                Yep, just like your mama, fuck nigga.

Tasia took a sip from Wade's glass and asked if he was ready to go.

"Damn right," Wade replied. He ordered a Uber on his phone, grabbed her hand, and headed toward the exit. Seth and Tasia locked eyes as she followed Wade. She flicked him off and laughed. They got into the Uber driver's black SUV and continued their tongue war as if the driver wasn't there. Tasia and Wade couldn't keep their hands off of one another.

After arriving at the front entrance of his two-story brick home, he fumbled the keys more than once, trying to open his front door. An antsy Tasia giggled. "I hope you don't fumble that dick like you are doing those keys."

Wade chuckled nervously and focused harder on the keys until he could open the door. He allowed Tasia to walk in first and slapped her on the ass as he closed the door behind her. He turned on the lamp and walked up behind Tasia, kissing her neck and rubbing her breast. They walked over to the couch, where Wade bent Tasia over and began pulling up her dress. He licked his fingers and gently inserted his index and middle finger inside her.

Tasia gasped and began to move her hips to his rhythm. Then, she stood up, leaned back on his shoulder, and sucked on his earlobe.

"Fuck. You are soaking wet," Wade whispered in her ear. He removed his finger from inside of her, spun her around to face him, and picked her up, holding her tightly by her butt. When her face met his face, Wade kissed her passionately. He then placed her in the middle of the couch, seductively undressed them both, pulled out a condom from his pants, and then kissed her. Tasia eyed Wade's skinny long penis and hoped it could get the job done. He positioned himself in front of Tasia and began kissing her left nipple while playing with her right one.

He looked up at Tasia and said, "You are so beautiful." He kissed her from her lips to her navel to her wetness. He scooted Tasia further down on the couch, softly kissed her inner thighs, put her legs over his shoulders, then went to work. Tasia came all over his face, and he continued to bring her to ecstasy.

Tasia's moans became louder and louder. She lifted Wade's head up and passionately kissed him. "Fuck me," Tasia whispered in his ear.

He licked her remaining juices from his lips, then rubbed himself against her opening and slowly inserted himself inside of her. "*Fucckkkk.*" Wade slowly exhaled. Tasia got wetter, and his strokes became faster. He put his leg on the couch to get deeper and found her G-spot. Tasia moaned uncontrollably, and then he suddenly climaxed. He lasted all of ten minutes, and Tasia was not satisfied. The sex was good but too fast for her liking. She decided that she would give him another chance since they were intoxicated.

"Are you good?" Tasia asked.

He chuckled breathlessly. "I'm great. Tasia, that pussy got some power."

She laughed. "Hey, what can I say?"

"Not a damn thing. I'm gone bring the freak out of you." He told her boastfully.

Tasia gave Wade a bashful smile.

The following day, Tasia stayed inside and got some much-needed rest. She also called Taylor to let him know she had moved to town, and after much teasing about her being there months before telling him, they agreed to meet soon. Shortly after she ended the call with Taylor, Josiah called her via FaceTime. Tasia was excited to talk to him and answered the FaceTime, smiling from ear to ear.

Josiah gazed at her with blissful eyes. "What are you doing?" He asked.

"Thinking about you!"

"Bullshit!" Josiah chuckled.

Tasia playfully rolled her eyes. "I'm for real. I miss yo fine ass."

"Same here."

"I got this week's flowers…I love them, as usual. You have no idea how it makes me feel to receive flowers from you." Tasia said as she spanned the camera around so Josiah could see the flowers neatly in their vase.

"Since you're so far away from me, I have to send you a weekly reminder that you're always on my mind."

"You're so sweet, Josiah. What did I do to deserve you?"

Josiah blushed. "Anastasia, you know I got you. What's been up in your world? We haven't talked in a few days. How is your dad doing? What's the latest update?"

Tasia sulked and took a deep breath. "He's not doing okay. One of his lungs collapsed a few days ago, and they had to rush him to the hospital. They stabilized him, and now he's back in hospice care at the nursing home."

"How are you holding up?" Josiah inquired.

"I'm okay for the most part. Just trying to stay distracted from the inevitable. It sucks that me and my dad didn't have the best relationship. I just don't know how to feel about everything. He's my dad, so yea, of course, I'm sad that he's dying. I feel as if I should be sadder and moping around. I just don't feel that low. Does that make sense?"

"I've never been in this situation before, so I can't tell you how to feel," Josiah replied sympathetically. "There is not a right or wrong answer. Have you thought about talking to a therapist to unpack everything you are going through?"

"I'm not ready to speak to my therapist just yet," Tasia stated reluctantly. "Everything will get better in due time."

Josiah looked disappointed. "I get it. But you have to promise me that you'll get help." Tasia softly nodded, and Josiah shifted the conversation to her blog. "I see your social media following is growing super fast! Check you out! You're doing promos and ads now. Random people are reposting your shit. I'm so proud of you!"

Tasia, shifting her emotions to positivity, smiled brightly. "Thank you, Josiah! I couldn't have done it without your constant push! Networking and posting consistently is finally paying off. I'm excited about the future opportunities!

"Me too! I have to come see you before you get too busy for me! I really miss yo sexy ass."

"Never that! I'm focused, but you know I will always make time for you!" They caught up a little longer and made plans for Josiah's visit before ending their call. Tasia loved the idea of Josiah visiting and was excited to show him around the city. She also couldn't wait to have sex with Josiah again. She was really grateful for Josiah's kindness towards her, however, he wasn't her man, so she didn't feel an ounce of guilt about her dealings with Wade. In fact, Tasia and Wade continued to have sex, which wasn't always the greatest. They had developed a routine. During the week, they would focus on their work. On the weekends, they would focus on one another. They also agreed to end things physically if they became serious with other people. Their friendship grew stronger, but Tasia still wasn't emotionally attached to him. He was just something to do.

Twenty-One

♡♡♡

"B
ITCCHHH!!" Fallon exclaimed through the phone. "I knew you and Wade were fucking! I knew it! I see the way he looks at you." Fallon laughed. "You stay calling that man your friend, but that's your nigga! You got a whole man and don't even know it."

Tasia instantly regretted opening up to Fallon about Wade. Annoyed at Fallon's presumptions, she sucked her teeth and said, "Girl, it's not like that. He's my friend, with a sprinkle of benefits here and there. He's cool and all, but I don't see us going any further than this. I'm not that into him."

"Sooooo…. you're having sex with him, but you don't like him? T, make it make sense."

"Listen, Fallon. A girl has needs. That's it. Nothing more, nothing less."

"Damn, you are one cold bitch. Teach me your ways, girl."

They both broke into laughter. Though their connection had blossomed, Tasia didn't trust Fallon. She thought she was cool for going out and networking with, but Tasia couldn't allow her to become any more than that in her life. After getting to know her, Tasia learned that Fallon was a user. Tasia understood that friendship was give-and-take, but Fallon had that Philly mentality. She made relationships for survival, not true connectivity. Tasia knew their relationship was strictly surface-level.

"Okay, okay. I'll shut up! But that's your man. You'll accept it eventually. Anyways, I was calling to see if you and Wade were coming out with me and Dee tonight." Dee was Fallon's man, the aspiring rapper who needed to consider getting a regular job. Tasia disliked Dee with a passion. He was cool to Fallon in public, but privately, he treated Fallon horribly. He was broke, insecure, controlling, and abusive toward her. Tasia hated it for her, but Fallon would not leave Dee. Tasia even tried offering Fallon help, but she made it clear that she didn't want Tasia's involvement in her relationship. Tasia realized that if Fallon was okay with arguing and fighting with a man all day, there was nothing she could do about it.

"What's going on tonight?" Tasia asked.

"My man performing on the Northside tonight! At a spot called Lou Suites. The rapper Big C gone be there too. He's hosting." Fallon proudly informed her. "Before your bougie ass say no, we got a VIP section next to Big C!"

A light bulb went off in Tasia's head. She could possibly get a few pictures of Big C for the blog. Big C had recently signed with a label, and his song had just gone viral. He was on the rise to stardom.

"Alright, alright." Tasia attempted to sound like Fallon had convinced her to go. "I guess you can count me in. Send me the deets, and I'll pull up. It'll just be me, though. Wade flew to New York this morning for work."

"No biggie. More drinks for us!" Fallon teased. "I'll send you the info now. See you tonight."

"Drip Too Hard" by Gunna and Lil Baby blasted through Tasia's speakers as she prepared for the club. Trap music was her choice while preparing for the night festivities. Tasia wore a black see-through long-sleeve crop top, high-waisted jeans, gold accessories, a Gucci belt, and heels. She teased her 28-inch middle part, body wave hair, and did her make-up until it was impeccable.

Tasia hated going to the club when unknown local rappers performed, so she smoked a blunt before heading out the door. She wasn't going to let the wack performances ruin her night. She had a goal to achieve, and she was going to the club to work. Around 11 pm, Tasia headed out and continued her trap music session in the car. A line was wrapped around the building when she arrived at the club. She texted Fallon to let her know she was outside, gave her keys to the valet, and walked right past the security line. Fallon emerged from the entrance and informed security that Tasia was with her. Security searched her bag briefly and allowed Tasia to join Fallon inside the club. Lou Suites was packed from wall to wall. Tasia could feel everyone staring at her as they walked through the crowd. With all eyes on her, her confidence spiked, and she strutted like she was the baddest bitch in the club.

Fallon and Tasia finally made it to the section, and

Dee and his friends were already there. Two guys got up so that Tasia and Fallon could sit down.

"Bitch, it's crazy in this muthafucka." Fallon yelled to Tasia over the music.

Before Tasia could respond, Dee walked over to them. "Wassup, T?"

"Hi." Tasia waved nonchalantly.

"Thanks for coming out to support the kid." Dee grabbed the Hennessy bottle off the table and asked the ladies to take a shot with him. They all took their shots to the head. After the shots, Dee stepped away to talk to the DJ.

"Girl, don't my man look good tonight? I dressed him for the performance!" Fallon looked at Dee with excitement. Tasia didn't find him attractive, but she had to admit he was fresh as hell for his show. Dee was a short, dark skin, husky man, and he wore his hair in a curly afro. Fallon had dressed him in a black Burberry button-down, black shades, black jeans, and a new pair of Jordans.

"Okay, Ms. Fashionista. Y'all both look good. Just'a matching."

Fallon giggled. She wore a sheer black jumpsuit with black heels, a Burberry purse, and heels to match. "Yep, real matchy. I need to let these hoes know that Dee is my man."

"Girl, don't nobody want Dee ass." Tasia chuckled. Completely ignoring Fallon rolling her eyes at her sly remark, Tasia bumped her head to the music and checked out the scene.

After Tasia and Fallon had been seated for about thirty minutes, the bottle girls approached their section with sparklers and more bottles.

"Oh, we gone be lit tonight!" Fallon exclaimed. Tasia agreed. The drinks flowed nonstop, and Fallon and Tasia were having a good time with Dee's crew. A few of Dee's homies tried to holla at Tasia, but she politely declined. She didn't want to have any dealings with Dee's friends. She figured if they were hanging with Dee, they were probably bums, just like him. Dee walked back and forth between the section and the DJ booth, ensuring that everything was just right for his performance. He was the second to last performance for the night.

All of a sudden, an excited commotion broke out near the exit. A crowd huddled by the door moved around with phones and cameras in the air. As camera flashes lit up the area, Tasia knew Big C had arrived. She brainstormed how to get his attention to get a picture for her blog, *The Realness*. Big C and his crew greeted a few people in the crowd and paused briefly for pictures as they made their way to their section. As Fallon promised, Big C's section was next to theirs. Big C and his crew took their seats, and Tasia was blinded by their jewelry. After Big C got a drink from his table, security escorted him to the stage to greet the audience.

"The niggassss are out tonight!" Fallon whispered to Tasia. Tasia agreed.

"Wassup STL!" Big C shouted on the mic. "The Lou is in the building tonight, and I 'preciate that! I'm turnt as fuck to be here wit my people. Check this out, I need to see drinks flowing, ass shaking, and everybody turnt all night long! If you with that shit holla, Hell Yeah!"

"*HELLLLLL YEAAAAHHH!*" The crowd shouted

back to Big C.

"Fucking right! That's what I'm talkin' bout. I got a cash prize for the artist with the best bars. We gone get into all that later, but right now, DJ, drop my shit!" As his lyrics blasted through the speakers, Big C rapped along, *"Shake that ass! Hoe, shake yo ass!"*

The crowd went crazy and shouted Big C's lyrics along with him. *"Stop playing, hoe! Gone shake that ass!"* The beat of the song was contagious. Tasia and Fallon couldn't help but get up and twerk. There wasn't a still body in the building. Men were standing, bobbing their heads, and peeping at all the women shaking to Big C's lyrics. Big C stopped rapping along and just gazed out into the crowd, viewing everyone singing along and enjoying his music. He returned to his seat so the next artist could come up before his big performance for the night.

"I'll be right back," Fallon told Tasia. "I have to get Dee right. He's up next."

"Cool, cool," Tasia replied. "I'm going to run to the ladies' room."

"Yeah, girl. Go ahead and do that now so you don't miss my man's performance." Fallon grinned as she rushed off to give Dee a pep talk. Tasia could care less about Dee's performance. She had to get seen by Big C. Tasia strutted off to the women's room to freshen up.

On her way back to the section, a few men tried to stop Tasia to talk to her, but she smiled politely and kept walking. Tasia was on a mission and could not get distracted. As she seductively walked back to the section, she intentionally slowed her pace near Big C's section. It worked, and she caught Big C's eye. He stared her down until she sat on the arm of the couch closest to his section. Tasia, fully aware that he was watching her, looked his way and smiled. They locked eyes, and Big C's bashfully smirked at her.

"Okay, T! He's about to take the stage! Watch my purse so I can go record my man!" Fallon interrupted their stare-down, and Tasia was irritated.

"Yeah, okay. I got you." Tasia stayed behind with half of Dee's crew while the others went to the middle of the floor to hype him up. When Dee's beat dropped, Tasia's ears perked up. It was actually pretty good.

"This shit right here is called Hustla. STL! Let me know if you fucking with it!" Dee shouted to the crowd on the mic. The crowd cheered, and everyone vibed to the beat and Dee's flow. While he performed, Tasia danced seductively on the arm of the couch. Big C was watching her, and Tasia gave him a show.

After Hustla ended, Dee yelled on the mic and told the DJ to drop his next hit, The Opps. Apparently, their favorite song by Dee, the crew he left behind got rowdy, stood up in the section, and bounced up and down, throwing up gang signs. Tasia was appalled and inched further away from them. She should have known they were gang affiliated because they all wore some type of green. Across the room, another group of guys wearing mostly black got just as rowdy, throwing up different gang signs. "Whew, it's getting hood in here," Tasia said, unimpressed. It looked like a recipe for a club fight, but Tasia wasn't afraid. She saw plenty of gang-related fights hanging out with her cousins in the SWAT's. She knew how to get out of the way well before things got too far.

After Dee's performance, he started shouting out his hood on the mic, yelling, *"Fuck the opps!* His crew loved every second of it. *"Fuck the opps!"* They yelled back at him, still contorting their fingers into gang signs in the air.

As Tasia watched them closely, she felt a tap on her shoulder. It was a guy from Big C's entourage. "Big C wants to know if you would join him in his section." He whispered. Tasia looked at Big C and eyed him up and down. He waved at her and gestured for her to join him. Tasia smiled and nodded to accept Big C's invitation. To not appear thirsty or in a rush, she took her time grabbing Fallon's purse. Finally, she followed Big C's wingman to the rapper's section. When she approached the table, other members of his entourage sitting around him moved, and Tasia sat next to him.

"Hey, pretty lady. What's your name?" Big C said once she got situated beside him.

"I'm Anastasia. It's a pleasure to meet you." Tasia introduced herself.

"I couldn't keep my eyes off you. You can't be from here. I've never seen you before." Big C said as he cozied up next to her.

Tasia shifted away from him a little and cut to the chase. Big C was handsome, but she wasn't trying to become a rapper's groupie. "Your music is pretty dope. I like it. You mind taking a few pictures for my blog?"

"Dang, lil mama. You about your business, huh? You ain't gonna trash me in your blog, are you?" He laughed.

"If you were trash, you wouldn't make *The Realness.*" Tasia quipped back with a smile.

"Aiight cool. *The Realness,* huh? I like that. I'm gonna

check you out. Let's flick it up!" Big C posed as Tasia snapped a few pictures of him, and he loved every second of it.

"So, tell me more about *The Realness*. What do you blog about?" Big C inquired.

"A little bit of everything, I---" Tasia began.

"Aye, ain't that yo people?" Big C asked as he pointed toward Fallon and Dee's booth.

Then, a loud commotion erupted in the club, and Tasia turned her head quickly to see what was happening. Dee and his homeboys were arguing with the group of dudes who were dressed mostly in black. The arguments quickly escalated to fist-throwing. Tasia watched as Dee got mushed in the face, and everyone in his crew started throwing hands with the other group of men.

People began to scatter out of the club as the fight worsened and the lights came on in the club. Some people stood around watching the fight, snapping pictures and streaming the fight live on social media. The DJ cut the music and asked everyone to pipe down and get back to enjoying the music. Security rushed to the scene of the fight and attempted to separate everyone. However, there were only four security men and about twelve men fighting. Dee's crew was smaller, but they were getting the best of the other crew. Suddenly, a guy from the other group pulled a 9-millimeter from behind his shirt, pointed it in the air, and fired it. The remaining crowd began to scatter. Fallon was searching around the club frantically for Tasia. When she saw her at Big C's section, she rushed to her, pushing and shoving through the crowds.

By this point, Big C's security was clearing a path to

get him out of the club, and Big C had grabbed Tasia's hand, pulling her along with him.

"*T! THEY ARE TRYING TO KILL DEE!*" Fallon shouted to get Tasia's attention.

Tasia heard her, turned around, and grabbed her hand through the swarming crowd.

They made it out of the club safely and hopped into Big C's bulletproof SUV waiting outside the exit. Tasia, Fallon, Big C, his manager, and two bodyguards waited anxiously in the car as his driver tried to maneuver around the other cars attempting to get out. "Oh my God, T! They trying to kill my man. Did you get my purse?" Fallon asked her. Tasia handed her the purse. "Wait, where are we going?" Fallon asked as she pulled out her .22 pistol. "I gotta go find my man! Come on, T. Let's go! Driver, stop the car!" Fallon demanded.

Everyone looked at her as if she was crazy. "Go where?" Tasia chuckled.

"The fuck you mean?" Fallon asked, puzzled by Tasia's lack of concern. "We need to find Dee!" "Are you crazy?" Tasia asked her. "They are shooting! I ain't going nowhere."

Fallon frantically took the safety off her gun. "T! You're seriously going to let me go out there by myself?"

"You shouldn't even be going out there!" Tasia exclaimed, shocked that Fallon wanted to risk her life for a man who treated her like shit. "A bullet has no name, Fallon. You really need to chill out. The police just arrived, so your man has probably already dipped or is about to get locked up. You need to think about yourself right now."

"I'm not no scary ass bitch! What makes you think I'm about to leave my man out here stranded! Now, are you coming or not?"

Tasia laughed sarcastically. She knew there was no getting through to Fallon. "You gotta gun. You a gangsta. Go ahead and handle it yourself, Thug Misses."

"Let me the fuck out of here!" Fallon shouted at the driver. He stopped the SUV and unlocked Fallon's door.

"Be safe, Fallon," Tasia shouted behind her as she rushed out.

"Go fuck yourself, bitch!" Fallon said as she slammed the SUV door.

"Ma, don't trip. She's a fool." Big C said to Tasia. "Let her thug it out since she 'bout that life."

"Oh, I'm not worried about her at all," Tasia assured Big C. "Them niggas finna go to war. Bodies gone be dropping left and right. This is St. Louis, Murder Capital, USA. Nobody is off limits. She out her fucking mind if she think I'm catching a bullet for anybody." Tasia quickly blocked Fallon's number and deleted her contact. It was fun while it lasted, Tasia thought to herself. She appreciated Fallon helping her get acquainted with the city, but Tasia wasn't signing up for street beef.

"So, what you got planned for the rest of the night?" Big C asked.

Tasia sighed. "Home. Tonight has been eventful enough for me."

"Nah, I don't think you should go home." Big C said slyly.

Tasia knew where this was going. Tasia said, "Really? Where should I go?"

"Back to the hotel with me. We can get room service, talk, and get to know each other."

Tasia rolled her eyes. "It's two in the morning. There's not that much to talk about. If you truly wanted to get to know me, you would take me on a date somewhere other than your hotel room."

"You're right, but I leave tomorrow and---"

Tasia cut him off. "So, the next time you're in town, you plan a nice date and see if I'm available."

"You're not with the shits at all!" Big C laughed. "I like that about you."

"Yea, yea. You tried it, Big C." Tasia said.

"Bet. Imma plan us a date." He said, laughing at Tasia's no-nonsense expression.

"We'll see."

"Did you need a ride home, or did you drive?"

"My car is in valet," Tasia replied.

Big C instructed his driver to confirm if the valet team were back outside. The valet was back, so the driver headed in that direction. "Damn, Ms. Anastasia. I don't want yo pretty ass to leave me." Big C said pitifully, attempting again to get Tasia to go back to his hotel room with him.

Tasia shifted further away from him. "You think I'm some kinda groupie bitch? I already told you I'm not going to your hotel. Chill the fuck out."

Big C was taken aback. "My bad. I'm sorry for coming on so strong. I'm feeling you, and I thought you were feeling me. Shit, you stared at a nigga all night. I thought you were just tryna play hard to get. I was willing to take another shot." Big C apologized remorsefully.

"Yea, I was staring. But that don't mean I want to fuck Big C." Tasia replied harshly, careful not to show any signs of weakness. She was in the car with a bunch of men she didn't know. Big C seemed harmless, but Tasia wasn't too sure. Also, she was genuinely not interested in Big C. He was tall and handsome, but she disliked how flashy and gaudy he was. "I just wanted a picture of you for my blog. This ain't that type of party, my nigga."

"Damn, it's like that? This was strictly business for you, huh?" Without giving her a chance to respond, he quickly grabbed her by her waist and pulled her near him. Tasia quickly went into attack mode.

Seeing Tasia get defensive, Big C put his hands up in surrender and waved his phone. "Woah, I'm not on that. I was just going to take a selfie with you."

Tasia looked at him inquisitively. "A selfie?"

He said, "Yeah. You about your business, right? I can help you get your followers up." She smirked, leaned into him, and they took the picture. "What's your Instagram?" Tasia gave him her Instagram name. Big C uploaded their picture into his story and tagged her. "No need to thank me. Now that business is handled, take me up on my offer. Not tonight, of course, but when I'm back in town."

"Sounds like a plan to me." Tasia smiled with satisfaction. They exchanged numbers as the valet brought Tasia's truck to the front. Big C hugged her and Tasia thanked him for supporting her blog.

"It ain't nothing. Text me when you get home." Big C replied.

"I'll do that," Tasia replied as she exited the SUV. She didn't know what would become of their connection, but she knew she wasn't letting Big C near her little c. Tasia planned to entertain him for business purposes only.

It was close to 3 am when Tasia finally made it home.

She sat on the sofa, rolled herself a blunt, and mentally unpacked the evening. Tasia couldn't believe Fallon expected her to risk her life over dumb gang stuff. Tasia was building a brand, and there was no way she could be associated with someone like Fallon. "What a bummer," Tasia said aloud. On the bright side, she got photos of Big C. She couldn't wait to see the buzz the photos would create for *The Realness*. Satisfied that she had accomplished her main goal for the night, Tasia finished her blunt and called it a night.

The following afternoon Tasia was awakened by phone notifications. Before she could take a look at her notifications, Lisa called.

"Hello," Tasia answered groggily.

"Bitchhhh! So this what we doing now?!"

Tasia sat upright in her bed. "What the hell are you talking about, Lisa?"

"ANASTASIA INGRAM! Don't play with me! I see how you doing it in the Lou!"

"Lisa, come on. What you on this morning?" Tasia was still half asleep and disoriented.

"Tasia, wake the hell up! You're all on the blog sites with fine-ass Big C!

"Say what? Stop playing with me! Wait a minute, let me check my phone!" Tasia perked up, and her fingers shook from excitement as she tried to maneuver through her phone. Tasia had a plethora of notifications. She was plastered everywhere on social media as Big C's girlfriend.

The whole world thought they were a couple. Tasia couldn't believe all the hype that had accrued overnight from a simple selfie. She was flabbergasted and excited. "Lisa! What the fuck! This is crazy."

"Alright, spill it! I need all the details, Tasia!" Lisa demanded.

"There is no tea, Lisa. I swear!" Tasia laughed. "It was just a selfie. Strictly business. Nothing more, nothing less." Tasia gave Lisa a play-by-play of the night's events, and Lisa was blown away. After catching up with Lisa, Tasia laid back down to take everything in. She had to strategize on how to use the attention coming her way. In celebrity gossip, the news becomes old fast, so she had to maximize the buzz before it died down.

She decided to upload the pictures she took of Big C along with their selfie to social media to fuel the flame. She captioned her post, "Go download Big C's newest mixtape. He's up next!" She would let people assume what they were. Next, she quickly whipped up a blog post for *The Realness.* She knew the views would be major since people assumed they were an item. People would read the blog to see if she discloses any information about their supposed relationship. She completed the blog post and set up her website to require a subscription to read new posts. If people wanted to be nosey, she at least wanted to be able to add them to her mailing list for future posts. Once she posted "What's Tea with Big C? to her website, she made another post on her social media page promoting the blog and tagged Big C in it. Her plan worked beautifully. Within an hour, *The Realness* had thousands of new subscribers. Many people commented on the blog with Big C and even checked out her other blog posts. Her email and social media notifications were going off so much that she decided to silence her phone. Tasia had done so much since Lisa's call she didn't realize it was almost 5 pm, and she hadn't showered or eaten anything. She stepped away from the buzz to shower and order a bite to eat.

Twenty-Two

♡♡♡

Tasia dug into her food from an Asian bistro close to her home and reminisced on her journey in St. Louis thus far. The night before was crazy, but it allowed her to reach a large milestone in her business. All her hard work was paying off, and she was ecstatic about the opportunities that were on the horizon. Excited to see if she had gotten more notifications about followers, reshares, and comments, she pulled out her phone and checked on her social media posts. Her blog posts and photos with Big C were still trending, and more and more people were following her and subscribing to The Realness. Browsing her newsfeed, she saw that one of her high school classmates, Kimmie, was on a romantic date in New York for her birthday. She briefly scrolled through her birthday pictures, liked Kimmie's post, and commented: *Happy Birthday!* She continued to scroll down her newsfeed and saw a post from Wade. Coincidentally, he had posted a similar dinner table as Kimmie. Since they all had gone to school together, Tasia realized it couldn't have been that much of a coincidence. She returned to Kimmie's post, then to Wade's post again, and confirmed they were in the same restaurant. Maybe they just linked up while Wade was in town, Tasia thought. Still on a high from her recent success, she continued to check her notifications and respond to new messages. However, jealousy and confusion grew as she thought about their dinner more. If it wasn't a big deal, Wade wouldn't have lied to her and told her he was going to New York for a business trip. His situation with Kimmie had to be pretty serious since he didn't inform Tasia.

She stood up from her kitchen table and began to pace back and forth. Wade wasn't her man, but she felt he could have been truthful with her since they made an agreement. "I can't catch a break with these men!" Tasia shouted out loud. After a few minutes of pacing, she flopped down on her couch and looked up at the ceiling. "God, why don't you love me? What did I do to deserve all this bad luck with men? Do you hate me or something?" She had too much to do to sit and be in her feelings. She decided that she would cut ties with Wade. He was clearly occupied with another woman. He was also a liar, and she could no longer trust him.

Tasia was getting ready to be petty and send Wade a cryptic text message when she was distracted by a DM from Seth.

So, you out here fucking with rappers now?

Tasia rolled her eyes. *Why the hell is he questioning me?* She wondered. Before Tasia could respond, Seth sent another DM.

T…real talk. I miss you.
What are you out here doing?
You know you are supposed to be mine.

"Nigga, please," Tasia said out loud. She was about to send Seth a hateful response, reminding him how much of a clown he was, until a lightbulb went off her in head.

Seth, I miss you too.

She replied, smiling devilishly to herself.

Can we talk? Face-to-face?

Tasia left him on read and took another shower. She put on a crop top and leggings and texted Seth that she was headed his way.

Perfect. Let me know when you are close by.

Instead of leaving immediately, Tasia took her time and worked on her blog for a few hours. Satisfied with her progress, she grabbed her purse and keys and texted Seth that she was nearby. Tasia knew Seth couldn't wait to see her and fill her head with lies, hoping to reestablish what they had. However, Tasia wasn't visiting Seth to hear another tired-ass apology. She was coming for vengeance.

When she arrived, Seth buzzed her in and greeted her at his door with open arms. She returned his big embrace with a standoffish church hug. Seth looked at her with guilt and told her that he really missed her. She ignored him and asked for a glass of water.

While he went to the kitchen, Tasia discreetly looked under his couch for the infamous shoebox. No luck. She took a seat and Seth came back with her water, turned on the TV, and sat next to her. She immediately hopped up and told Seth she had to use the restroom. Tasia dashed to his bedroom and softly closed the door behind her. She needed to find that shoebox and fast. While in his room, she began her search by looking under the bathroom sink, his bed, and his sofa. Still no luck. She then darted to his walk-in closet and there were clothes and shoes everywhere. Tasia scanned his items and said to herself, "If I was stolen credit card numbers, where would I be?" There were no Adidas shoeboxes on his shoe shelves, so she began looking under the clothes on the floor. She came across a mountain of clothes in the corner and started throwing them to the other side, finally revealing a tattered blue Adidas shoebox. She frantically went through it and took pictures of the documents before returning to the living room.

"Yo, you good?" Seth asked while Tasia took a seat on the couch.

"Yea, I'm straight," as she wiped a bead of sweat from her forehead. He moved next to her and slowly put his arm around her.

"T, I'm dead ass serious. I miss you and want to make things right." He looked at her intently, waiting on a response.

"Seth, you know what I miss?"

"What?"

"Riding your face. That's what I miss."

Seth licked his lips. "Oh, yea? Come take a ride then."

Tasia stood up and was already dripping wet. He slid down the couch and leaned back. Tasia removed her leggings and climbed on top of him. She positioned herself on his face and rotated her hips slowly until she found a rhythm with his tongue. Seth went to work, licking and humming on her clitoris hungrily until she came. He pleased her until Tasia couldn't take it anymore and trembled uncontrollably. Seth gripped her hips so she couldn't move and continued to drive her crazy with ecstasy.

After she came again, Seth released her hips and helped her down from his face. He attempted to kiss Tasia, and she jerked her face back.

"What? You don't want to kiss me?" Seth looked at her with confusion. Tasia shrugged her shoulders, looked at the floor, then told him no.

"I made a mistake." Tasia finally said as she grabbed her leggings and slid them on. She intentionally brushed up against Seth and realized he was rock hard. "I wasn't supposed to hook up with you. I have to go. I can't do this." Pretending as though she was about to cry, she grabbed her purse and scurried to his front door.

"Tasia, wait. What's wrong, baby? Let's just talk." Seth stood in disbelief, watching her fidget with the door knob.

Tasia looked back at him with fake regret and almost laughed at the sight of her juices still running down his face. "I-I-I- I just can't!" She dramatically flung herself out of the door and walked quickly as she headed toward the elevators. The biggest smirk spread across her face when she made it on the elevator. Not only did she get what she came for, but she had finally curated the perfect idea to punish Seth for all he had done.

When she made it home, Tasia went straight to her laptop. She created a fake shoe page on Instagram and uploaded exclusive shoes and apparel to the page. Next, she messaged her blog's page from the fake page. Tasia created a conversation between the two, making it appear that the shoe enthusiast had been purchasing shoes from Opulent Kicks STL, only to learn that the shoes were fake. She wrote a blog post called EXPOSED. The focus was that Opulent Kicks STL had been rumored to sell fake shoes from China and that Seth, one of the store's salesmen, was a scammer and had been stealing customers' credit cards for personal use. She used the pictures of the documents in the shoe box and the fake conversation as her evidence. Once done, she made a graphic about her new blog post and crafted the perfect post for social media. The caption read: *"Hey Real Crew! A shoe fanatic (who will remain anonymous) dropped some piping hot tea in our DM's about one of STL's most "opulent" shoe boutiques. Check out the screenshots and let us know what you think below!"*

"Checkmate, bitch!" Tasia laughed to herself as likes and comments flooded in about the boutique and Seth being a scammer. Tasia knew it would work. Her page was still trending and at the top of everyone's algorithm since her picture with Big C went viral.

Since Seth hurt her, she decided to hurt his reputation and pockets. It's the internet, so people would automatically assume the rumors were true. If people weren't buying shoes, Seth would no longer have access to customers' credit cards to use for scamming. She wanted Seth to learn she was no one to mess with. Tasia scrolled through the comments and laughed as she read people's reactions.

"I knew that shit was fake! The prices were too low."

"Oh, hell naw! Let me go check my bank statements right now! #SethTheScammer"

"I am NOT surprised! Homeboy always seemed a little too shifty to me!"

"Wow, really?"

"Damn! I just copped some shoes from there! I'm taking them back first thing in the morning. #OpulentIsFradulent" People began to tag Seth, Chris, and the shoe store in the comments asking them if the post was true. Tasia was even more pleased when her phone dinged. She knew exactly who it was.

"Let me see what this clown has to say." Tasia took a deep breath, grabbed her phone, and read the text.

I hate your fucking guts.

Tasia replied back to Seth with a kiss emoji.

You're a trifling ass bitch!

I've been called worse.

Tasia put Seth on Do Not Disturb and continued to read the comments. Even though she had accomplished her goal, the very reason she had moved to St. Louis, it didn't feel as satisfying as Tasia thought it would. She thought ruining his reputation would make her feel better, but it made her feel even worse. Also, the pain of what Seth had done to her still sat heavily in her chest. Tasia looked up to the ceiling. "God, I'm sorry. Please forgive me." Tasia began to second-guess her actions. She rolled up a blunt and sat in her thoughts. How the universe was set up, she knew karma would soon be knocking at her door. She had stooped too low.

The following day, Tasia woke up to over a dozen texts and calls from Seth.

Woowww! So it's really like that Tasia?
You got me fired!!
You're messing with my life.
You better pray to God that I don't go down for this!
I can't show my face, it's people out here threatening me.
I thought we were better than this?
You know I never meant to hurt you!
You got your lick back, let's call it a truce.
Answer my calls!
Baby stop ignoring me.
I'm sorry! Please delete that shit off your page!

Tasia didn't respond but deleted her entire text message thread with Seth and blocked his number. She knew he wasn't truly sorry. Besides, the post was bringing her more new followers. So many people had sent her DM's requesting to work with her, to do promo and collabs for their brand. Looking through her messages, she knew social media would become very lucrative for her. There was no way she was taking it down.

After responding to a few messages and setting meetings for the following week with new connections, Tasia decided to get out of bed and run errands. Her last stop of the day was at the supercenter. It was on the more urban side of town, so she hated shopping there and only came for their large candle and home scent section.

While browsing the aisles, Tasia had everything except what she came for in her cart. Finally, she decided to wrap up her shopping and head to the candle aisle. While she was smelling candles, an older, clean-cut gentleman approached her.

"Excuse me, ma'am. I'm sorry to bother you, but my daughter's car is outside getting towed. It's seventy dollars to get them to stop towing her. I only have sixty, and I have to pay the tow company. I'm embarrassed to ask, but I left my wallet at home. Do you happen to have ten dollars? I would let you hold my phone, and after I pay them, I would leave and come back with your money."

Tasia completely understood his dilemma and didn't hesitate to give him the money. "Keep your phone. Here's the ten."

The gentleman smiled from ear to ear. "Baby girl, bless your heart. I really appreciate you. I'm so embarrassed. I can't believe I left my wallet."

"Don't be. I hope you and your daughter get everything taken care of." He thanked her once again and left the aisle.

Tasia selected a few candles and headed to the register to check out. While passing an aisle, she heard two men talking. One of the voices belonged to the gentleman she had given ten dollars to earlier. He was telling the same sob story to another customer. Tasia reversed in her tracks, walked down the aisle, and approached them. The man tried to avoid eye contact with Tasia and began to stutter.

Before he could get another word out, Tasia looked at the customer and told him to keep his money because the man was lying. Tasia put her hand out. "As a matter of fact, give me my money back! I will follow you around the store if you don't. Nobody will get the chance to hear yo fake ass sob story. You're too old to be doing this."

He sighed. "Okay. You got me. I'm sorry." He then pulled out a wad of cash and handed Tasia her money back.

"Unbelievable," Tasia replied as she took her money.

The other man stood in disbelief. "Damn, OG. You out hurr doing it like that?"

The swindler apologized and walked off swiftly.

"*Gah damn!*" Tasia exclaimed. "Welcome to the Show Me State, I guess. Just another city full of scammers."

The man laughed and asked Tasia where she was from because of her accent.

Tasia giggled and said, "Not you talking about accents when you out here sounding like you should be in a Nelly video. But I'm from Atlanta."

"You're funny, but I see you don't play no games."

"It's just the principle for me."

"You're right. His story sounded pretty legit. I was getting ready to give him a twenty. Meanwhile, he got racks in his pockets."

"Y'all St. Louis folks are something else."

"Everyone isn't like that. Now I feel like it's my duty to show you we're not the same."

Tasia looked him up and down. She hadn't noticed how fine he was. He stood about six feet tall, had a light complexion, and an athletic build. His hair was faded with waves, and he had the prettiest green eyes.

Tasia smiled at his offer. "I don't even know your name."

"My name is Stefon. And you are?"

"Anastasia."

"Well, Anastasia, you should let me take you out. I think you will enjoy yourself."

"I might take you up on your offer." Tasia bashfully replied. They exchanged numbers, agreed to talk later, then parted ways.

A few days passed, and Tasia and Stefon had been texting and calling to get to know each other. Tasia was digging him, but she didn't want anything serious. Tasia wanted to focus on her brand, build her blog, and meet new people. When Mr. Right came along, she would know. Until then, she decided to focus on herself.

Twenty - Three

♡♡♡

Weeks passed, and Tasia was seemingly in a better mental space. Tasia's blog was taking off in the city, and she was becoming a bigger brand on social media. She was nominated for the STL's Top 30 under 30 Influencer Award, and Lisa, Brittany, Josiah, Kyle, and Morgan surprised her by visiting St. Louis to celebrate with her. Tasia felt special and appreciated by her friends. Everyone except Josiah stayed in an Airbnb while they were in town. He stayed with Tasia because they had some catching up to do. Their rendezvous was better than their last encounter.

Tasia also took Josiah as her plus one to the award ceremony. He was happy to be with her and especially excited to see Tasia win and accept her award. During their visit, Tasia took the ladies out for drinks while the fellas visited Anheuser-Busch Brewery for a tour. She wanted to catch up with her girls and didn't want the men in their business. While they were out for drinks, Tasia ran into Stefon and decided to introduce him to her friends. He paid for their drinks before leaving the ladies to enjoy their night. Her friends liked Stefon and thought he was handsome, nice, and generous. They could tell he was really into Tasia and felt he was a good fit in her life. While her friends' stay was short, Tasia was so grateful and blessed to have such thoughtful friends. She enjoyed them while they were there and was happy to show them around her new city.

St. Louis didn't compare to Atlanta, but Tasia was finding her path and making a name for herself. She was now making enough money from her social media brand to hire an assistant and writers from Atlanta, Los Angeles, and New York. Her employees gathered the latest gossip from celebrities and socialites. Content for The Realness improved tremendously, and her following grew to nearly 400k. Tasia was featured on a several podcasts to showcase her brand and blog. *The Realness* was becoming a threat to the bigger blogs, and most began to copy her content, adding small details to distinguish themselves. Tasia was flattered. She knew she was doing something right if bigger platforms were copying her.

Since Tasia's business was growing, she contemplated quitting her writing job with the magazine in Atlanta. She and Mrs. Julie had talked about that some day happening, and Mrs. Julie had promised to support her, but Tasia wasn't sure if it was time. She wanted to make sure she was going down the right path. Her job in Atlanta was her safety net, and she was scared to let it go. As the blog picked up more traction, Tasia got busier and knew she would have to decide soon. Tasia had even restarted therapy and coping with her past traumas. It seemed as if everything was finally falling into place for her. She was making new genuine connections and was finally getting over Seth in a healthier way. Tasia still had a soft spot for him, but she knew the feelings would subside with the assistance of her therapist. She realized she was happy that things didn't work out with Seth. If they did, she wouldn't have been in St. Louis and met Stefon, who she was slowly falling for.

Stefon gave her butterflies. Tasia acted like a young schoolgirl when she was around him. Stefon made her nervous and anxious at the same time. She had never felt like that before. He was different. Stefon was sweet, affectionate, generous, attentive, and expressive. He was older and much wiser, so he mentally stimulated Tasia. He turned her on so much, but she took things slow and hadn't taken things there with him yet.

One evening, after Tasia was done working for the day, she noticed that she hadn't received a call from Stefon that evening. So she called him, and it went straight to voicemail. It was strange, so she called again. Stefon answered immediately but hung up without talking to Tasia. She tried to call again and got his voicemail. Tasia was concerned about Stefon and didn't know what to do. As she thought about multiple worst-case scenarios, Stefon texted her.

Sorry, babe. I can't talk right now.
I have a toothache. Wyd?

Aww, babe. I'm so sorry to hear that.
Do you need to cancel for tomorrow?

No, not at all. My mouth just hurts when I talk.
I will be fine tomorrow.

Perfect. Get some rest.
I will see you tomorrow. Goodnight.

Goodnight.

The following evening, Tasia arrived early to their date at a Michelin Star restaurant. A few minutes later, Stefon entered with the most precious little girl Tasia had ever seen. He had brought his four-year-old daughter, whom Tasia knew about but had never met. The little angel's name was Justine, and she was beautiful. Stefon was all smiles as he hugged and kissed Tasia on the cheek.

"Bae, I wanted to surprise you, but you beat me here. I know we discussed it briefly and never set a time, but I really felt like it was time for you to meet my daughter."

Tasia bent down at eye level with his daughter. "Hi, Justine. My name is Anastasia. It's so nice to finally meet you."

Justine smiled at Tasia and immediately gave her a hug. "You are pretty."

Tasia bashfully thanked her. "You are pretty too! I love that cute dress."

"Thank you!" Justine said in her adorable little voice. "Are you my daddy's friend?"

"Yes, I am."

"Can you be my friend too?"

"If you would like me to."

"Daddy, can Annastacy be my friend too?" Tasia and Stefon chuckled at Justine's pronunciation of Tasia's name.

The three of them sat down and had a marvelous night. Tasia enjoyed Stefon and his daughter and could see herself playing step-mommy. She adored how he treated his daughter. Justine was clearly a daddy's girl, and Tasia was delighted in watching Stefon and her interact.

Tasia wished she had the same loving relationship with her dad. Tasia knew she had to accept what she and her father shared and stop blaming herself for how her father treated her. Josiah had been stopping by the nursing home to give updates on his condition, and Tasia was very appreciative. Josiah always came through for her and never let her down. She was dating and having fun, but Tasia knew Josiah would always be around. Tasia felt horrible for keeping him as a backup, but she just couldn't let him go.

"Bae? Bae?" Stefon waved his hand to get Tasia's attention. Tasia slightly shook her head and blinked a few times. "Is everything okay?"

"Yeah, I'm sorry." Anastasia was slightly embarrassed.

"Damn, TT, you're over there daydreaming. What are you thinking about?"

Tasia giggled and whispered, "Dreaming that you were my zaddy too!"

Stefon blushed. "You are something else."

Their night couldn't have gotten any better. I could get used to this, Tasia thought. The three of them felt like one big happy family. From that day forward, Stefon brought his daughter around more. He also brought Tasia around his circle of friends and close family members. She became more infatuated with him and began to fall in love.

One stormy night, a tornado warning was released. Parts of the city were already flooded and without electricity. Tasia and Stefon had made plans to get dinner and a couple's massage but canceled due to the bad weather. So, Tasia planned to watch movies and eat snacks all night. While she was halfway through a Netflix movie, Tasia got a text message from Stefon asking her to open the door. She scrunched up her face, confused that he had driven to her place in such a nasty storm. She frantically got up and looked around her home to ensure everything was tidy because she wasn't expecting company. She checked herself in the mirror to make sure she was decent. Tasia was wearing a two-piece loungewear set with her hair in a messy bun. She peeped through the blinds, and to her surprise, Stefon was already parked outside.

She turned on her porch light, cueing him to run inside. Tasia opened the front door as Stefon jogged from his car to her house with a handful of bags. Once inside, he slid off his shoes to avoid tracking water and mud throughout her home. Tasia helped Stefon with the bags, removed his jacket, and then he hugged her tightly.

"Is everything okay? What are you doing here?" Tasia asked.

"I really wanted to see you, and I know how much you

wanted to get those massages today. So I brought dinner and the massage to you." Stefon explained, showing her the Chinese food and body oils he had in the bags. Then, he went into his jacket pocket and pulled out a jewelry box. "And, the truth is, I had something I planned to give you tonight. I copped this for you a minute ago." Tasia smiled from ear to ear, anxious to see what he got her. "Open it." He requested excitedly.

Tasia opened the box, and it was a diamond-studded pendant that read, "The Realness." Tasia gasped and squealed with excitement.

"You are so thoughtful!" Tasia exclaimed as she gave him a passionate kiss. "I feel so special and lucky to have you."

"TT, I'm the lucky one. I don't know what I did to deserve you, but I'm glad I did. I'm falling for you. You are my confidante and my best friend. I feel you were placed on this earth to be my soul mate. I'm happy that I met you." Stefon replied. He looked into her eyes, and they kissed passionately again.

"What do you want to do first? Do you want to finish your movie? Eat? Or, get your massage?" Stefon asked.

Tasia grinned. "I want that massage." Stefon set up her bedroom with the massage items as Tasia took a shower. You're in for a surprise tonight, sir, Tasia thought as she lathered her body. After she got out of the shower, she dried herself off in her bedroom and lit the numerous candles she had spread throughout her room. She laid down and placed a towel over her butt. She yelled downstairs to Stefon, who had stepped out of the room to give her some privacy. "I'm ready for my massage, babe!"

Stefon entered the room, connected his phone to her Bluetooth speaker, and played the playlist he had made just for Tasia. "Relax. If you want me to stop or apply more pressure at any time, just let me know."

"Okay." Tasia giggled at Stefon's fake masseuse voice. Stefon took off his shirt so oils wouldn't get on his clothes. He poured some oil into his hands and went to work on Tasia's body. His touch was so relaxing that Tasia dozed off. She was awakened when she felt his hands rubbing up and down her legs, close to her butt. When she didn't object or move, his hands went deeper between her legs, closer to her entrance. Her insides began to tingle, and Tasia was ready for him to make a move, which she knew was coming. She didn't want to seem to eager, so she allowed him to lead the way.

"May I remove the towel, Ms. Ingram?" Stefon asked, still roleplaying as her masseuse. She nodded, and he gently removed the towel and tossed it to the side. Her butt was now exposed, and Stefon gently caressed it, which turned her on. Then he separated Tasia's cheeks, and she felt Stefon's tongue lick her up and down.

"Do you want me to stop?"

"No," Tasia murmured. Stefon spread her butt cheeks wider and started to massage her butthole as he continued to lick her, easing Tasia into ecstasy. He slapped her ass while she orgasmed, and Tasia moaned with delight. Stefon stood up, pulled down his pants, and positioned himself behind her. "Aht aht," Tasia stopped him and handed him a condom from her nightstand. She noticed Stefon manscaped and was also packing. His penis was thick, and it had length.

Stefon saw her checking him out. "Do you like what you see?" He asked her, intentionally making his manhood jump. Tasia bit her bottom lip. He put the condom on, grabbed her face, and gave her a wet, sloppy kiss. Then, he laid her on her back and gently inserted himself inside her. Tasia exhaled with satisfaction. Stefon's stroke game was impeccable. Stefon pinned Tasia's legs to the bed and stroked her to the beat of the music. She was in spread eagle. Then, mid-stroke, he stopped. "Get up," Stefon commanded. Tasia scrunched up her face. "Trust me." Stefon chuckled. He walked her to the wall. "Put your hands on the wall and spread your legs." Once Tasia was in position, he knelt and licked her from the front to the back.

He was putting in work, and Tasia's knees buckled. "Bae, I'm about to cum." She moaned as she began to lose balance.

"Cum, baby." Stefon egged her on. "Cum all over my face." Tasia did just that. After she climaxed, Stefon turned her toward him, lifted her up, and pinned her up against the wall. He inserted himself inside her, and Tasia wrapped her legs around him. Tasia had never been fucked that good, and she loved every minute of it. He stroked her deep and passionately kissed her until they both reached ecstasy. After Stefon put her down, they sat beside each other, panting hard to catch their breath.

"Are you okay?" Stefon asked.

"I'm more than okay." Tasia smiled seductively.

"You like that freaky shit, huh?"

"Damn right, I do," Tasia assured him.

"I could get used to this," Stefon replied as he kissed

her.

"Me too, baby," Tasia admitted.

Stefon stood up, grabbed her hand, and asked if they could shower together. They washed each other in the shower, ate, and watched movies for the rest of the night. After that night, they agreed to be exclusive with one another.

Twenty-Four

♡♡♡

Stefon and Tasia's sex-capades became a weekly reoccurrence. After a while, she began to notice red flags. On certain nights of the week, she would call Stefon, and he would always be unavailable. He either had a sore throat, his battery was low, he didn't get the call, or his all-time favorite, a toothache. His funny behavior began to make Tasia put her walls back up. Her last straw was when she called him on a Sunday evening, and he told her he was at the DMV.

"Stefon. The DMV? On a Sunday? Nigga, go find you somebody else to play with." Tasia ended the call and blocked Stefon's number.

Tasia sensed that there was another woman. Just my luck, Tasia thought. She just couldn't catch a break. She really liked Stefon but refused to lose her sanity over another man. She had been down that road before and wasn't returning to her old ways. She thought they were perfect for one another and building a bond, but their relationship was short-lived.

A week after she blocked Stefon, someone was at her door around ten that night, banging as if they were the police. Startled, Tasia grabbed her bat from the closet and discreetly looked through her blinds. Stefon was standing on her doorstep.

She rolled her eyes. "What the fuck?!" She stormed to the door and abruptly opened it. Stefon looked pitiful and could barely hold his balance. Tasia looked at him in disgust. "What the fuck are you doing here?"

"Can I come in and talk to you?"

Annoyed, Tasia moved to the side to let him in. Stefon staggered to her couch, sat down, and motioned for her to sit beside him. Tasia could tell immediately that he was drunk, and she was irritated.

"Stefon, what the hell do you want? We are NO longer a thing. You cannot come to my house unannounced."

"Baby, why did you block me? What did I do? I don't like that you shut me out."

"And I don't like liars, Stefon. Nowadays, I remove myself from situations before I do something irrational. I just can't fuck with you no more."

"TT, I haven't done shit to you except be a stand-up guy." Stefon grabbed her face with both hands and expressed his love for her. "Tasia, you are my best friend. I love you, and I want to be with you. There's so much shit going on in my life that I want to tell you about, but it's complicated, and you won't understand. I wish I could leave the city and start my life over. I want to move to Texas." Stefon slurred over his words. "Tasia, do you want to go on a trip to Texas? We can go next month. I want you to be my wife. I want you to have my son. I want to build a life with you."

Tasia snatched her face from his hands. Stefon sounded like a broken record from her past, and she wasn't the least bit moved. "What's so complicated that you can't tell me?"

"You'll hate me if I tell you." Stefon slurred. "Come on, TT. Let's run away together."

"Stefon, you're full of shit. I ain't doing a damn thing with you. It's best that you leave. I have no idea what you got going on, but I don't want any parts of it. I'm emotionally drained, and I just don't have time for this. Are you able to drive yourself home?"

His face scrunched up. "Tasia, I'm fucked up. I barely made it here. I want to stay here with you." He slowly lowered himself back onto Tasia's couch.

"Aye, my boy. That's going to be a no." Tasia pulled him back upright. "Let me see your phone."

Stefon gave her his phone, and Tasia ordered an Uber to pick him up.

"Here." Tasia snapped, returning his phone. "Your Uber is four minutes away. It's best that you stand outside and wait for your ride."

"Damnnnnn, it's like that?" He whined drunkenly. "Tasia, you really kicking me out?"

"Yep. I do not need this energy around me." Tasia grabbed his hand, escorted Stefon outside, and locked her front door. Since he was drunk, she made sure he got into his Uber. Tasia didn't know what to think of the unexpected visit. She didn't know why he wanted to move to a new city.

A few days later, Tasia was on the phone with Brittany, who asked how she and Stefon were doing. Tasia updated her on their last encounters, and Brittany agreed it was weird.

"Did you check his social media? There might be some clues on his pages."

"Nah, he really doesn't do social media. He's never active."

"Girl, what's that nigga's last name?" Tasia gave Brittany his information, and she ran a search on Facebook. Moments later, Brittany gasped. "Bihhhh!"

"What, Britt? What did you find?" Tasia asked anxiously.

"Tasia, you're not going to believe this." Brittany sent her screenshots.

Tasia fumbled her phone when she received the pictures. Brittany called her name, but Tasia was too taken aback to respond.

"Brittany! What the hell?!" Tasia screamed, finally coming back to her senses. The pictures were of Stefon and his wife at their wedding a week ago. Tasia couldn't believe his deceit. It was the same weekend Stefon had confessed his love to her. Tasia began to laugh uncontrollably. She figured this was her karma for seeking revenge on Seth. Brittany was convinced Tasia was losing her mind. This go around, Tasia's feelings weren't hurt. She just couldn't believe Stefon was living a double life.

Tasia ended the call with Brittany. She looked at the dozen screenshots Britt had sent of the newlyweds and shook her head. "Karma is a bitch." She said out loud. Nothing added up or made sense, so she conducted her own investigation. She had only known about Stefon's inactive page. She typed in Stefon's full name on Facebook and got no results. She searched for him on her internet browser, and two social media accounts populated, including Facebook. Since she wasn't searching for his name under any of her social accounts, she could see his pages. That's when she realized he had deliberately blocked her. "Niggas ain't shit." Tasia declared aloud. She decided to unblock Stefon and text him. "Stefon? Is that even your real name? Congrats on your marriage! You're a fucking liar. Oh, and another thing, the Bible says it best. I will not take revenge. I will leave room for God's Wrath. For it is written, 'It is mine to avenge. I will repay, says the Lord.'"

Tasia planned to take her L in silence and move the hell on. This time, she was determined to take time to heal. She had been jumping from one situation-ship to the next. She decided it was time to focus more on herself, her brand, and her business and remove all distractions from her life.

Tasia started marketing more and putting out more content on her social media. Her following continued to grow. She went to more events in the city and built relationships with other creators. Tasia always ran into Stefon when she attended the events she promoted on her social media. Someway, he found a way to be in her presence. She tried to avoid him, but he was becoming very stalkerish. Tasia just couldn't duck him.

One particular night, Stefon was waiting outside the club at her Jeep. When she approached him, she took out some pepper spray and prepared to spray him. "Stefon, get the hell away from my whip. Tonight is not the night."

Stefon blocked her from getting inside her truck. "Anastasia! Please hear me out! When you came into my life, everything was going bad. You were the sunshine that took away my rainy days. My wife and I were engaged then, but everything was rocky. I just didn't know how to tell you. We were too far in. I really didn't want to get married. I'm miserable without you in my life. If I could turn back time, I would choose you."

Tasia stood there dumbfounded. "Nigga, you can't be serious. I'm so disappointed in you. I barely want to look at you. I don't have shit to say to you. Erase me from your memory and get the fuck out my way before I make a scene." She pushed him out of the way, hopped in her Jeep, and sped off.

The following day, Tasia headed to run errands, and walked outside to Stefon leaning on his car with flowers. Tasia ignored him and walked toward her car. He approached her calmly. "Can we talk?" He asked politely.

"No! I don't have shit to say to you. You can say sorry all you want, but you will always be a sorry-ass nigga in my eyes. Stop popping up. Go home to your wife!"

"Please hear me out, TT."

"No, you hear ME out. Leave me the fuck alone!" Tasia smacked the flowers out of his hand. Stefon grabbed her arm and pulled her near him. Tasia knew it was time to make a scene. "Help! Help! Help me! He's trying to kill me! Don't hurt me!" Her neighbors rushed outside with their phones out.

Stefon released her abruptly. "Fine, Tasia, have it your way. I'll leave you alone." He scurried away before her neighbors could intervene.

"I'm good, everyone. False alarm." Tasia assured her neighbors. Instead of running errands, she went to the local police department and filed a restraining order against Stefon. If anything happened to her, he would be the main suspect.

After that incident, Stefon's pop-ups ceased, and Tasia moved forward with her life. By removing all of her distractions, Tasia's life was finally flourishing. She began to make enough income to comfortably quit her writing job in Atlanta. Tasia was mentally, emotionally, physically, and spiritually in a better space. She was very proud of how far she had come since moving to St. Louis. She forgave herself for putting herself in situations that didn't serve her any good. Tasia also forgave those who hurt her. She paused dating and figured God would send the man she needed on His time.

In the meantime, Tasia planned to elevate every aspect of her life in her new city. She learned from her past mistakes and didn't regret anything that had happened. She was thankful. Tasia knew that she wouldn't have achieved as much without those lessons. She was blessed and overly joyful that things were finally going her way.

Epilogue

Ring! Ring! Ring! Tasia's eyes were still closed, but she grabbed her phone from her nightstand and groggily answered without looking at the Caller ID.

"Good morning. Is Ms. Gram available?"

"Who?!" Tasia asked.

"Ms. Gram. Is she available?" The man asked again.

"Do you mean Ingram?"

"Oh, yes. Sorry, Ms. Ingram."

"This is she." Tasia opened her eyes and sat up.

"This is Devon from Garden Manor Nursing Home. I was calling to inform you that Mr. Antonio Gram was pronounced deceased around six this morning. Garden Manor and I offer our most sincere condolences to you and your family. We are deeply sorry for your loss."

Tasia cleared her throat. "How many fucking times do I have to tell you that the last name is Ingram. I-N-G-

R-A-M! INGRAM! If you call someone about their dead family member, you should at least get their last name right! Thank you for the call, but they should never have you calling families about their deceased loved ones! You need sympathy training with your rude ass!" She ended the call, threw her phone across the bed, and slid under the covers. Tasia stared at the ceiling. She didn't have any emotions.

She was numb. She knew her father's time was near, but everything was finally going good in her life. Now she had to tackle this obstacle. Tasia was confused because her emotions weren't the same as when her mom passed. When her mom passed, it felt as if her heart shattered. With her dad, she felt nothing. Tasia shed no tears. She was the only one alive from her immediate family. Now, she really felt like an orphan. She couldn't fully understand why God would leave her in the world alone and abandoned.

Tasia sat up and grabbed her phone to text Lisa and Josiah the news. They both sent their condolences. Lisa promised she and her parents would help with the arrangements, and Josiah booked her a ticket to Atlanta for the following day.

For the remainder of the morning, Tasia smoked two blunts back-to-back and moped around the house. She was vulnerable and wanted to talk to someone who could relate to what she was going through. But she only knew one person who would fully understand her. So, Tasia went through her phone's block list and unblocked a familiar phone number. She knew she was the last person Seth wanted to talk to, but she needed him. She needed someone.

Within minutes, Seth responded to her text.

Anastasia, I'm sorry for your loss
and even more sorry for how I
treated you. I never meant to hurt you.
If possible, let's meet in Chesterfield
for lunch.

Tasia mustered up the strength to get ready for lunch, and after her shower, she put her hair in a bun and threw on leggings, a t-shirt, Retro Jordan 1s, and a blue jean jacket. Seth was already inside when she arrived, waiting for her at their table. The host escorted her to Seth, and he stood to embrace her. They hugged for quite some time. Shockingly, their lunch date wasn't awkward.

Tasia apologized to Seth for sabotaging his job and reputation, and Seth also apologized. Then, he asked if they could be friends again and put everything in the past. Tasia agreed to start fresh and to let bygones be bygones.

While they were catching up, Tasia got a call from an unfamiliar number. She had ignored calls all day, but Tasia knew she would have to start talking to people and getting her dad's funeral arrangements in order. She figured it was someone associated with the nursing home because they kept calling her. Tasia excused herself from the table and told Seth she was stepping away to take a call.

"Hello... Hello?" Tasia could barely hear the other caller. "Umm, hello?" she sucked her teeth as she got ready to hang up.

"Hello, is this Anastasia?"

"Yes, it is. May I ask who's calling?"

The woman on the other end cleared her throat and

began to stumble over her words. "Anastasia, my name is Angelique."

A light bulb went off in Tasia's head. It was the unknown woman who was visiting her dad at the nursing home.

"I know you don't know me, but I know of you." Angelique continued.

"How so?" Angelique became quiet. Tasia asked if she was still there.

"Yes, I'm still here. Anastasia, my maiden name is also Ingram. I'm your older sister." Tasia froze. "I heard the news about Antonio earlier this morning, and I was calling to give you my condolences. If you need any help, I can assist. Hopefully, after the funeral, we can get more acquainted. I also have a son, whom I would love you to meet as well….

Tasia's phone slipped from her hand and shattered on the floor. She stood there distraught as tears rushed down her face. *Little did she know, her true karma had just begun.*

About the Author

drienne Denise was born and raised in St. Louis, MO. In her younger years, she fell in love with reading and began secretly writing short stories. After high school, she attended Alabama A &M University and earned her degree in Communicative Science Disorders. While attending college, she pledged Alpha Kappa Alpha Sorority Inc., and became her Chapter's Ivy Leaf Reporter where she submitted public announcements for all of their functions. After graduation, Adrienne began a career in Real Estate and Home Staging. While marketing her Real Estate, she created a weekly blog about home tips, décor, lifestyle, investments, and achieving goals. Her blog lit a fire under her and she picked up her pen again and began to write her first Urban Fiction, but life happened and she moved down South to further her career in Real Estate.

After moving, the pandemic hit and during that down time, she began working on a new book idea and was able to finally complete her first work of art. Her debut book, *Detached Lover*, is the first of many published works Adrienne will release. She hopes to gain new readers with every release and have them to connect with her characters and their relatable stories.

When Adrienne is not creating, in her free time, she loves to travel, read, create fashion looks, and decorating.

To learn more about Adrienne, visit
www.AdrienneDenise.blog

Printed in the USA
CPSIA information can be obtained
at www.ICGtesting.com
LVHW090827091123
763156LV00023B/51/J